WITHDR AWN

D0384230

Praise for *Miss Dreamsville and the Collier County Women's Literary Society*

"One can feel the immense joy of Amy Hill Hearth's engagement in her first novel. It radiates through every scene and through every page. Sometimes, an exceptional writer finds an exceptional premise, and the result is a truly exceptional book. Such is the case with *Miss Dreamsville* . . . The writing is brilliant, especially the dialogue through which the characters are defined."

—*Southern Literary Review*

"Amy Hill Hearth's first novel is a charming and funny snapshot of life in a tiny Florida town in 1962. It's also a sweet-tart reminder that those good old days weren't so good for everybody."

—*Tampa Bay Times*

"Funny, insightful, poignant, and uplifting."

—*The Cleveland Plain Dealer*

"You may already know Hearth's name—the former journalist wrote the nonfiction book *Having Our Say: The Delany Sisters' First 100 Years*, which was a bestseller and play. Her fictional storytelling is just as captivating."

—*The Durham (NC) Sun*

AVON PUBLIC LIBRARY
BOX 977 / 200 BENCHMARK RD.
AVON, COLORADO 81620

"Throughout this engaging tale, which sweeps smoothly from humor to touching to horrifying—just as life does—the words of Hearth's 80-year-old narrator fall as true as a plumb line."
—*The Berkshire Eagle*

"Hearth's characters are instantly likeable and there for each other as they take bold chances . . . A book that rings with authenticity."
—*The Daytona Beach News-Journal*

"Hearth has done very well with her first work of fiction. The characters are endearing, and she has a good understanding of the American South in the 1960s. I recommend it."
—*Historical Novel Society*

"Amy Hill Hearth's delightful first novel is a rollicking, provocative tale about how reading and meeting others who are different can be the most subversive of acts."
—Ruth Pennebaker, author of *Women on the Verge of a Nervous Breakthrough*

"Amy Hill Hearth honors and humanizes people and their wonderful diversities. She astutely weaves pertinent, factual histories into her debut novel. What a laudable book!"
—Camille O. Cosby, PhD, educator and producer

"Segregation, feminism, gays coming out, inter-racial dating, it's all in *Miss Dreamsville*, written as it happened in small towns everywhere. And wisdom; you could learn a lot about life from reading this book. Most of all, be daring, be friends, be true to

AVON PUBLIC LIBRARY
BOX 977 | 200 BENCHMARK RD.
AVON, COLORADO 81620

yourself. By the end, I cried and I must say, I wouldn't mind hearing more about each of the richly painted characters."

—Patricia Harman, author of *The Midwife of Hope River*

"*Miss Dreamsville's* cast of characters includes a postmistress, a librarian, a convicted murderer, a northern transplant, a lone African-American girl, and an even lonelier gay man, among others. Set in Naples in the early 1960s, its local color and plot will surprise Florida natives and visitors alike."

—Enid Shomer, author of *The Twelve Rooms of the Nile*

ALSO BY AMY HILL HEARTH

Having Our Say: The Delany Sisters' First 100 Years

The Delany Sisters' Book of Everyday Wisdom

On My Own at 107: Reflections on Life Without Bessie

In a World Gone Mad

The Delany Sisters Reach High

"Strong Medicine" Speaks:
A Native American Elder Has Her Say

Miss Dreamsville and the Collier County
Women's Literary Society

Miss Dreamsville

and the Lost Heiress of Collier County

~ A NOVEL ~

AMY HILL HEARTH

ATRIA PAPERBACK

New York   London   Toronto   Sydney   New Delhi

ATRIA PAPERBACK

An Imprint of Simon & Schuster, Inc.
1230 Avenue of the Americas
New York, NY 10020

This book is a work of fiction. Any references to historical events, real people, or real places are used fictitiously. Other names, characters, places, and events are products of the author's imagination, and any resemblance to actual events or places or persons, living or dead, is entirely coincidental.

Copyright © 2015 by Amy Hill Hearth

All rights reserved, including the right to reproduce this book or portions thereof in any form whatsoever. For information, address Atria Books Subsidiary Rights Department, 1230 Avenue of the Americas, New York, NY 10020.

First Atria Paperback edition September 2015

ATRIA PAPERBACK and colophon are trademarks of Simon & Schuster, Inc.

For information about special discounts for bulk purchases, please contact Simon & Schuster Special Sales at 1-866-506-1949 or business@simonandschuster.com.

The Simon & Schuster Speakers Bureau can bring authors to your live event. For more information or to book an event, contact the Simon & Schuster Speakers Bureau at 1-866-248-3049 or visit our website at www.simonspeakers.com.

Manufactured in the United States of America

10 9 8 7 6 5 4 3 2 1

Library of Congress Cataloging-in-Publication Data

Hearth, Amy Hill, date.
    Miss Dreamsville and the lost heiress of Collier County : a novel / Amy Hill Hearth.—First Atria Paperback edition.
        pages ; cm
    1. Life change events—Fiction. 2. Literature—Societies, etc.—Fiction.
3. Florida—Intellectual life—Fiction. I. Title.
    PS3608.E274M58 2015
    813'.6—dc23   2014040719

ISBN 978-1-4767-6574-7
ISBN 978-1-4767-6575-4 (ebook)

In loving memory of my niece,
Anna Katherine Hill
(1980–2012)

Miss Dreamsville

and the Lost Heiress of
Collier County

One

Dolores Simpson was a woman with a past. Now, depending on your age and where you're from, you might interpret that in a number of ways. Let me assure you, however, that in the southern part of the United States of America, in a certain era, this could mean only one thing: *man trouble.*

This affliction spares few women. Even maiden ladies and great aunties—the ones who smile and nod on the porch, contentedly snappin' peas—have stories of youthful turmoil and shattered dreams.

Dolores Simpson, unfortunately, had what my mama used to call *serious* man trouble. After leading a questionable life in Tampa, Dolores came back home one summer day in 1939 with all her worldly goods in a satchel under one arm and a brand-new baby boy in the other.

Yes, indeed. Serious man trouble.

Home, for Dolores, was one hundred and twenty miles south of Tampa in God's forgotten paradise, Collier County, which is bordered by the Gulf of Mexico on one side and the edge of the Great Everglades Swamp on the other. In those days, Radio Havana in Cuba was the only station that could be heard on the wireless and alligators outnumbered people by at least ten thousand to one.

Dolores's destination was an abandoned fishing shack that once belonged to her grandfather. The shack sat on stilts on a tidal river which was so wild and forbidding that no one with an ounce of sense would try to live there. Still, it was all Dolores knew. She had failed at city life. She had failed at pretty much everything. The river was a place where she could protect her secrets and nurse her frustration with the world.

And there she stayed, alone except for the son she raised, for twenty-five years.

I, TOO, HAILED FROM COLLIER County, but instead of the river or swamps I was raised nearby in Naples, an itty-bitty town with a sandy strip of beach on the Gulf.

I barely knew Dolores Simpson. She was, shall we say, reclusive to an extreme. My only knowledge of her was that she had once been a stripper but now hunted alligators for a living. If she had been a man she would have been admired as a fearless frontiersman.

I wouldn't have known even this much, nor would I have met her, if not for her son, Robbie-Lee. In the late summer of 1962, he and I became friends when we joined a new book club called the Collier County Women's Literary Society. To its members, the club provided a sanctuary of sorts. Each of us was a misfit or outcast in town—in my case, because I had come back home after a divorce—but in the book club we discovered a place to belong.

It is one of the ironies of life that being part of a group can, in turn, lead you to find strength and independence as an individual. That's exactly what happened to Robbie-Lee and me. After a year in the book club, we decided it was time to follow our dreams.

For Robbie-Lee, who loved the theater, the only place on his mind was New York City. He spoke endlessly of Broadway and was determined to get a job there, even if it meant sweeping sidewalks. Dolores, whose maternal instincts kicked in with a mighty roar at the idea of him leaving Collier County, objected to his planned departure, but lost the battle. Robbie-Lee caught a northbound bus on a steamy August morning in 1963.

At the same time Robbie-Lee went north I set off for Mississippi. I was hoping to learn more about my mother, who was born and raised in Jackson. Mama had died without telling me certain things. She never talked about her family, or how she met Daddy, or when and where they got married. All I know is they got hitched at a Methodist church because Mama insisted on having a bona fide preacher conduct the ceremony. They left Mississippi and came to Florida because Naples was Daddy's hometown.

What I hoped to find was kinfolk. An aunt or uncle, perhaps. Or maybe a cousin. Since I was a small child, Mama and I had been on our own. It's painful to say, but Daddy up and left us. At least I hoped to find out why my name is Eudora Welty Witherspoon—"Dora" for short. I could only guess that Eudora Welty, the famed Mississippi writer, had been a friend of Mama's when she was growing up.

As I said, Mama never told me certain things.

I figured I'd go to Jackson for a few weeks or at most several months, but before I knew it I'd been away from Florida for a year. I had made more progress finding out about Mama and her people than I ever could have imagined. All I needed was a little more time to wrap things up and settle them properly. I had a job shelving books at the Jackson Library and I rented a small room in the home of a widow named Mrs. Sheba Conroy. I planned on giving proper notice—I didn't want to leave anyone in the lurch—then head home to Naples.

And then the telegram came.

Two

Poor Mrs. Conroy, my landlady in Jackson. I can still picture her face when she saw the Western Union man through the glass panel of her front door. Even under the best of circumstances Mrs. Conroy was nervous as a rat terrier, and with the arrival of a telegram she was likely to need her fainting couch.

To her generation, a telegram was how they usually found out somebody had died, and even though the modern era had arrived and you could make a long-distance telephone call—especially to a city as large as Jackson—plenty of folks still relied on the Western Union man to deliver urgent news.

I couldn't believe it was for me. I'd never gotten a Western Union in my life and had hoped I never would. For a moment I was tempted to tear it up, unread, and toss it out the window right into Mrs. Conroy's Gulf Pride azalea bushes. But sooner or later, I knew I'd be outside on my hands and knees searching for the pieces and trying to put them back together. I'd have to know what it said.

Mrs. Conroy was so worked up I thought she was on the

verge of an apoplectic fit. She was quivering like Aunt Pittypat in *Gone with the Wind* when the Yankees were shelling Atlanta. "Well?" she shrieked, even before I could read it. "What does it *say?*"

I didn't answer at first. Finally, with my voice all aquiver, I blurted out, "It's bad news."

"I knew it!" Mrs. Conroy wailed. "Somebody died! Oh, Lord! Sweet Jesus . . ."

"Well, I don't know about that," I said, trying to calm us both down. "It just says *something's wrong*. But it doesn't say what."

"Let me see that," she said, yanking it from my hands. "'Big trouble. Come home now.'" She read the words aloud then looked at me. "What does that mean?"

"I don't know," I said.

"Oh, Lordy, Lordy." Poor Mrs. Conroy was wringing her hands. I'd never actually seen anyone do that, but sure enough, that's what she was doing.

"Mrs. Conroy," I tried to sound respectful, but firm. "Could you leave me alone for a moment so I can think? Just for a moment, please?"

She left reluctantly. I heard her moving pots and pans around in the kitchen. Then she began singing "The Old Rugged Cross," which is a nice old hymn but not great background music when you're trying to figure out who sent a Western Union that upended your life and why.

The sender was none other than the stripper turned alligator-hunter herself, Dolores Simpson.

A horrible thought occurred to me: Maybe something had happened to her son, my friend Robbie-Lee. But he was still in New York City and had just written to me that he was well and happy.

One thing was for sure. Whatever was going on was very serious. If there was ever a woman who didn't rattle easy, it would be Dolores. If she said there was trouble, you can bet grandpa's pet buzzard it was the Gospel truth.

But what kind of trouble? *Whose* trouble?

All of a sudden I wanted to go home. I *had* to go home. And I hated myself for staying away for a whole year, even though it had been a good year and I'd found out some things about Mama and her family that had turned my way of thinking upside down. But I had been fooling myself to think that nothing would change in Naples and that I could go back anytime I wanted and everything would be just as it was.

Most likely, someone had died, just as Mrs. Conroy feared. Since my social life had revolved around my book club, I went over the list of members in my head. Besides Robbie-Lee there was Jackie Hart, who had started the book club and was in good health as far as I knew. Jane Wisniewski, known to all as "Plain Jane," was a poet who made a living writing sexy stories for women's magazines under the name Jocelyn Winston. She was in her late fifties and had never mentioned any health concerns. Priscilla Harmon, who at nineteen was the youngest member of our book club, was at Bethune-Cookman College in Daytona Beach. Miss Lansbury, the librarian who helped us choose our book selections and kept the library trustees from interfering, had gone off to live with her kinfolk, a tribe of local Indians. And then there was Mrs. Bailey White, who, come to think of it, was quite elderly. Ten years older than God, as Mama would have said. But why wouldn't Dolores just say that in the telegram? "So-and-so died. Come home."

Instead, it said "big trouble."

Which led me back to Jackie. She'd been a newcomer to

Naples, having moved from Boston, of all places, when her husband was hired to work for one of our wealthiest residents, Mr. Toomb. Jackie was glamorous and witty but she had a special talent for upsetting the status quo. If they'd been able to get away with it, the town fathers would have had her tarred and feathered and shipped back north.

The book club upended the grapefruit cart, but that wasn't all. Jackie had also started a secret radio show she called *Miss Dreamsville* on WNOG, "Wonderful Naples on the Gulf." This was the first late-night radio show in Naples. I don't know what goes on in Boston, but in Collier County, Florida, a middle-aged wife and mother like Jackie had no business having her own radio show, especially if it involved the deliberate cultivation of a secret, seductive persona (or to use Jackie's favorite term, "temptress").

Then, Jackie came up with her wildest idea yet. She volunteered to take care of a baby so that its unmarried mother—our book club member, Priscilla—could go to college. Plain Jane and Mrs. Bailey White agreed to help. Now this was an extraordinary offer that would have been considered an act of great Christian charity except for one thing. Priscilla and her baby were colored.

Oh, that was more than enough to cause "big trouble."

And yet it didn't make sense that Dolores Simpson would send the telegram. She held a grudge against Jackie. Why would she care if Jackie was in trouble up to her ears?

Mrs. Conroy had moved on to another hymn, "Up from the Ground He Arose," never my favorite, but at the moment, hearing it sung by Mrs. Conroy with her machine-gun vibrato, made me want to beg for mercy. Although I could have borrowed Mrs. Conroy's telephone I slipped out the front door and scurried to the phone box on the corner. I thought I'd try to call Jackie since Dolores didn't have electricity let alone a phone. As luck would have it, the long-distance operator could not get through to anyone in Collier County. A storm had knocked down the lines in Lee County, north of Collier, and it would be another day or two before calls could go through.

So this is what I did: I borrowed money from Mrs. Conroy. And I took one Trailways bus after another all the way back to Collier County. It was the same route I'd taken a year earlier, only in reverse.

The last stretch from Tampa to Naples on the Tamiami Trail was the longest, or so it seemed. I asked the driver to drop me off at a little side road that led to an area known as Gun Rack Village. It was a sorry excuse for a road, but the only way to get to Dolores Simpson's fishing shack unless you had a small boat with a shallow draft.

The bus driver made me promise to be careful. His warning that I better watch out for swamp things was good advice. I whistled and sang, or banged my hand on my little suitcase, just to keep from catching any snakes or gators by surprise.

I found Dolores sitting on the step to the rickety dock that led to her two-room fishing shack. She was whittling a stick into a small weapon known as a "gig." At any other time and place I would have been wary of someone crafting a spear, but seeing her there, knife in hand, made me feel downright nostalgic. I realized I'd been gone too long. This was the Everglades, the River of Grass. To the Seminole Indians, it was "Pa-hay-okee."

To me, it was simply home.

Three

Dolores spat out a big stream of tobacco juice. "Well, it's about time you got here," she barked, barely glancing up from her handiwork.

This was not the greeting I expected. "I left as soon as I could," I said, thinking that the least she could do was be impressed, maybe even grateful, that I'd done what she'd asked. "You know, Jackson, Mississippi, is a long way from here. I had to borrow money—"

"I don't care about that," Dolores said.

"Well, are you going to tell me what this is about?" My voice was high and squeaky. I hated that, especially when I was trying to sound confident and mature.

She kept whittling.

"Look, Dolores, I think you owe me an explanation."

She still didn't answer.

"Is this about Jackie Hart from the book club?"

"That woman's a damn fool, and so is old Mrs. Bailey White

and that other gal—what's her name, Plain Jane—who are helping raise that baby."

I had a terrible thought. "Is Priscilla's baby all right?"

"Baby's fine," Dolores said.

"Then what is it?" I must have been on my last good nerve because I spoke sharply. "You sent me a Western Union! What in tarnation is the 'big trouble' you were talking about?"

She finally stopped whittling and looked me eyeball to eyeball.

"Your ex-husband," she said.

"Darryl?"

"Well, that is his name, isn't it?"

I felt my face flush. "I'm surprised, is all." Darryl was a pain in the hindquarters, to be sure, but I would never have put him in the category of "big trouble."

"Well, let me be the first to tell you," Dolores said. "He wants to build houses on my land. And a shopping center! And maybe even a golf course! He's going to fill in this whole stretch of the river and run us all out of here." She dropped her head and took a sharp breath. Maybe, I realized, to cover up a sob.

I felt light-headed. "Darryl doesn't have that kind of money," I said finally. "Besides, he's dumb as a post. He doesn't have the smarts to dream up a project like that, or make it happen."

Dolores scoffed so loud she startled a night heron nesting halfway up a tree about thirty feet away.

"Aw, shucks," Dolores called over to the heron, "I ain't going to hurt you. Now just settle down on yer ol' eggs and stop your frettin'."

I looked over toward the mama night heron, my eyes searching until I saw the familiar shape of its beak and the markings on its little head. They were odd-looking birds on account of their yellow eyes with red irises. Plus, they didn't sing. Instead, they made a sound like the cranky old crows that used to raid Mama's sunflower garden the minute we turned our backs.

"Your Darryl has got hisself help—people from up north will be paying for it."

"He's not 'my' Darryl."

"You were married to the idiot for a few years. I thought you could try to talk some sense into him. Besides, who loves this here river more than you do?"

Well, that was true. I was known for bringing all kinds of swamp and river critters home with me, which Mama, amazingly, tolerated. After a while, folks around the county had gotten to recognize I had a special talent with turtles. After I rescued an Everglades snapping turtle the size of a truck tire from the middle of U.S. 41, folks started calling me the Turtle Lady. From then on, people brought turtles to me that needed help. Three of them stayed on as pets—Norma Jean, Myrtle, and Castro.

I looked again at the mama heron. A heron nest was a messy-looking pile of sticks, and I remembered, with a flush of shame, that years before I had made fun of one when I'd been out for a walk with Mama in these very swamps. She'd said to me, "Now, it may not look like much to you but no doubt it is perfectly suited to the heron. The heron knows what it's doing, rest assured."

Dolores followed my gaze. "Huh, she's giving you the stink eye," she said of the heron. "She don't like being stared at, especially by a stranger."

This seemed a surprising side of Dolores. It didn't fit with her reputation. It was hard to imagine tenderness of any kind in her heart, but then again, she had raised Robbie-Lee and he was the nicest man I ever met. Go figure.

"Dolores," I said, trying to get back to the problem at hand. "What do you expect me to do about it? About Darryl, I mean?"

"Don't you go rushing me, girl," Dolores snapped. Her raised voice was met with two sharp squawks, like warning shots, from the heron.

"Aw, will you just stop worrying yourself to death?" Dolores called to the bird. "Do you think I'm going to cook you for my supper? If I was going to do that, I'd have done it already."

"Dolores, look, I want to help, but I don't know if I can stop Darryl," I said. "I'm just one person, and I haven't even lived here the past year, and—"

She hurled her whittling to the ground and jumped up with clenched fists, her arms flailing like a toddler having a tantrum. For a split second I thought she might run straight for me and strangle the life out of me, so I stepped backward, tripping over my suitcase and landing on my rear end. The heron, apparently unhappy with the commotion, burst from its nest, wings a-flapping, in what struck me as an almost-perfect imitation of Dolores.

"You can't let him do this!" Dolores screamed. Half sprawled in the sand, I felt like a turtle that finds itself upside down. I heard the sound of fast-moving footsteps heading away from me—thank you, Jesus. A door slammed, and I felt momentarily relieved. She'd gone inside.

Then it dawned on me that I was in a fine pickle. Soon it would be dark in the swamp, and I wasn't about to walk back to the Tamiami Trail with no flashlight or torch. Moonbeams had a way of illuminating sandy paths that weren't visible during the daytime, making it easy to get confused—and lost—at night.

I'd been so eager to talk to Dolores I'd scurried right over to see her, right off the bus. I guess I thought she'd invite me inside and we'd talk. It hadn't occurred to me that we'd have a big fuss and she'd leave me outside all night.

The fall had knocked the wind out of my lungs. I spent several long moments just looking around me. Dolores had made some improvements to the fishing shack since her son had left home. The front door, if you could call it that, had been painted shocking pink. A hand-carved sign, stuck in the ground and tilting wildly like a forgotten grave-marker, read Home Sweet Home. Off to the right, brush had been cleared away from the outhouse which now featured the words "Powder Room" painted in a girlish script.

But the 'Glades were coming alive with evening sounds. I soon decided that gators, snakes, and panthers were, in fact, scarier than Dolores—although frankly I wasn't 100 percent sure. I struggled back to my feet and edged my way carefully along the dock toward the shack, which sat like a little island on rough-hewn pilings. As I knocked, I ducked to one side, just in case she answered with a shotgun blast.

When she didn't respond, I called out, hoping she could hear me. "Dolores, you know I can't stay out here all night. I need to borrow a flashlight."

Nothing. Quiet as a grave.

I tried again. "Dolores, what would Robbie-Lee say if he knew you weren't looking after me?"

The latch clicked and the door swung open.

"Don't you go saying my son's name," Dolores said. "He ain't here anyway. He up and left me. Went to New York City."

"He'll be back," I said gently. "He's young, and just wanted to see a little more of the world. Just like I did."

"See the world," she harrumphed. "I guess the 'Glades ain't good enough for the likes of you, or him." She paused. "Why would anyone in his right mind go to New York City?"

I couldn't argue with her on that point. Mississippi wasn't exactly a stone's throw away, but at least it was the South.

I noticed she had a drink in her hand. I wasn't sure if this was a good sign or not. "You must hear from him—right? Does he send letters? He should be sending letters," I said, taking her side.

"Yes, he writes me letters but he doesn't tell me much of anything. Says a whole lot of nothing in them letters. Just things about pretty parks and big, tall buildings." Suddenly, she brightened. "He saw Liz Taylor outside some theater on Broadway."

"Really?" I asked, forgetting my problems. "Robbie-Lee saw Elizabeth Taylor in person?"

"Yes, he did," Dolores replied proudly. "She was going to see a play, and he said he was maybe ten feet from her, with him working in the theater and all."

"Well, ain't that something?" I said. "Was she just as purty in person? Did he say in the letter?"

"Oh, purtier!" Dolores replied, as certain as if she'd been there herself. "Can you imagine seeing a Hollywood person like Elizabeth Taylor in the flesh?"

"She was my mama's favorite movie star," I said softly.

"Mine, too," Dolores said wistfully. "Ever since I saw her in *Father of the Bride*."

Now I was really seeing another side of Dolores Simpson. I had trouble imagining Dolores in a movie theater at all, let alone watching such a sweet and charming movie. Of course, that film had come out fourteen years ago, in 1950, and it made me wonder what Dolores must have been like when she was younger.

Then I had a memory of Mama, talking about forgiveness and how hard it was for her to get past the fact that Elizabeth Taylor stole someone else's husband. My mind was a thousand miles away when suddenly I realized Dolores was peering at me as if she'd never really seen me before. All this talk about Elizabeth Taylor had altered the air we were breathing.

"Come in," she said finally.

THE NEXT MORNING I WOKE up on an ancient horse-hair couch that smelled like spilled beer, stale cigarettes, and low tide. An old metal spring was poking into my back.

She had left me a note, written in pencil in all capital letters. THIS HERE CORNBREAD IS FOR YOU. TAKE IT AND EAT. TAKE A COKE, TOO. SORRY IT BE WARM. COME BACK AFTER YOU'VE TALKED TO DARRYL.

Talk to Darryl? Oh Lord, in my disoriented state, I'd almost forgotten. Honestly, I'd rather have met the devil before daylight but I had agreed the night before that this was the next step. If it was true that he was going to pave over this part of the 'Glades, I needed to hear it from the horse's mouth. And give him a piece of my mind.

And find out where he got the money to pull off such an idea.

And find a way to stop it. Or at least, keep it from happening right here.

I washed down the cornbread with Coke and was revived enough to start walking back to the Trail. I noticed, as I left, that the mama night heron was using the Home Sweet Home sign for a perch. She stared at me warily as I walked past. I was tempted to say howdy but thought better of it. Poor thing had been through our ruckus the night before. As Mama used to say, "When it comes to Nature, leave it be."

The thick smell of the 'Glades made me feel drugged or a little feverish. I wasn't used to the overwhelming clash of plant life anymore, some of it quite stinky in its own right but bunched together, almost nauseating. Mixed in was a vague scent of decay, helped along by humidity that was almost indescribable, though a high-school friend had come close when he said it felt like being caught in a downpour, only it was raining up. On particularly hot days, Jackie, in her wry Northern way, would say, "How refreshing! Essence of Swamp!" which was funny but always made me feel inferior. However, having been away for a year, I could see her point.

As I marched along, I tried to picture my friend Robbie-Lee making this same trek day after day for years, just to get to school or the library or anywhere. And I wondered how in the world he had survived growing up with Dolores as his mother.

After disturbing several snakes along the way, I finally reached the Trail where, mercifully, I got a ride from a truck driver heading south to Everglades City. I guess I was a pathetic sight, walking down the side of the road with a suitcase in my hand. I offered him a dollar when he dropped me off by the Esso station, but he wouldn't take it. Told me I'd better take good care of myself, and that's when I realized that I must've looked like death warmed over in a saucepan. I didn't want anyone else to see me like that. Pride is a sin and so is vanity, but who wants to return to her hometown looking like a wilted orchid?

It was still early, and Naples was not fully stirring. I walked quick as I could, hoping I wouldn't run into anyone. It was already hot as Hades, and I had to catch my breath twice. While I was confident that Judd Hart, Jackie's teenage son, had been taking good care of my pet turtles, I was eager to see them. I managed to half run the last hundred yards to my little cottage with my little suitcase bumping against my thigh at every step.

I opened the gate and stepped into the yard. Nothing stirred, so I whistled and stayed still. I whistled a second time and heard some rustling. Slowly, they came out from their hiding places, their heads poking out, curious. And then they lumbered toward me, picking up speed, with Norma Jean, always the boss, in the lead. When they got close they stopped short. They didn't have the greatest eyesight in the world but as soon as they heard my voice they knew it was me.

I wanted to spend the next hour right there in the front yard but I had to go inside and pull myself together. Happily, the cottage did not need airing out. Judd had clearly been following my instructions.

I unpacked my suitcase and showered. Only then did I allow myself to settle into Mama's favorite chair. How I missed her. In the year I had spent away I had often imagined sitting in her chair and feeling comforted, and I did. But I also felt a deep stab of sadness.

I was born right here in this little cottage. There wasn't a nickel to spare for a doctor, not that there was usually one available, especially with the Depression going on. Thankfully, Mama had been trained as a nurse and so she birthed me herself.

Mama used to say that at least Daddy left us with a roof over our heads. Not that it was much of a roof. Every time we had a hurricane it leaked in a new and mysterious way, and Mama and I would spend the duration of the storm moving mop buckets from place to place until we were too tired to care. The year I turned fifteen, Mama finally had enough money set aside from her part-time nursing jobs to have it fixed proper.

When I married Darryl, a local boy I'd known since child-hood, we set up housekeeping all the way up in Ocala. I wasn't happy about it, but Darryl had landed a good construction job. Before long Mama took sick, and I began spending more time with her in Naples than with Darryl in Ocala.

That's when I found out that Darryl had a mean streak. He didn't like me being away from him, even for a good reason. The sicker Mama got, the more petty and irritated Darryl became. Later, I spent a lot of time trying to decide if he'd changed over-night or if he'd always been that way and I had failed to notice.

Mama and I both thought she had glade fever and it would pass once the weather turned. But even when the rains ended, she was still feeling puny. I knew things were bad when she gave up all her part-time nursing jobs, one by one, including her favorite, her twice-daily visit to check on Miss Maude Mobley, who was ninety-three and lived alone. Miss Mobley had out-lived all her friends and kin. She didn't need to be in a state home; she just needed someone like Mama to make sure she was taking her liver pills and eating proper. Mama wouldn't rest easy until I went to Miss Mobley's church and asked the preacher to find someone to take Mama's place.

Not that anyone could take Mama's place. I always knew that was the case, but imagining and living it are two different things. Her final decline happened sooner than I expected. Without telling me, Mama slipped out one morning while I was shop-ping at the Winn-Dixie. She took the bus to Fort Myers, where she saw a blood doctor. When she came home, she told me she had cancer and they couldn't fix it. Two weeks after Mama saw the doctor in Fort Myers, she crossed over to the Spirit World in her sleep.

After the burial, I went up to Ocala, packed up my things,

and came home. Now it was just me at the little cottage on the Gulf. Me and my turtles.

Returning home to Naples as a divorced woman was even harder than I thought it would be. People I'd known my whole life—even old pals from school—avoided me. I got a job at the post office and was thankful for it, but on the days I was assigned to counter duty I found myself having to make small talk with people who looked down on me. If not for Jackie Hart and her book club, I'd have remained friendless.

These memories were exhausting, and I was tempted to let myself fall asleep in Mama's chair. The deep, soft cushions still smelled of her.

But my mind was too restless. Part of me wanted to handle Darryl on my own to show everyone that little Dora Witherspoon was more independent and confident than she used to be. This was plain foolishness, however, and I could practically feel Mama glaring down at me from the Other Side. Mama would have said there was no shame in asking for help, in which case I had only one place to turn: my old book club. If anyone could stop Darryl, it was the members of the Collier County Women's Literary Society. Especially, an outspoken woman from Boston named Jackie Hart.

Four

Dolores Simpson sat on the dock that led to her fishing shack and wondered how she'd ended up here, alone, on the edge of the 'Glades with no one to talk to except a nervous night heron. Nothing in her life had gone right. She wasn't even sure who she was anymore. Truth be told, she wasn't even Dolores Simpson.

Her real name was Bunny Ann McIntyre. She always wondered what her mama had been thinking when she wrote those words in the family Bible. Of course, when she became a grown girl and was working as a stripper (she preferred "fan dancer") in Tampa, Bunny was a perfectly suitable name. At least she didn't have to come up with something new and catchy like all the other girls. The funny thing was, girls named Mary, Elizabeth, and Susan who became Safire, Sugar, or Bubbles were annoyed that she was, in fact, an actual Bunny. Why this bothered them was a mystery to her, but then women in general had always seemed more complicated than men.

When she fled from that life and moved back to the Everglades, she wanted a new name to go with a new life. On the bus heading south from Hillsborough County, a lady in a tailored navy suit left a magazine on the seat next to her. Dolores picked it up and flipped to a random page where she began reading about a woman named Dolores Simpson who owned a six-bedroom home, an Olympic-sized swimming pool, a maid, and even a Lincoln Continental. And she hadn't done it by marrying some man. No, according to the story, she had started her own business. She was even quoted as saying she *didn't need* a man in her life. Incredible! How she wished she could be that woman, and if she couldn't, well, at least she could borrow her name.

Good-bye, "Bunny." Hello, "Dolores."

But a lot of good it had done her.

She spat a stream of tobacco juice, taking care not to hit the pink bougainvillea that Robbie-Lee had planted at the foot of the dock. Dolores had learned the hard way that bougainvillea, which was generally quite hardy, would shrivel up and die if it had an unlucky encounter with tobacco spit. While she wasn't partial to flowers, Dolores couldn't see the sense in ruining a perfectly good plant. Besides, Robbie-Lee was fond of it, and she wanted it to be here looking purty when he came back.

If he came back.

"*Oooh*, my son is gone. Gone to see the world," she moaned softly. Adding, "Fool. Dang fool."

She wished she could direct that nasty stream of tobacco juice right at the feet of the folks who had created her problems. First was Jackie Hart, that trouble-making redhead from Boston. Robbie-Lee had been doing just fine until Jackie came along. The boy had a promising future which he now had thrown away. He'd managed to get hisself the rarest kind of job, one in which he didn't get his hands dirty. As the sole employee for Sears, Roebuck & Company in Collier County, he'd helped folks place their orders from the catalog. It didn't matter that the Sears Center where he worked was the size of an ice cream stand. He wore nice clothes to work and he wasn't going to age overnight the way most of the menfolk in Collier did, either from the fishing industry or farming melons and sugarcane.

But then all of a sudden he left for New York City. Just like that. New York City! Inspired by that awful woman, Jackie Hart, who put it in his head that he was missing something. Well, dagnabbit, if he wanted to go north so badly he could have gone to Fort Myers, or Sarasota, or maybe even Apalachicola. At least he would have still been in Florida. He'd have still been squarely on Confederate turf. But why New York City? It wasn't even part of the United States, as far as Dolores was concerned.

She looked over at the night heron. "Oh, just you wait and see," Dolores said mournfully. "Being a mother is hard. When they grow up, they gonna do what they gonna do. Your young'uns will do the same to you that my boy did to me.

"But he'll be back one day," she added, this time to herself. "I know he will."

The second person who had messed up her life was Darryl Norwood, ex-husband of that little gal, Dora Witherspoon. She hoped she'd gotten through to Dora. The telegram had worked to bring her back here. Maybe there was some hope that the river could be saved.

If not, she would have nowhere to go. "Things won't be so peachy for you, either," she called over to the bird. "You're going to be the last night heron in Collier County. What we have here is a mighty bad situation. At least you can fly away. You can start over. I can't. I'm good for nothin'. I'm stuck."

Dolores examined her hands. Twenty-five years working

in the 'Glades, and they looked like the skin of the alligators she caught. But that was the least of her worries. Back when she'd been a dancer, the owner of the club had complained that her breasts were too small. Unless she allowed liquid filler to be injected into her breasts, she would lose her job. She'd gone along with it. Now they were lumpy, and hard, and hurt in ways she didn't think possible. How stupid she'd been when she was young. Some mistakes you pay for, forever.

Her first mistake was thinking she was in love. She was fifteen and had just finished eighth grade. When her belly started swelling, she thought maybe she had worms, or possibly a hernia. But her mama and daddy knew otherwise. They threw her out.

She'd hitchhiked to Tampa on the back of a tomato truck in pouring rain. She still didn't know what was wrong with her or why her parents made her leave, but a stranger on the streets of Tampa took one look at her and walked her to a hospital emergency room. Three hours later she had her baby. The nuns convinced her she was racked by sin and not worthy to be a mother. She never had a chance to hold the baby. She wasn't even sure if the baby was alive or healthy, and there were times when she wondered if she had dreamed the whole thing.

She left that hospital four days later on her own two feet, alone. She hitchhiked to the beach in St. Pete and survived by stealing picnics from tourists. Being so young, her body bounced back quickly, and soon she got herself a job at a nightclub. It was only after she showed up on her first day of work that she found out she was to be a dancer, not a waitress. She went along with it, thinking she'd do it just for a while, but "a while" turned into seven years. And that's when she got pregnant again.

The owner of the nightclub suggested an option that would,

as he said, "fix" the situation but Dolores was too scared to consider it. One of the other dancers—a sweet-faced girl from Alabama—had gone to an underground clinic and died.

Surrendering another baby to the State of Florida was out of
the question, as far as Dolores was concerned. This baby was a
keeper, come what may. She had him at the same hospital as the
first one, only this time she was prepared. She scooped him up
and took off out of there before somebody could thrust papers in
her face and hand her a pen. She named him Robbie-Lee after
a crop reporter she liked to listen to on the radio. A man who
sounded nice, day in and day out, whether he was discussing the
worrisome possibility of a January freeze in the orange groves or
warning listeners about a fierce storm that had popped up over
the Gulf on a summer day. Sometimes the friendly voice asked
questions which he quickly answered himself. For example: *Did
you know that Tampa is the lightning capital of the United States?*
(Well, it is!) Or: *Did you know that many historians believe our city
gets its name from the Calusa Indians, or the Shell People, because
"Tampa" means "sticks of fire" in their ancient language?* (Well, it
does!) So her radio announcer was smart as well as nice, a qual-
ity which Dolores admired.

Within hours of leaving the hospital, she fled the area with
Robbie-Lee curled up like a kitten under a silk scarf she'd
snatched years earlier from a Canadian traveler, or "snowbird."
She skipped out of Dodge without so much as a fare-thee-well
to anyone, not wanting to alert her landlord, who would have
had her sent to jail for being late on the rent. Never mind that
her baby would be taken from her.

All she could think of was to head back down to Collier
County. That's what people do when they're almost out of hope,
right? Head home? She had heard through the grapevine that

her parents were dead, so at least she didn't have to face their scorn again. And Collier County was familiar. As for making a living, her granddaddy had hunted gators in the 'Glades back in the day, and she thought, *Well, heck, I can do that. I watched him do it. I helped him do it.*

Besides, she figured, huntin' gators couldn't be any harder or more dangerous than working in some old strip club. In fact, it might be easier.

The years slipped by like the hidden currents in the river. She wouldn't have said she'd been happy—she wasn't sure what that felt like—but she wasn't miserable. She got by, and folks left her alone. Most importantly, Robbie-Lee had grown up handsome, clever, and nice, just as she'd dreamed.

If only Robbie-Lee had stayed away from that book club he would be here, helping her with the gators. She hated to admit it but she had come to rely on Robbie-Lee to lend a hand with the big, unruly ones. Since he'd left, she'd pretty much given up the gator business altogether. Especially after an odd thing happened: She had started feeling sorry for the critters. She'd never sympathized with the big ones, which would just as soon eat her up, but the little ones—the only kind she could now grab hold of these days—well, they were almost cute! This had come as a shock to her, and she had quietly started retiring her gear.

She was living on fish she could catch from her dock. She sold grunts—minnows, the Yankees called 'em—to the bait shops, always setting aside a healthy portion for herself. She rolled the tiny things in flour and fried 'em up whole, just like her granddaddy did, and served 'em with a mess of grits. Indeed, there was nothing Dolores liked better than a big ol' plate of grits and grunts.

And now someone wanted to take it all away. To some folks

it probably wouldn't have seemed like much. But to her, it was a little slice of heaven.

How could a man grow up in the 'Glades and fail to see its beauty? How could he look at it and see only money? She'd run into plenty of men like Darryl in her life. They thought of no one other than themselves. They weren't any different from the school-yard bullies who used to pick on Robbie-Lee, calling him "homo" and other names. Darryl and those just like him, she decided, were evil.

The person who was harder to understand was Jackie. She had a nice home, a husband with a steady job, a couple of kids, and a Buick convertible. What else could a woman want? *If I had that kind of life*, Dolores thought wistfully, *I would be busy living it. I wouldn't waste my time creating problems and meddling in other people's business.*

Dolores had never met anyone from Boston and wondered if they were all like Jackie. First of all, that peculiar accent that was near impossible to understand. Plus the bizarre urge to speak your mind and have everything upfront and out in the open. And the worst Yankee trait of all, a missionary zeal to fix everything Southern.

Not that Jackie was a bad person. She wasn't evil like Darryl. She was just a Yankee and, typical of the Northern born, couldn't leave well enough alone.

Five

"There's something I need to tell you, Miss Witherspoon," Judd Hart was saying, and I noticed he wouldn't look me in the eye. When he heard I was back in town, Judd made a beeline to my cottage to say hello. With his red hair and blue eyes, it was easy to see that he was Jackie's son. He was thirteen now and about four inches taller than when I left. We were sitting on the bottom step of my porch, feeding pieces of honeydew melon to my snappers. Of course, this meant having to scold Norma Jean from time to time. She was such a piggy, and I could see she hadn't changed a bit.

"Judd," I said, "you don't have to call me Miss Witherspoon. You can call me Dora."

"I can't call you Dora. You're a grown-up."

"Well, then, call me Miss Dora," I said.

Judd frowned. I guess that was too Southern.

"Well," I prompted him, "what is it you want to tell me?" I tried to hide the nervousness from my voice. "Is it about all this business with my former husband and the development he wants to build?"

"No, not that," Judd said. "I just wanted to warn you that when you see my mom, she'll look a little, um, different."

All I could think of was that maybe Jackie had changed her hair, or gained weight.

Judd looked away. "She'll be wearing black," he mumbled.

"What?"

"Black. You know, mourning clothes."

"Oh, Judd! Someone in your family went to Glory? No one told me! I'm so sorry! Who was it?" My heart went into a tailspin of pity and sorrow. Poor Jackie!

"Well, no one in our . . . family." Judd looked miserable.

"Then . . . who?" I asked.

"President Kennedy."

Hmmm. Jackie had been wearing mourning clothes—for President Kennedy? Since the previous November? In three months it would be a year. I had figured she took it hard but I didn't think she would carry on this long.

"She says she's going to wear them for one year and a day," Judd went on. "I just didn't want you to be surprised."

"Judd, let me ask you something, and it might seem like a silly question," I said. "You know I've never been up north. What I want to know is, is this something all Yankees do?" In my head, I was picturing everyone in Boston walking around in black.

"Nope," Judd said. "I don't think so. I'm pretty sure she's the only one in America, other than the Kennedy family, of course. This is just Mom being Mom."

"Oh," I said, at a loss for words. So wearing black for a year, for a president not everyone liked (especially in the South), would be considered odd even in Boston. There were times like this when I got a hint that Jackie was over the top even for a Yankee. "Well," I said, finally finding my voice, "as the saying goes, 'To each his own.'"

Judd suddenly seemed defensive. "I guess with her being from Boston and all, and she's such a fan of Mrs. Kennedy, and all that . . ." His voice trailed off. He tried to grin but it came off as a lame little smile, so he shrugged instead. "I didn't want you to be, you know, caught off guard. Because when I told her I'd heard you were back in town, she ran to get dressed and I know she's headed over here any minute now."

We'd run out of melon strips to give the turtles. Castro and Myrtle had gone into the shrubs to take naps. Norma Jean was still begging for goodies. She stared at us and made munching movements with her mouth. "Yes, we see you, Norma Jean," I said, laughing. It was hard to miss an Everglades snapping turtle the size of Mama's divan.

"You know what, Judd?" I said. "You've done a fine job here, looking after my friends."

Judd beamed at my compliment. "I really mean that," I added. "I wouldn't have gone off to Mississippi if you hadn't been here to take care of my turtles. And check on my little cottage. But everything looks swell. Did you have any problems?"

"No, ma'am," he said, and I was pleased to hear the "ma'am" roll off his tongue, since a Boston boy wouldn't survive down here for long if he didn't learn the basics. Seems like he'd settled in fairly good.

And then he asked me a question I didn't know the answer to. "How long are you going to be back for?"

"I don't know, Judd." I sighed before continuing. "I've still got something I need to do back in Mississippi. But I've got to see if I can help Robbie-Lee's mother. She's going to lose her home if my stupid former husband"—I paused for a moment, regretting that I had referred to Darryl in such a mean-spirited way in front of Judd—"uh, if my former husband fills in the swamp over there."

Judd was quiet for a moment. "But where would all the turtles, and the gators and everything, go?" he asked.

I was thinking Judd might be a great ally when we both heard brakes squeal. Before you could say "Sweet Jesus, protect me from whatever that is," Jackie's convertible slid to a halt in the wind-driven sand that always seemed to pile up on the street directly in front of my cottage. There was no one else in Naples who drove quite like that. And, there was no other car like that south of Tampa: a completely impractical, two-door, banana-yellow 1960 Buick LeSabre for which she had traded, in a moment of pure rebellion, her dull and matronly station wagon.

We loved that car. Oh, how we all loved it. No one else in our book club owned a car, and Jackie had enjoyed driving us around. It was wonderful to see her again, right behind the wheel, which is how I usually pictured her in my mind although the effect was altered somewhat since she was indeed wearing black. A black head scarf. Black gloves. Black cat-eye sunglasses. And, of course, a black dress that was tasteful but not especially demure. Probably, from that store she was always talking about, Filene's.

Black is not an easy color to wear in Florida under the best of circumstances and, in Naples, it was always a signal that someone had up and died. Black was for grieving and condoling only. Of course, that might not have been true, say, in Miami or some other place where they had bona fide nightclubs. Here in Naples the only place was the Shingle Shack, and I doubt any woman ever wore black unless she was coming straight from the kind of funeral that drives a woman to drink.

Jackie leaned on the car horn, a Yankee habit that made me want to reach for smelling salts. Why in the name of Our Sweet Savior did she think this was necessary? Did she think we couldn't see her? She was smiling and waving her arm with the kind of jaunty Northern confidence that annoys the beeswax out of Southerners. Plain Jane, the poet from our book club, was sprawled in the backseat like she was sunbathing on a chaise lounge. I almost hadn't noticed her.

"Woo hoo!" I called out, once I had recovered from the car horn. "So great to see y'all! Git yourselves out of that crazy car and come set on the porch with me and Judd for a spell!" But as soon as I raised my voice, I could feel Mama's disapproval coming straight down from the Spirit World like a bolt of lightning, since hollerin' was "not nice." Mama was always talking about things that were either "nice" or "not nice." That was pretty much how she saw the world. Judd, Jackie, and Plain Jane were probably wondering why I sprang up, rabbit-like, rather than shout again, but I knew better than to disrespect Mama. It didn't matter than she was six feet under at the Cemetery of Hope and Salvation over by the Esso station.

Jackie and Plain Jane had both climbed out of the car, and I thought we were going to have a bear-hug reunion, but when I got to the gate and started fussing with the latch, Jackie started screeching like a banshee on a coconut-milk binge. "Don't open it!" she pleaded.

I had plumb forgot that Jackie was scared to pieces of my turtles. It was a wonder she let Judd look after them while I was away. For the sake of friendship, and to keep Jackie calm, I climbed over my own fence. Jackie, Plain Jane, and me had a three-way hug like a football huddle. You know you like some-one, and truly missed them, when you don't mind embracing them in the suffocating heat of Florida in August.

I wasn't sure about other book clubs, but making a decision, even with just three of us present, required more discussion than Khrushchev and Kennedy probably had during the entire Cuban Missile Crisis. Plain Jane wanted to sit on my porch and sip iced tea and get caught up. Jackie balked on account of my turtles which (a little rudely, in my opinion) she kept referring to as "those dreadful things." She suggested we go to her house and drink mimosas. I knew what I wanted to do, but I waited for the two of them to talk their ideas to death. Finally, there was a lull. "Where's the baby?" I asked. "I'm dying to see her."

Instantly, it was agreed that we would all go to Mrs. Bailey White's house, where the baby spent most of her time.

Judd was obviously relieved that we were leaving. Jackie called to him, "Honey, I made some chili for you and the twins. Go ahead and eat if I'm not home in time for supper. And there's a special honeydew melon that I bought just for you."

As we were driving away, two things occurred to me. One was that the aforementioned honeydew melon was, in all likeli-hood, the same one Judd and I had just fed by hand to "those dreadful things."

The second was that I was thrilled to be back with Jackie and Plain Jane in the Buick. On the radio, the Supremes were singing "Where Did Our Love Go?" and for the moment, all was right with the world.

Six

Mrs. Bailey White's house was haunted. How could it not be? Someone had died an unnatural death there. That someone was Mrs. Bailey White's husband. Although what really happened was a topic of popular debate in Collier County, and Mrs. Bailey White insisted it was self-defense, she had been convicted. And she went to prison for decades.

I have to admit I was scared of Mrs. Bailey White when she showed up at Jackie's book club at the library two years before. We all got the creepy-crawlies but were too polite to ask her to leave. It never occurred to us that we would grow to like her.

Now we were on the way to her house, which had become a familiar place to me. I rode up front with Jackie; Plain Jane stretched out again in the back. There was a time when people scowled at the sight of Jackie's outrageous car, but that was before the town discovered she was Miss Dreamsville, the incognito radio star. Now people smiled, a few waved, and some children even called out "Miss Dreamsville! Miss Dreamsville!" as we drove past. The impossible had happened: The town now tolerated Jackie as one of its own. She'd made Naples famous with her radio show, and even though she had quit the show (it wasn't as much fun, she said, now that everyone knew who she was), she would always be thought of as Miss Dreamsville, just as people would always call me the Turtle Lady, and Mrs. Bailey White would always be the Black Widow of Collier County. Like it or not, in the South, nicknames stick like bare feet in a clay pit.

Mrs. Bailey White's house was tucked back from the road. I still got a little *thumpety-thump* in my heart as we approached it, but when we rounded the bend of the long private drive I was surprised. Why, the old Victorian house looked almost present-able. The serpent-like vine that had gone up one side of the house, across the roof, and down the other side had been re-moved. There was a fresh layer of paint or stain, and the broken window on the third floor had been replaced. I wouldn't say the old house looked spiffy. There was still something about it that wasn't quite right, and I found my eyes searching for flaws. It simply looked tired, as if it were an older lady trying to reclaim her glory days by wearing an excess of Maybelline.

I'm pretty sure I'd never actually been hugged by Mrs. Bailey White, even when I climbed on the bus bound for Mississippi the year before, so I was a little shocked when she greeted me with a ferocious little embrace. This, despite her appearing more delicate. She didn't look older but somehow gave the impression of being more fragile, and yet I could see she hadn't given up in the way that some older ladies do. Her clothes and hair were tidy and there was a toughness in her manner that was hard to de-scribe. She was in a battle against decline, much like her house.

She excused herself to locate a bottle of wine she'd made from her rose blooms the previous year. I don't know what impressed me more, the fact that she was able to grow roses in Collier County or that she'd managed to make wine out of the faded blooms before they turned moldy. There was no telling what an old-timer like Mrs. Bailey White had stashed away in that mind of hers.

We were interrupted by a shrill sound, and for a second I thought a bird got itself caught in the chimney and couldn't find its way out.

"She's awake from her nap," Plain Jane announced, and I realized she was talking about the baby. "My turn," she said, clapping her hands together, and then practically ran up the stairs. Plain Jane looked thinner than I remembered, at least from behind. They were all getting older, I thought, a bit startled. Since I was past thirty I wasn't anyone's idea of a spring chicken but I wasn't in the same league. Plain Jane, as I said, was more or less sixty; Jackie had crossed the most dreaded boundary of all—forty. Mama would have lumped them all into the category "ladies of a certain age," which is a courteous way of referring to a woman past her "prime," a term which I'd always found annoying on account of it making you sound like a side of beef.

I didn't know about up north—I could ask Jackie someday, at a delicate moment—but here in the South, women were said to peak by twenty. By the time you were in your late twenties, it was said that the bloom was off the rose. While I was busy brooding over the unfair burdens placed on womankind, Plain Jane, beaming, appeared at the top of the steep staircase with a sleepy infant cuddled in her arms.

Eudora Welty Dreamsville Harmon—Dream, for short—lifted up her head when she spied a stranger—me. She was wearing a starched pink dress with matching pink hair clips and little white leather lace-up shoes. But what impressed me most were her eyes, large and soft and intense like a doe's, exactly like her mama's. She couldn't stop staring at me the whole time Plain Jane walked carefully down the stairs, until the moment I put out my arms to take her. Then she began to wail, and buried her face in Plain Jane's neck.

"That's okay, she doesn't know me at all," I said cheerfully, although I was—truth be told—a little sad. I hadn't seen Dream since she was four months old, and I knew she would have no memory of me. Still, the fact that she was so comfortable with the others made me feel like a fifth wheel. The baby was partly named after me—the Eudora Welty part—and Dream was a nod to Jackie being Miss Dreamsville. But I hadn't been around to watch her grow.

Mrs. Bailey White appeared with what I presumed to be the rose wine and ushered us into her parlor, which was dripping in lace and velvet and featured a horsehair sofa that no one wanted to sit on. With great care, she set up a neat little row of crystal glasses, nicer than anything I'd ever drunk from, that's for sure. When Dream turned her head and smiled right at Mrs. Bailey White, we all cooed with delight—even Jackie, who had never struck me as the cooing type. Considering that neither Mrs. Bailey White nor Plain Jane had children, and Jackie wasn't exactly June Cleaver on *Leave It to Beaver*, it was a pleasure to see they'd all got the mothering bug and were not just doing a perfunctory job.

Jackie offered a toast. "To Dora, who has returned to us. At least for now."

Mrs. Bailey White settled herself into a fine-looking rocking chair and stretched out her arms. "Let me have her," she said.

"Oh, all right," Plain Jane said reluctantly.

As I watched Mrs. Bailey White settle herself in the rocker

with Dream on her lap, I wondered to myself, *Why does this seem so strange?* And it dawned on me that I had never before seen a white woman with a colored baby on her lap. Negro women took care of white women's babies, not the other way around. And yet it seemed perfectly normal. No doubt it would upset plenty of white people to see this, but how could they object? It was love, that was all. Just love.

"Can you believe this, Dora?" Jackie asked, interrupting my thoughts.

"What?"

"That we're taking such good care of Dream? Aren't we just the most devoted mommies you've ever seen?"

"You surely are," I said. "How old is she now?"

"Sixteen months," Jackie said between sips of wine.

"Sixteen months and three weeks," Plain Jane corrected.

Mrs. Bailey White laughed. "And two days. Not that anyone's counting."

"Priscilla must be very happy with the job you're doing," I said.

"You just missed her," Jackie said. "She was here for three days, on one of her visits home."

This was disappointing news.

"But don't worry, I'm sure she'll be back soon," Jackie added, seeing my long face. "She comes home as often as she can."

"Is she doing well in school?" My mama would have said that was a "none of your business" question but I couldn't help it. I prayed that this arrangement was working out for Priscilla. I'd never been so surprised in my life as when I learned that she was expecting a baby. She wasn't married and there wasn't even a beau in the picture as far as I knew, and I thought we'd been pretty good friends. She was focused, mature, and diligent in the way she lived her life. But she was also very young, just nineteen when Dream was born, and, as they say, it only takes one mistake. No one—not even our Priscilla—was perfect.

If there was anyone who deserved a second chance in life, it was her. Although she had hoped to go to college, and shared her dream with us at book club meetings, on some level she never truly believed it could happen. A person gets tired of aiming for a dream that most folks think is pure foolishness, she said. One day she met a man and made what Mama would have called an "unwise choice." In a single moment of weakness, she nearly ruined her whole future. That is how she explained it—that it was a mistake—but in my own heart I wondered if she had allowed the pregnancy to happen as a way of giving up—of sabotaging her own dream—because she could not stand the strain.

And, indeed, that gal was under pressure. It wasn't until later that we understood that her community had placed its hopes on her shoulders. She was the one who showed the most promise, and she was expected to succeed. It wasn't just "Priscilla is going to follow her dream and go to college." It was, "Priscilla is going to make all *our* dreams come true by showing the other young folk how it's done."

When her disgrace became known, the most excruciating scorn was from those who felt let down. Then there were the jealous types who thought she'd been reaching too high, anyway. The way Priscilla told it, she had to endure the sneers of those who said, "I told you so" and "Ha, she's no better than the rest of us." When Jackie came up with her wild idea, giving Priscilla the chance to go to college anyway, part of her motivation, she confided in me, was to get away from her own people who were judging her. The other factor was that she really did want to go to college, and with Jackie and the others looking after Dream, she figured it must be part of God's plan. But it all hinged on whether she could make the adjustment—being away from home, the first person in her family to go to college, and leaving a baby behind might prove too much. While she'd written me several letters, I felt there was a lot she wasn't saying.

"She's doing great in school," Plain Jane said. "So far she's had perfect grades."

No surprise there. Priscilla was the smartest person I'd ever known.

"But how is she doing with . . ." I searched for the right words.

"With missing Dream?" Jackie said, finishing my question. "Well, as good as could be expected. I mean, she cries for hours before it's time for her to catch the bus back to Daytona Beach."

"But she wants to keep going?" I asked, saying aloud what I feared most to ask.

"So far, so good," Jackie said. "We're trying to make it as easy on her as possible by taking very good care of Dream. And they'll be reunited when Priscilla graduates."

To myself, I thought, *That's three more years. I hope Priscilla can hold on.*

"Well, all we can do is the best we can," Jackie said cheerfully. "And we are getting expert guidance from Priscilla's grandmother." This had been part of the deal: Priscilla's grandmother, who lived a few miles away and made a living working in the fields, would see the baby regularly.

"Now, let us hear about *you*, Dora," Plain Jane said warmly, "and why you are here. Not that you need a reason."

"Oh, I tell you *what*, being back home makes me realize how much I missed it," I said with a rush of emotion. "How much I missed *y'all*. But I have a little more I need to do in Jackson. And I can't leave my landlady hanging on forever."

"Well, however long you're here, we are happy to see you," Jackie said.

"We were just about to write you a long letter, just to let you know what's going on," Mrs. Bailey White said. She sounded a little uneasy.

"About Darryl," Jackie added, in her direct, Yankee way.

"Thank you," I said, suddenly feeling self-conscious. "But I got a telegram about it."

This raised a few eyebrows. "Really?" Jackie demanded. "From whom?"

I told them how Dolores Simpson had contacted me, hoping I would come home and talk some sense into Darryl. "Her house is right smack in the middle of where he plans to build," I said.

Jackie looked surprised and maybe a little impressed. So did Plain Jane and even Mrs. Bailey White. They'd all encountered Robbie-Lee's mother in the past and concluded they were no match for the former stripper turned alligator hunter who lived back in the swamps.

"So you saw her?" Jackie asked. "I mean, you've met with her since you got back?"

"Last night," I said. "Went straight to see her after getting off the bus. By the way, Mrs. Bailey White," I added, trying to divert the conversation away from Dolores Simpson, "have you looked at the maps? I'm worried that your house isn't all that far from Dolores's, at least as the crow flies. I hope you're not in the way of Darryl's plans."

A moment of dread seemed to settle in the room like a cloud of decades-old dust. "Not to worry," Mrs. Bailey White said. "I cornered the mayor when I was at the bank recently. He wouldn't give me any details but he said I wouldn't be affected. He said I'm near the development but not directly in the way."

"But Darryl couldn't take your house, anyway, unless you wanted to sell," Plain Jane said.

"Oh, who knows what he could do, now that he seems to have the town fathers behind him," Mrs. Bailey White said in a voice that sounded world-weary.

"Who, exactly, are these 'town fathers'?" Jackie asked.

"The powerful people in town," Plain Jane said. "The mayor, of course, but also the high school football coach—he could probably burn the town down and get away with it—and also the preacher at First Baptist, plus the core group of people who come from good families with *old money*."

"My family was 'old money' people with a good name, except I kind of made a mess out of things," Mrs. Bailey White said sheepishly. "I mean by going to jail and all," she added, as if we didn't know what she meant.

"I think we need to look into Darryl's money source, 'cause he's getting financing from somewhere," Plain Jane said.

"Well, it's not from Mr. Toomb," Jackie said, referring to her husband's employer.

"How do you know that for sure?" I asked.

"A few weeks ago Ted was talking on the phone late at night with Mr. Toomb, and I picked up the extension in the kitchen and listened," she said. "Mr. Toomb was saying that he didn't like Darryl Norwood one bit, and that the young scallywag—that was the word he used—was too big for his britches. I think Darryl angered Mr. Toomb by not kowtowing to him. Mr. Toomb would expect a young man like Darryl to come to him first and let him know what his plans were."

"Well, then Darryl is getting his money from outside the county, and probably out of state," I said. "From people who won't care one bit about what happens here."

"Carpetbaggers," Mrs. Bailey White said ominously.

"What, like Sherman's march?" I asked. "Wrecking everything in his path? That was a hundred years ago, up in Georgia."

"Yeah, and there's been carpetbaggers in one way or another ever since," Mrs. Bailey White said gravely. "Always some Yankees sniffing around the wreckage and making money off the suffering of their Southern brethren."

"Oh, for Pete's sake!" Jackie said. "So Darryl may have Northern investors. That doesn't make them evil."

"The problem is that when money comes from somewhere else, there seems to be a lack of concern about the, uh, repercussions locally," Plain Jane said. "And there is a history of that in the South."

"*Ugh*, and what a bad combination!" I cried out. "A heartless local boy—*Darryl*—and Yankee investors! They'll probably pave over the whole Everglades."

"Is it really going to be all that bad?" Jackie asked. "It's just one project and I, for one, wouldn't mind if this town got a little larger. We sure could use some new people around here, maybe some new restaurants! And shopping . . ."

"*What?!*" I almost yelled. Dream, still cuddled in Mrs. Bailey White's lap, jerked her head around and studied my face. She looked like she was trying to decide if she should cry, or not. I surely was getting off on the wrong foot with Dream.

We all hushed, realizing we were disturbing the baby. Finally, Jackie spoke. "I'm sorry, Dora," she said softly. "I didn't realize how much you cared about Robbie-Lee's mother and the thought of her losing her house."

"It's not just about her and her house!" I said, trying to keep my voice level. "It's about the river, and all that precious land around it. Those swamps are not just empty space, you know."

Plain Jane interrupted. "Dora, you need to prepare yourself," she said in a tone that was both firm and kind. "A lot of folks around here see this as a good thing. It means lots of new jobs. The Chamber of Commerce is behind it, and they keep talking about construction jobs which will pay better than working in the fields or fishing. Plus, once the development is built, there will be jobs in retail, at restaurants, all kinds of new opportunities."

"Well, I'm all for new jobs but at what price?" I said, my tone bitter. "You want opportunity, go to a city! You need a job, then go to where the jobs are. Why ruin what we have here? What about nature? And what about the people who live back there and would have to leave?"

Back at my cottage later, I thought about all those who would lose their way of life, and have nowhere to go. All of them were already dirt poor. To my knowledge they weren't bothering anybody. It was almost as though the folks who ran Naples were upset that those poor folk *existed*. I'd heard it over and over again while I was coming up: Why don't *they* go somewhere *else*?

"They" were hardscrabble white folks like Dolores Simpson, a few Indians, and a small village of colored people who had been there since slavery days ended. The Negro settlement included Priscilla's grandmother. If poor, backwoods white folks and Indians were seen as a nuisance, Negroes were considered a threat, and there had been a not-so-subtle effort to relocate them where they could be watched and contained, notably, the construction of a complex of nine buildings called McDonald's Quarters in downtown Naples near the train depot. Every progressive Southern town had its Negro quarters, and in this regard, Naples refused to be left behind. The new complex was presented to the Negroes as a step up—a safe, modern environment with indoor plumbing and running water. Truth be told, it operated more like a prison, especially at night, since a curfew kept Negroes off the streets of Naples after sundown.

Some of the Negroes had refused to go to McDonald's Quarters, however. It wasn't lost on them that the place was called the Quarters, which was reminiscent of the slave quarters of yesteryear. Their rejection was denounced by the rich folks as sheer folly and a lack of gratitude. Occasionally there was some fussing about the "renegade" Negroes who had insulted the good people of Naples by refusing the town's hospitality and generosity.

And then it would die down again. I confess I didn't pay much attention unless Mama brought it up, which she did often. Mama always took the side of poor folks, regardless of color.

I wondered what Mama would have said about Darryl's project, and the words came through strong and straight from heaven. *Darryl's a shortsighted and greedy jerk*, I heard her say inside my head, and just thinking those words made me almost laugh out loud.

Was I imagining Mama's words or did I have a direct line to her, reposing as she was, beyond the pearly gates? It didn't matter. Her words rang true either way. The fact is I'd been assuming that moving poor folks away from the river would be a *consequence* of Darryl's project. Knowing my hometown, I now realized it was possible that getting rid of them was an underlying reason for the groundswell of support for Darryl in the first place.

Seven

Judd Hart showed up at my cottage the next morning with a small snapper whose shell had been damaged, probably by a lawn mower.

"Look, I fixed him up," Judd said, beaming but a little hesitant. He had used gauze and first-aid tape, and I wondered aloud if it would do the job. "Oh, I've been studying," Judd said. "Not that you were doing anything wrong," he added quickly, "but I read a copy of *National Geographic* magazine, and it said the shell has to breathe. We should never use any kind of epoxy, or heavy tape."

I had used anything I could think of over the years, even duct tape in emergencies, to hold an injured turtle's shell together. And here was Judd, at thirteen years old, showing me something new. I was humbled. He bit his bottom lip, and I realized he was afraid he might have offended me. Truth be told, I was a little embarrassed, but my instincts told me that Judd's need for praise was greater than my need to protect my pride. It couldn't be easy having Jackie for a mother, plus a dad who traveled a lot as the business manager for Mr. Toomb. This was a boy who might have benefited from having a brother, but instead he had two older sisters—identical twins—who were in their own little world. I'd never actually had a conversation with either of them.

"Judd," I said, "you're very wise and I'm sure you will go places in life. I am very impressed, and, on behalf of turtles everywhere, thank you."

He blushed a shade of red that nearly matched his hair. I realized if this conversation went on any longer it would be excruciating for him, so I changed the subject. "So, when does school start?" I asked.

His face fell. "Two weeks," he said sadly.

"Um, well, what grade will you be in?"

"Eight," he said, not sounding any happier.

I racked my brain for a better topic. I was not used to conversing with teenagers. "Oh," I said, "your mother mentioned that you joined the Civil Air Patrol."

"Yes!" he said, almost bowling me over with his enthusiasm. "I'm too young to fly but I can go along as a spotter. I'm going to keep doing it during the school year, though I'll have to cut back my hours. I had to persuade Mom that it would be okay, and convince my dad that it was something important I should do."

He was right: It was important. The Florida coastline was so vast that even the Coast Guard couldn't patrol every inch. The Civil Air Patrol filled the gap, with volunteers flying their own small planes to check for boaters in trouble. But the Naples Civil Air Patrol didn't just fly over the Gulf. They followed the rivers and streams into the Everglades. In recent years, the volunteer group had taken on an additional role that seemed straight out of a James Bond movie except it was real—to keep an eye out for suspicious activity since Collier County was so close to Cuba.

Judd told me about the things he had seen. There was a fishing boat that ran out of fuel and was in danger of sinking because of a problem with its bilge. And a tourist who fell asleep on a float and drifted too far from shore to swim back. "I saw something really strange last week," he said. "A lot of trees being cut down by the river a ways behind Mrs. Bailey White's house but further down."

If I'd had anything in my hands, I'd have dropped it. "*What?!* Wait, are you talking about where Darryl is planning his project? Are you saying he's already *started?*"

Judd looked panicky. "Well, I don't know . . . I mean, I don't know if it's his, or if something else is going on. But every day it seems like there's more trees cut down."

He was sorry he had brought it up. I could see it in his eyes. "Judd," I said, trying to be calm, "have you ever seen a map of the plans? I mean, Darryl's development plans?"

"No, ma'am," he said. "There ain't any map as far as I know. Oh, don't tell Mom I said 'ain't,' okay? She'd ground me for a week."

"There must be a map," I said, thinking aloud. "Judd, I'm going to leave you with the turtles and go see if I can find someone who will know what's up."

Judd nodded. As I turned to leave he added, "There's a trailer. I saw it from the air. It's in a clearing about a mile from the Trail. Maybe that's where you'll find your, uh, former husband."

I COULDN'T FIND ANYONE DOWNTOWN who would talk to me. I went to the mayor's office; I went to the hardware store and the Book Nook. My little town was usually a gossip mill but not when it came to this subject.

Judd had drawn a rough map showing the way to get to the trailer. It was much too far to walk, and, anyway, I needed reinforcements. I hated to do it but I called Jackie from the pay telephone inside the Rexall. Would she take me over there? Would she keep me company, in case we found Darryl and he got ugly? If there was one thing Jackie loved, it was intrigue. That, and the possibility of some surefire excitement.

"Of course, Dora dear," she said, "I believe I owe you an apology. I was thoughtless and selfish about the construction in the, um, swamps. I was thinking about it and I believe you are right that the creatures, uh, *critters*, as you say, have a right to be here, too. Mankind is nothing if not arrogant. And, anyway, if I can help you, I would like to."

I couldn't resist. "Even if it means you won't get new restaurants and stores?" I asked, needling her.

She sighed. "Yes, if it's the right thing to do. Besides, I'm mad at your former husband. I don't like the way he's handling this."

"That makes two of us," I said. No disagreement there.

"I can't go over there right now, though," Jackie said. "Can you wait an hour?"

"Surely can," I said. "I'll be at the post office."

I was reluctant to see my former colleagues because I wasn't ready to answer questions about my year away, and they had a way of flustering me. Working there wasn't so bad, but as the only woman I'd always felt I was a bit of an intruder. Too bad Marty, my second cousin on Daddy's side, had been relocated to the post office in Plant City.

I found three of my former colleagues having a smoke break in back. They had been looking at a girlie magazine and when they saw me, they quickly put it away. Of course, this made it even more awkward to speak to them.

Maybe because I'd caught them doing something they shouldn't—and feared I would tell their supervisor—they were friendlier than I expected. I learned there was a lot of support in town for Darryl's project, and, just as Plain Jane had said, it was all about jobs. One of my former colleagues put it this way: "My son has no future here. The only hope I have of him coming back to Collier County after he graduates from Gainesville is that there will be new opportunity here. Otherwise, he'll move away."

Great, I thought. What I didn't say was, *Why don't you move with him, to some place that's already paved over?* But since I was trying to get information from these fellas, I couldn't afford to alienate them. They were trying to be honest with me. The smartest thing I could do was listen. So far they'd been pretty forthcoming. But when I asked if Darryl had permission from the mayor and the council, they either didn't know or didn't want to give me a straight answer.

"There have been some legal formalities," one of them said, choosing his words carefully. "I'm pretty sure, from what I hear, that he's already started work."

A car horn blasted out front. "That's my ride," I said. "Thank you, but I've got to run." I wanted to hurry so that Jackie wouldn't honk the horn again.

The youngest of the three men followed me. He'd been in the Navy, and I always thought he might be sweet on me. "Dora?" he called out.

"What?"

"I don't think things have been done properly," he said. "By Darryl, I mean. I went to one of the town meetings and it seemed like it was a done deal. Important enough to be rushed through. Please be careful, Dora."

His comment almost took the wind out of my sails. I climbed

into the passenger seat, grateful that the convertible top was up, on account of it looking like rain. I didn't feel like seeing anyone—or being seen—at the moment.

But Jackie was on a tear. "I just learned the most amazing thing," she said breathlessly. "Ted is on the road—up in the Panhandle or whatever it's called—and he phoned me because he won't be home tomorrow, even though he said he would. Anyway, it seemed like it just kind of slipped out—like he wasn't going to tell me—but when he's on the road he gets tired and I think he let his guard down—"

"What?" I said.

"He said that Mr. Toomb is going to . . . well, I don't know how to say this, it sounds so ridiculous."

"Jackie! You're killing me!"

"Mr. Toomb is starting an airline." She hit the accelerator.

I thought I must have misheard. "An *airline*?"

"A regional airline. You know, Naples to Miami. Naples to Tampa. Jacksonville to Tampa. But the major ones in place by the end of this year."

First the real estate development, now an airline? What next? I said a quick prayer that the ultimate goal was not like the plans rumored for Orlando, where someone widely suspected to be Walt Disney was said to be buying up huge tracts of land. Walt Disney himself was thought to be waiting for the right time to make a big announcement about his "Florida Project."

I finally found my voice. "Jackie," I croaked out the words, "do you think this has anything to do with that project planned by Walt Disney?"

"Sure," Jackie said. "I think old Mr. Toomb is positioning himself to ride on Walt Disney's coattails."

"What about Darryl?"

"Oh, I think Darryl is an opportunist just like Mr. Toomb. I asked Ted if he knew anything and he says Darryl's money is coming from New Jersey. Some suburb in New Jersey—I think it's called Basking-something. Basking Ridge, I think. Anyway, Darryl's investors may be trying to capitalize on Disney too, same as Mr. Toomb is."

"But we're *so far south* of Orlando," I said. "Heck, that's almost two hundred miles north of here!"

"Doesn't matter," Jackie replied. "That's the way investors think. Florida is 'hot' right now. Everything's on the table. That's what Ted says."

I could see it all now. Naples would be connected to the outside world in a way it had never been. "Won't they have to improve our airport?" I said, thinking that would take some time. All we had now was a little cement runway good enough for the Civil Air Patrol to take off and land. Just a few private planes, that's all. A commercial airline would change everything.

"Oh, they're already doing that," Jackie said. "Judd said something to me about it the other day, but I wasn't really paying attention."

This was bigger than I had even imagined, and beyond anything I could prevent. I might as well try to part the Red Sea. What was the point in confronting Darryl? But a funny thing had happened to Jackie. Now that I was tuckered out, she was full of that unstoppable Jackie energy.

"Well, we can't stop Walt Disney, and there's not much we can do about Mr. Toomb," she said. "But I don't think we should raise the white flag to Darryl—not without a fight, anyway."

Eight

*D*ang, thought Dolores Simpson, the former Bunny Ann McIntyre. *Why was it taking that little gal, Dora Wither-spoon, so long to meet up with her ex-husband and talk some sense into the man? When was she going to come back here and tell me what in tarnation is going on?*

Dolores was not accustomed to feeling impatient. Living in her fishing shack all these years meant she had none of the stresses and deadlines of ordinary life. There's no reason to be in a hurry when you have nowhere to go. The fish would bite, or they wouldn't. The night heron sat stoically on her messy ol' nest. Five minutes could have passed, or five years.

"Hey," she called, "how many eggs you got there, anyway? Three? Four?"

The small heron stared back. Sometimes, she'd shake her head just like a person but today she wasn't going to be bothered.

"I wonder when yer ol' eggs are going to hatch," Dolores said half to herself. "I hate to break it to you," she added, calling over to the bird, "but in case no one told you, your little night heron chicks are going to be ugly as a toad's hindquarters. Now, don't take it real personal; that's just the way it is. If this is your first nest of eggs, I don't want you to be surprised, that's all. But Lawd knows there ain't nothing uglier in this world than a night heron chick."

The bird stretched its neck and let out a sharp squawk.

"Oh, you didn't like that, huh? Well, I'm sorry. I didn't mean to upset you. Just teasin' you, is all."

Dolores swallowed a mouthful of porch-brewed tea from an old canning jar. Beside her on the step was a basket overflowing with swamp reeds. Marylou, a Seminole Indian, had taught her how to make baskets years before. It was a miracle, watching Marylou turn reeds into a work of art—a usable work of art that the tourists would buy. Marylou had died a long time ago—ten years? fifteen?—and ever since, Dolores didn't have the heart to make baskets. But with all this mess going on with new development, something made her start again. Maybe it was the easy rhythm of weaving the reeds. Worst thing in the world, waiting for news. And maybe even harder when you're all by yourself, 'cept for a night heron to keep you company.

She remembered how quickly Marylou's hands moved when she was making a basket. Why, she could make one in a few hours, depending on the pattern. Of course, Marylou had been making baskets from the time she was four years old, maybe even younger.

She worked for about an hour, then rested. Was she getting lazy, or was it just old age comin' down the pike? *Hard living catches up to a person real fast,* Dolores thought. *You think you're doing purty darn good, next thing you know you look like somethin' that washed in with the tide.* When she'd gone into town and sent that telegram to little Dora Witherspoon, she'd been shocked at her own reflection in the big plate glass window at the five and dime. *Who the heck is that?* For a second she thought someone was sneaking up behind her but it was time—just time—that had caught up with her.

Well, one good thing about getting older was that the men didn't bother her anymore. Whenever that thought passed through her mind, she got religion. "Thank you, Jesus!" she'd say aloud. She didn't miss men—at least, the bad behavior of men—one bit.

Funny thing was, her nearest human neighbors were men. Billy and Marco were brothers of undetermined pedigree who shared a pickup truck and several bad habits. Because of their antics, usually fueled by moonshine, the area was called Gun Rack Village by the uppity types who ran Naples nearby.

There was a fellow who never spoke a word and wore clothes like Tarzan. Dolores kept her distance from him, especially once she'd learned that Billy and Marco called him Sing Sing, after the prison up north from which he'd got loose and swum across a big river—the Hudson, maybe.

More recently, an older man had set up camp near a huge clump of mangrove trees. He told Dolores, when she'd encountered him on the river one day, that he'd had enough of the modern world and intended to live and die right there. She'd agreed to bury him if she came across his body.

And then there was Weird Sam. He lived in an old trawler that had washed up the river in one of the bigger storms and had stuck fast between two cypress trees. No one knew the details, but according to the grapevine, Weird Sam was from a well-off family that had him put in an institution. At some point he either escaped or was let out; regardless, his family wouldn't have anything to do with him. So he lived back in the swamps with a cat named Fish, a dog named Freedom, and a parrot called Mrs. Roosevelt. He did not entertain visitors.

But he did reach out to Dolores when his cat stepped on something sharp and got a deep cut in its paw. He showed up crying with the parrot on his shoulder, the dog by his side, and the injured kitty in his arms. For some reason he thought Dolores could help him, and she did. He held the cat tightly while she poured some moonshine down its throat—just enough to make it woozy—and then stitched up the poor little paw. The cat was right as rain in no time, and Weird Sam started to consider Dolores a friend, or something close to it.

Scattered among the ragtag white residents were Seminole Indians, though how many there were, and exactly where they were, Dolores did not know, even after living on the river all those years. Dolores had only known Marylou, who had taught her how to weave baskets.

Further south on the river was the small village of colored folks. There was one spot on the river where they were known to gather on a Sunday once or twice a year. The first time Dolores had seen them there, she thought she was seeing haints. She hid behind a small grove of mangroves and watched as Negro women, dressed in white robes, walked single file toward a natural clearing by the river. What was most startling to Dolores was the women's absolute silence. They paused while a group of small boys dashed ahead, poking sticks into reeds and banging drums up and down the water's edge. No doubt they were scaring off gators and snakes. Not until Dolores saw two preachers wade out into the water, with one holding a Bible high in the air so it wouldn't get wet, did she realize this was a baptism ceremony. The women were dunked under the water one at a time and came up spluttering. There was much hugging and joyful weeping as each newly baptized woman joined the others on the sand. Only after they were all baptized did they begin to sing. Their voices were lush and glorious as they sang their praise music in perfect harmony, accompanied by the 'Glade's own peculiar sound, a constant, low droning that seemed to come from deep within the earth.

Dolores didn't have any deep love for the Negro race, but witnessing their ceremony seemed to soften her a little around the edges. It was hard to stay angry and brittle in the presence of such joy and beauty.

She was raised with the firm belief that was hard to shake, though, that white folks without a bank account or an education had it just as hard in life as Negroes. She did not see any advantage in being white if you were, as she was, at the bottom of the pile.

Yet Dolores had to admire the gumption of this particular group; they weren't any different from her in one respect: All they wanted was to be left alone. They'd refused to move to Mc-Donald's Quarters. The Negro "renegades," as they were sometimes called, included Priscilla Harmon—before the miracle of her going off to college—and her grandma. Robbie-Lee had mentioned once that Priscilla's grandma worked in the fields for one of the families that grew sugarcane and watermelons. Most of those colored children did not go to school, but Priscilla had taught herself to read and write by studying an old Sears catalog and an illustrated Bible, according to Robbie-Lee. The girl was so smart that the teachers at the Negro high school enlisted the help of the town's librarian to find her new and challenging books to read. This was how Priscilla came to know about Jackie's book club, which met at the library. She had just finished high school and was working as a maid for mean old Mrs. Burnside.

Then she let everyone down by getting pregnant, a disaster that Dolores understood only too well. White girls who were poor like Dolores were in the same boat as colored girls. All it took was one mistake and that was the end of your dreams, assuming you had any in the first place. Meanwhile, white girls who came from money simply disappeared for a while, came back home, and were allowed to act like nothing had happened. They'd been taken out of state—"gone to Georgia" was the phrase—to bide their time at a maternity home, and their babies given away to a well-to-do Protestant couple, or sometimes kinfolk.

As for the young man or boy who helped create the heartbreaking situation, he usually got off scot-free. Once in a while, some irate daddy would insist on a shotgun wedding—marry my daughter or else. But the better off the family, the more likely they were to try to hide the girl's mistake.

Much as Dolores disliked Jackie Hart, there was a small part of her that admired her for figuring out a way to help Priscilla. But Dolores felt something else, too: a flash of envy. No one had helped her, back in her time of need and confusion.

Now she found herself in trouble again—a different set of circumstances, of course, and yet familiar in the way it made her feel. Once again, she was treated as a person who didn't matter, who had no say. Once again, the world wanted to take what she had and give her nothing in return. She was forty-seven years old and all used up; some of it was her own fault, some wasn't. Regardless, all she really wanted was peace. Was that so much to ask?

This is why she had to fight to protect the river. For herself and her way of life, yes, but it was more than that. This place—the 'Glades—felt eternal. In its own way, it was sacred, like the Grand Canyon, or that place in California with the giant trees.

Unfortunately, since the 'Glades featured gators, snakes, bugs, and poisonous plants, folks didn't always recognize its beauty. Outsiders seemed to think it was a wasteland. If that was where your people were from, you got used to strangers acting like you crawled up out of the swamp yourself. You felt cursed being born there.

Only once had she heard anyone say anything nice about the 'Glades, and it had stuck with her. Her family was not churchgoers. But once, curious as a cat, she'd sneaked over and hid in the bushes near the tent revival at the Colored Adventist Church, just to have a listen. At the end of the service, the preacher gave thanks "for the 'Glades and the life that sprang from it." This got her attention. "We sometimes don't appreciate this here swamp," he'd said, "and we be skeert at some of the things that live in it and around it. It ain't an easy place to live. But thank you, Lord. The swamp be worthy because you designed it, Lord. You put the swamp here at the same time you hung the sun in the sky, and for this we are grateful, Lord."

She memorized those words and they came to her often over the years. This was not a wasteland. Far from it. She would fight for the little night heron, the mangrove trees, the flowing water, and the wild grasses. Surely, the river had a right to survive.

Nine

"Here, read this while I drive," Jackie instructed, and I was only too happy to oblige since her driving style, which never seemed to include both hands on the wheel, often made me wish I'd stayed at home in the company of my turtles.

Judd had drawn his map on the back of a piece of paper he must've torn from a school notebook. On one side was a to-do list that included "Mow Miss Turnipseed's lawn," "Ask Dad: bike tire," "Fishing worms," and "iron uniform." The latter, I supposed, referring to the Civil Air Patrol outfit that made teenagers look like miniature grown-ups.

"Not that side," Jackie said, glancing my way. "Flip it over."

Why was it that I so often felt stupid around Jackie? Sure enough, the reverse side was Judd's rendering of where he thought the new road had been carved into the swamp, based on what he'd seen from the air. Jackie had already gotten us to the Tamiami Trail and from there she headed north. Our first turn from the main road was supposed to be about a half mile past a combination bait shop and liquor store called Gin and

Bare It. Judd had told Jackie it was easy to spot from the air on account of a gigantic painting of a naked lady on the tin roof, a revelation which, Jackie recalled, had left her momentarily speechless.

Jackie wrinkled her nose when we passed by, then slowed down so we could find the side road. "Hasn't anyone in this county ever heard of a street sign?" Jackie complained. "Wait," she added. "That must be it."

Sam Cooke was singing "Another Saturday Night" on the radio, but the signal was already fading and Jackie turned it off. The side road was a lot like the one I took to Dolores Simpson's fishing shack, only more remote. "Oh, rats, why did I get the car washed. Remind me next time I buy a car to get one of those surplus Jeeps from the war."

The road showed signs of being heavily used, and recently. This was unusual. Even Jackie, city girl that she was, noticed the broken tree branches on either side, and she remarked about ruts in the road, which she maneuvered around rather expertly. I started looking for the next road, where we were supposed to make a right turn. "If we get stuck out here, we're in trouble," Jackie announced, as if it wasn't obvious. Just as I was about to suggest we turn back, we came upon the right turn, or what we hoped was our right turn.

"Maybe we should have told someone we were heading out here," I said.

"Judd knows," Jackie said.

Of course he did. He'd made the map. And, knowing Judd, he was looking at his watch right now, trying to estimate our location.

"Jackie, you look to the front and I'll look back," I said.

"Of course I'm looking to the front, I'm driving the car!"

I paused. "Jackie, I guess no one ever told you this," I said, choosing my words carefully, "but when you're driving on a dirt road this far back in the swamp, it's pretty easy to run over a snake. If you see one and you think you hit it, it's important to say, 'I think I just ran over a snake.' And your passenger—that would be me—will need to be prepared to look back and see if it's behind the car after you ran it over."

"Well, where would it be if it isn't behind the car?" Jackie asked.

"Could be it's climbed in the car. But more likely underneath and wrapped around the axle."

"*Oh my God, that is disgusting!* Ew! Ugh! *I hate this place . . .*"

I was sorry I'd said anything.

Jackie continued driving with her hands clutching the wheel. "How come nobody told me this before?" she whined.

"I have no idea," I said. "I guess I should have told you. I mean, all the times you've driven to Priscilla's grandma's house, someone should have mentioned it. I guess we all thought you knew."

Jackie made a sound like *harrumph*. "Whenever I learn something like this, it makes me wonder what *else* I don't know," she said. I was afraid she might turn around but she didn't.

Another ten minutes, however, and she hit the brakes hard. A brand-new gravel road, twice as wide as the little unpaved side roads, appeared in front of us. Was it a mirage? I couldn't have been more shocked if a UFO plopped down in front of us. Unlike the twisty, haphazard roads we were used to, this one was straight as a crow flies. It wasn't paved like the Tamiami Trail but it still counted as bona fide by Collier County standards since an actual engineer, rather than Billy Joe down at the so-called highway department, seemed to have designed it. For example, it appeared to be properly graded. And gravel? That took planning. And money.

Jackie took a long drag on a cigarette. "How far do you think we are from home?" Her mood was serious, and I was grateful for it.

"A couple of miles," I said. "Four or five, maybe. What does the odometer say?"

Jackie, for once, looked sheepish. "I didn't check the odometer before we left."

"Well then the only way to tell would be to climb a real tall tree." Jackie gave me one of those "you've got to be kidding" looks.

"I'm not climbing a tree, and neither are you," she said. "There are *things* in those trees. Horrible bugs! Snakes!" She shuddered, and I turned my head to the side so she wouldn't see me hiding a smile. Poor Jackie. She was so far out of her element here that it was hard not to be amused.

And yet, fear was not a bad companion to have, back in the swamps. Distances were so hard to figure. At times, the marsh acted like a giant sponge that swallowed noise. Visually, it was even more confusing. You might come across a place that was wide open and meadow-like, with rabbits running around, or a stretch of open water with little islands where gators dozed on the banks and spoonbills perched in low-slung trees. In many parts of the 'Glades, though, you couldn't see farther than the nose on your face, as my mama used to say.

"Let me see that map," Jackie said. "If Judd is right, this new road is not more than a mile long, and the construction trailer should be right at the end of it." She hit the gas a little too hard, causing the rear wheels to dig into the gravel and sending a thousand tiny pebbles flying. A hundred yards later, we saw something in the roadway: A gator not much bigger than a hound dog had parked its lazy self in the middle of the road. "Look at that disgusting *thing*!" Jackie said, slowly bringing the Buick to a stop. She pounded her fist on the horn, a loud blast that was completely ignored by the gator, which didn't so much as twitch at the sound.

Jackie hadn't yet accepted the fact that gator encounters were inevitable. Why, in Collier County, if you weren't careful you could step on one dozing on your front steps. In fact, that's how Mama's friend Miss Fern Tootin died. Not that Miss Tootin got chomped by a gator. She tripped over it and fell. But it wasn't the fall that killed her, either. It was on account of her being so annoyed at the gator that she fired a shot from a .22 caliber pistol, only the bullet ricocheted off her wrought-iron fence post and struck her dead.

Jackie honked again. "What the heck is wrong with it? Do you think it's dead?" she shouted.

"Aw, come on, Jackie, it's just a baby."

"I should run over it," she said.

"Jackie! How could you say that?!"

"Well, it's not as if there aren't a million of them around here. I don't think anyone would miss one."

"Jackie Hart, that little gator has more right to be here than *you* do! They've been here since time began, and you just got here in 1962."

Jackie sighed and lit another cigarette, the fourth or fifth one since we started on this little journey. I noticed she was using a lighter I hadn't seen before. "That's nice," I said quietly.

"What's nice?"

"The lighter. Is it new?"

"Ted got it for me as a birthday present." She handed it to

me to look over. "It's just like the one that Elizabeth Taylor owns. Well, not exactly, because hers is probably solid gold and mine is gold plate."

This was getting to be a little peculiar. It was the second time in three days that Elizabeth Taylor, bless her heart, had unknowingly intervened and saved the day for me. Dang, that woman must have some mighty powers. She was clear across the country, in Beverly Hills, and just bringing up her name could change the course of a conversation all the way over here in the Everglades.

"It's gorgeous," I said. I didn't smoke but even if I did I knew that a lighter like that would be out of my league. Jackie was one of those women who always looked good; my mama would have said it was on account of her having good cheekbones, though to be honest I never really understood what that meant.

"Look, Dora," she said, "I'm sorry. Of course you know I would never have run over the, um, creature."

"I'll get out of the car and chase it to the side of the road," I offered.

"Oh my God, Dora, don't!"

"Jackie, it can't be more than four feet long."

"I'll drive around it."

"Well, then drive around the tail end of it, not the front end." "Huh?"

"Always drive behind an alligator's tail end," I explained patiently. "If you drive in front of it, it's more likely to panic and run right in front of the car."

"Oh for Pete's sake!" She ground out her cigarette in the ashtray. "I'm not going around him! He's going to have to get out of *my* way." Jackie leaned on the horn again but the critter didn't budge.

She lowered the power window and stuck her head out. "Get out of the road!" she shouted.

The poor beast, unmoved by the threat of a Buick weighing two tons or even the Yankee-style horn honking, was startled into action by Jackie's hollerin'.

"Look at that," Jackie said proudly. "It's moving." Sure enough, the gator, now wide-eyed and apparently sensing a true predator, started to creep forward, then move swiftly to the edge of the gravel road, where it vanished.

"Must have been the Boston accent," I said. "He never heard one of those before."

Jackie laughed. "What do you say we find that stupid trailer, and with any luck, your stupid former husband, and get this over with?" Before I could answer she pounced on the accelerator, fishtailing that Buick and giggling like a half-mad schoolgirl.

"Jackie, stop that! You must be damaging the road!"

"Oh, so what?" Jackie said. "Why can't we have a little fun. Besides, you hate the road! It shouldn't be here, right?"

I hung on for dear life, hoping Jackie wouldn't lose control of the car and land us in the swamp. I had never known a married woman who acted like Jackie. I knew a few girls in high school with a similar wild streak but they'd changed overnight once they'd said their "I dos" and "I will obeys" at the altar.

There's a saying that if marriage don't change a woman, motherhood will. Well, that was not the case with Jackie, either. Many times the thought had gone through my head that her twin daughters and especially her son, Judd, were more mature than she was. When they'd arrived in Naples, the kids were wise, taking their time to adjust, but with Jackie, it was like she'd been shot out of a cannon. The womenfolk in town were appalled; the men were scandalized. Her fashion taste was more Ava Gardner than Florida matron, her intelligence was intimidating, and her tendency to speak her mind was shocking. She not only had opinions, she shared them.

The fact that her husband Ted was old Mr. Toomb's newly hired business manager had given her some leeway. She and Mr. Toomb had their differences but they had buried the hatchet, for the time being at least. Of course, that's what I hoped, but I also knew that Jackie was the kind of person who burned up goodwill in a hurry.

Jackie finally calmed down and began driving like a normal person. I tried to focus on the possibility that I might be seeing Darryl. I was grateful that Jackie was with me; even though I never knew what she was going to do next, I could count on her friendship.

The road began to curve gently and suddenly there it was: a brand-new construction trailer. One vehicle, a pickup, was parked nearby. A man was hunched over slightly, studying something—maps maybe, or construction plans—that had been spread out on the hood.

Darryl.

My heart switched places with my stomach. I wanted to beg Jackie to turn around but somehow I summoned the courage to stifle the urge. I had to get this over with.

But as we drove closer, I soon forgot all my troubles. Jackie slammed on the brakes, and the car lurched to a stop. We were close enough to read the lettering on a sign that read Welcome to Dreamsville!

Ten

Now I was sorry. Oh, was I sorry. I wish I'd never come home. I wish I'd never been born. Most especially, I wish I wasn't with Jackie Hart at that precise moment.

Jackie's reaction was nothing less than I expected. "I'm going to kill him!" she screamed, and I was hopeful we were still far enough away that he didn't hear her, though he looked up and stared in shock when he realized a strange car was sitting a piece down the road.

"He can't do this!" Jackie hollered, hurting my ear. "He's stealing my name! I'm going to call my lawyer!"

"Jackie, let's turn around and go home and talk this over," I said quickly. My instinct was to retreat, plan, and return to battle another day. Jackie's instinct was to fight first, think later.

Instead of gunning the engine, however, she drove like a civilized person (which, frankly, almost scared me more) until we were close enough to pull up a few feet from him. I could see that he recognized the car—of course he did. Everyone in southwest Florida knew that car.

"Excuse me, *sir*," Jackie said, like she was about to ask for directions.

I almost felt sorry for Darryl. He was entirely flummoxed. "I thought I heard a car horn a while ago," he said. "I guess that was you?"

"Might have been," Jackie said with that same edge to her voice.

"You're Miss Dreamsville, aren't you?" he asked. "Mrs. Jackie Hart?"

"Yes," she said icily.

"Oh, I see you're in mourning. I'm sorry for your loss."

"And I see that you have chosen to call your development 'Dreamsville.' The implication is that I am endorsing this project. You will be hearing from my attorney."

This was a side to Jackie I hadn't seen. Although she was so mad I sensed she was quivering beside me, she had reined in her temper.

"Well, actually, it's going to be called Dreamsville Estates," Darryl said without emotion. "Our slogan is Welcome to Dreamsville!"

"What nerve you have!" Jackie said, struggling to maintain her dignity. "I am aghast! Never have I seen such audacity!"

Darryl smirked. "All's fair—"

"—in love and war?" Jackie said, finishing the old saying for him.

"And—when it comes to Florida real estate," he added. "But you wouldn't know that, would you? Since you're not from around here."

"I'm not brand-new here," she snapped. "I've lived here for two years."

"Well, whoop-dee-do," Darryl said. "Two whole years. Lady, if you lived here for twenty years, you'd still be an outsider."

"Go ahead and laugh at me, sir," Jackie said, lighting a cigarette and blowing a stream of smoke directly into his face. "You will be sorry."

"Is that a *threat*?" Darryl asked, pretending to be taken aback.

"Take it any way you like," she said, "but don't say I didn't warn you. Never underestimate a woman from Boston, or do so at your own peril. Oh," she added, suddenly remembering I was there. "I believe that Dora here"—she gestured to the passenger seat—"would like to have a word with you before we leave."

Darryl leaned down and looked in amazement at me, hunkered against the far door. "Dora!" he said, clearly stunned. "What are you doing way out here?"

I took this as my cue. My knees were wobbly, but I got out of the car. Now was the time. I was hoping Jackie would understand that I needed to be alone with Darryl for a few minutes, and despite her distress, she got the hint. "Dora, shall I come back later?" she asked.

"No, Jackie," I said quickly. "Just wait here." We weren't at the Dairy Queen, for pity's sake, and while I wasn't particularly afraid of Darryl, I didn't want to be stuck out here with him, either. She nodded and moved the car a respectful distance away.

"Do you want to talk in the trailer?" Darryl said, still looking shocked. "Or we can talk in my truck."

"Truck is fine," I said. I could tell he was having trouble reading my mood. Angry? Sad? What? Well, the truth was that I was nervous as a rabbit at a hound dog convention but I was determined to hide it.

He opened the door for me, then went around to the driver's

side and climbed in. The windows were lowered already, or the truck would have been hot enough to fry bacon. Even so, the seats were roasting.

"Dang, it's hot," Darryl said, buying time.

"Surely is."

"It's *really* hot."

"Darryl, I need to talk to you about something other than the weather."

"Okay," he said. "I thought you were in Mississippi. I didn't even know you were back."

I cut to the chase. "Darryl, why are you doing this?"

"Doing what?"

"Ruining the swamp! Paving over the river! And on top of it, calling it Dreamsville! That's not fair to my friend!"

Darryl laughed. "You came all this way to fuss at me about that?! Let me tell you something, Dora, you're just as nutty as your friend there. If you'd stayed with me, you could have been a rich woman."

"Darryl, what in tarnation has happened to your *soul?*"

"Oh, so now it's my soul we're talking about. Gee, Dora, I never thought of you as being the Bible-thumping type. You trying to get me back to church? You weren't there yourself every Sunday, if I remember correctly."

We had fallen back into our old pattern, the kind of fighting that makes you get madder and madder and gets you nowhere. "Darryl, let's stay on the topic," I said, trying to sound calm and mature, although I surely didn't feel that way. "You and me—we grew up around here. We played here. You helped me rescue turtles, do you remember that? I knew you had changed. That's why I couldn't stay married to you anymore. But this—this *development*—well, I'm shocked, Darryl. Not only are you going to wipe out the animals and the birds, there are people living here, too. They don't have anywhere else to go. If you do this, Darryl, there's no going back. The 'Glades have been here forever; you're going to change that?"

Darryl was silent. "There's a lot more 'Glades than just the part I want to build on," he said finally. "This is just one piece of the 'Glades. Besides, if I don't build on it, someone else will. Trust me on that, Dora."

"Well, I don't trust you, Darryl. And it makes me very sad to say that."

"So you came here to try to persuade me to change my mind?"

"Well, yes, Darryl. I thought it was worth a try. For old times' sake."

"There's something you should know, Dora," he said, and his voice sounded different. "I was going to write to you in Mississippi. I'm getting married."

"I see," I said as calmly as I could manage. I wanted to say, *Well, that was quick, Darryl*, but I curbed my tongue. "Oh," I managed to say faintly. "Well, good for you, Darryl. What's her name?"

"Celeste," he said, without providing a last name. "I met her in New York on a business trip. Well, her folks live in New Jersey. In Basking Ridge."

Basking Ridge, I thought. I couldn't remember where I'd heard that before but at the moment it didn't matter. "That's nice, Darryl," I said simply. "Thank you. I mean, thank you for telling me." I suddenly felt tears stinging the corners of my eyes. Did this mean I still loved him? Or were they tears of a different kind—humiliation that we had failed as a couple and he had found someone new? I climbed out of the truck without looking at him, hoping he wouldn't see. As I walked back to Jackie's car, though, I realized he was following me. I figured he just wanted to get the last word. All I wanted to do was hightail it out of there.

"Dora, you shouldn't judge me!" he said, and now he sounded angry. He was right on my heels. "Aren't you going to wish me good luck on my marriage?" This was said with so much bile that I was sorely tempted to turn around and slap him.

"Now, you two settle down," Jackie called out. She must have heard the last exchange of words, maybe more. I kept my stride steady and marched to the passenger side, got in, and locked the door.

He muttered and fumed, then surprised me by turning and walking around to Jackie's side of the car. "You know what?" he shouted in Jackie's face. "If it hadn't been for you and your *Miss Dreamsville* radio show, I wouldn't have been able to get the financing. You put us on the map! So thank you very much for helping me get rich!"

Jackie looked stricken. She opened her mouth but no words came out. Darryl turned his back and stomped arrogantly toward his truck. A second later he was gone, tearing down the road at a reckless speed.

I wondered if he knew how lucky he was. After taunting Jackie, he had walked right in front of her car. If she had recovered faster, my former husband could easily have become a brand-new hood ornament on the flashiest car in town.

Eleven

I hope Seminole Joe catches up to him," Mrs. Bailey White said. We were sitting in her parlor, having skedaddled from Darryl's construction site for a place to talk things out. Jackie was worn out, collapsed on Mrs. Bailey White's good sofa after a marathon weeping session that was fueled by pure rage and peppered with threats and oaths about high-powered Northern lawyers and what they would do to Darryl for having the nerve to steal her name.

"Who is Seminole Joe?" Jackie asked wearily.

Mrs. Bailey White and I locked eyes, and Plain Jane, slouched in an oversized leather chair near the fireplace, looked up from the book she was reading and chuckled softly.

"What's so funny?" Jackie demanded.

"Nothin'," Plain Jane said, returning to her book.

"Seminole Joe is a haint," I said simply. I was sitting on the floor, trying to get better acquainted with Dream, who was having a good ol' time with a set of alphabet blocks that Plain Jane had purchased at the Junior League yard sale.

"A ghost," Mrs. Bailey White added, translating for Jackie.

I didn't want to get onto the topic of Seminole Joe, not after the day I'd had, and surely not in Mrs. Bailey White's parlor, where her kinfolk were lined up in jars on the mantel. Or, rather, the ashes of her kinfolk. The way I was raised—along with just about everyone else in Collier County—your body was supposed to be buried, not reduced to dust and placed in your home *on the mantelpiece* like a 4-H trophy. I had never got myself used to their presence.

But Jackie, being Jackie, was not going to be satisfied with our skirting the topic. "I never heard of this 'Seminole Joe' before," she said crossly. "Is this some kind of local secret?"

"Seminole Joe is our boogeyman," I said simply. I watched as Dream toppled the blocks by piling on one too many. She chuckled and clapped her hands in delight. "Maybe," I added, "we shouldn't talk about Seminole Joe until Dream has her nap."

"She's too young to understand what we're talking about," Jackie said.

"I wouldn't count on that," said Plain Jane, looking up from her book again. "It's time for her nap, anyway," she added. "I'll take her up."

"So, who is this Seminole Joe person?" Jackie asked again.

"As I said, he's Collier County's very own boogeyman," I replied.

"I hate that term, 'boogeyman,'" Jackie said, lighting a cigarette. "And I don't believe in ghosts," she added between puffs.

"You live around here long enough, you'll believe in 'em," Mrs. Bailey White said under her breath.

"Well, what does this have to do with Darryl?" Jackie asked. "You said something about Seminole Joe catching up to Darryl. It may not be necessary after my lawyer gets through with him."

"Oh, it was just wishful thinking," Mrs. Bailey White said. "I mean, that would solve all our problems."

Jackie said nothing. I could see she was taking this all in, though how she was interpreting it, I wasn't sure.

"Don't you want to know who Seminole Joe was, I mean *is*?" I asked.

"Okay, I'll bite," Jackie said.

I looked at Mrs. Bailey White. Since she brought up the subject, it was her story to tell.

Mrs. Bailey White took a ladylike sip of iced tea, cleared her throat, and began. "A long time ago, when white folks first showed up here, the Indians didn't know what to think," she said in a tone that reminded me of a schoolteacher talking to her pupils. "They were Spanish, and they showed up one day in their sailing ships. Before long they discovered there was a fresh-water spring on Marco Island and they'd stop there, regular-like, on their way to whatever they were doing. Exploring, I guess, but also raisin' Cain.

"Anyway, an Indian named Joe was killed by a pirate. Some say the murderer was the famous pirate Gasparilla, but no one knows for sure. After that, the ghost of this poor Indian fellow, Joe, started to attack them in their sleep and feed their body parts to the alligators. Or so the story went. After a while, the Spanish started avoiding Marco Island and the area we call Collier County altogether. As long as they stayed away, Joe was at peace.

"During the War of Northern Aggression, deserters from both sides—Mr. Lincoln's army as well as our Rebs—found their way to South Florida. They hung deserters in those days. The more skeert they were of getting caught, the farther south they ran. So here in Collier County we had the worst ones—the kind that had gone plumb jack crazy. In the First World War, they called it 'shell shock' but I'm not sure they had a name for it back in Mr. Lincoln's War. And that's when the stories about Joe's ghost started up again. From that time on, folks started referring to him as Seminole Joe.

"If you were in the swamp after dark, he might come after you with a hatchet. Lots of folks went missing on account of old Joe. He didn't seem to bother the Negroes. He only went after the whites. Especially our Confederate soldiers, because they reminded him of General Andrew Jackson from South Carolina. If there was one person the Seminole Indians hated, it was General Jackson. Before Jackson became President of the United States, he made his name fighting the Seminoles. To this very day, don't ever hand a twenty-dollar bill to a Seminole Indian or he will refuse it and spit on the ground, because Andrew Jackson's picture is on the twenty-dollar bill."

Mrs. Bailey White paused for dramatic effect, then went on.

"Old-time Collier County folks don't like to talk about Seminole Joe because it was considered bad luck to say his name aloud. He was still roaming around when I was a young girl. The most famous case in my day was when a moonshiner named Gerry Brevard made the mistake of setting up his equipment right where Seminole Joe and his people are buried. Normally, Seminole Joe wouldn't bother with a loser like Gerry Brevard but Seminole Indians are mighty particular about their burial grounds. Gerry Brevard had to go.

"My daddy and Judge Harvey P. Decker are the ones who found him. He ran straight out into the road, and they almost hit him, but he was half-dead anyway. In his final breaths, he pointed to the swamp and said, 'Seminole Joe.' There was a sound in the swamp and my daddy looked up and there he was—the old Indian haint hisself, watching them. Next thing they heard was Gerry Brevard's rattle of death, so they turned their attention to him. When they looked back at the swamp a moment later, Seminole Joe had vanished."

Mrs. Bailey White picked up her knitting, which was her way of letting us know she had finished her story. Jackie looked at me, started to say something, but changed her mind. I was trying to hide my excitement. Mrs. Bailey White had told the story of Seminole Joe in more detail than I'd ever heard it.

After a few moments of silence, except for the little clicking noises from Mrs. Bailey White's knitting needles, I couldn't stand it any longer. "Mrs. Bailey White," I said breathlessly, "I can't believe you knew someone—your own father—who saw Seminole Joe!"

"Oh, well, I saw him, too," Mrs. Bailey White said, pausing in her knitting. "I was in the car. In the backseat."

"Sweet Jesus!" I said, jumping to my feet.

"Oh, for Pete's sake, Dora, cut it out," Jackie said. "It's just a story."

Plain Jane came back down the stairs, having finally settled Dream for a late nap. "What's going on down here?" she asked. I filled her in, and noticed that she was watching Jackie carefully.

"So, Jackie, what do you think of all this?" Plain Jane asked, although surely she anticipated the answer.

"I don't believe any of it," Jackie declared, "but I suppose it would serve Darryl right if he ran into old Seminole Joe." She laughed at her own little joke.

Mrs. Bailey White and I looked at each other, a little alarmed. No matter what Darryl did, he didn't deserve that fate. Plain Jane, settling back in her favorite chair, sighed and shook her head.

"What book is that you're reading?" I asked, hoping to change the subject.

Plain Jane held up the cover for me to see. "*To the Lighthouse* by Virginia Woolf. I've been hearing about this book for years and years, and then Jackie suggested we read it."

"It's a book club pick?" I said, feeling left out once again. I had wondered if the three members of the club who'd stayed in Naples would keep choosing and discussing books.

"Why, Dora, we should have told you what we've been reading, and you could have been reading it, too," Plain Jane said guiltily.

"It's okay, I read it anyway, a few years ago," I said, adding, "I thought it was beautiful."

"Aw, everyone says they love *To the Lighthouse*," Jackie complained.

"You didn't like it?" I asked, surprised.

"Not as much as the others did," Jackie sniffed. "I think it's one of those books you're *supposed* to love."

"What do you mean?" Plain Jane cried.

"It's one of those books people talk about at cocktail parties," Jackie said. "Everyone trying to sound so *terribly sophisticated* says, 'Oh, *To the Lighthouse* is my favorite!' but half of them haven't even read it."

"Oh, Jackie!" Plain Jane said. "I think you are so wrong. I just read it again and frankly it is unforgettable. There's a passage I'm looking for . . ."

"Dora, Plain Jane is right—shame on us for not letting you know what we were reading," Mrs. Bailey White said. "We just thought you were busy with your adventure in Mississippi and we didn't want to interfere."

"Ah, yes," Jackie said. "Speaking of your adventure in Mississippi, are you going to tell us what you found out about your family?"

"Oh," I said, completely off guard. I started to say something evasively Southern but stopped myself. I could learn *something* from Jackie, couldn't I? So I tried my hand at Jackie's signature bluntness. "I'm not ready to talk about that yet," I said, and although it sounded Yankee-rude it also felt surprisingly good to say what I meant.

The others looked a little surprised. "Well, Dora dear, whenever you're ready," Plain Jane said, rescuing me. "For the moment, we need to figure out what we're going to do about Darryl, anyway."

"What, other than hoping Seminole Joe goes after him?" Jackie chortled. "Seriously, I'm beginning to think that old ghost could help us in some way."

"Jackie, you are going to get us into some serious trouble," Plain Jane said uneasily.

"Oh, don't be silly!" Jackie said, lighting yet another cigarette. "What do you think I'm suggesting? Summoning the ancient spirit of Seminole Joe and asking for his help?"

"Well, I suppose one of us could dress up like Seminole Joe and sneak up and bop Darryl over the head, not to hurt him but just to scare him," Mrs. Bailey White said thoughtfully. "Maybe then he'd be afraid to go ahead with his project?"

I swallowed hard. "I don't think that's funny," I said.

"I wasn't joking," Mrs. Bailey White replied. I looked at her for a long time, trying to reconcile this sweet-looking little old lady with the woman who had done time in jail and was now suggesting that we hit my former husband over the head "just to scare him."

"Mrs. Bailey White," I said, my voice all squeaky and trembling, "this is out of the question, and I do not want to be part of this conversation."

"Oh," Mrs. Bailey White said, looking a little chagrined. "Sorry I upset you, Dora."

"Now, girls," Jackie said, trying to diffuse the situation. "I have a better idea. You know how I used to do some copyediting over at the newspaper, before I had my radio show? Well, I've been asked to do some writing—a column, as a matter of fact!"

"How exciting!" Plain Jane said, and I might have detected a touch of envy in her voice. "Jackie, you're just full of surprises. Why didn't you tell us?"

"I'm telling you now. And, besides, they only just asked me last week."

"What's the column going to be called?" Plain Jane asked. That was a question I wouldn't have even thought to ask but, after all, Plain Jane had written for some of the big-name magazines in New York.

"Chatter Box."

"Chatter Box?"

"Meaning little bits of news and delightful gossip," Jackie said. "And my byline will be Miss Dreamsville." After a pause, she said, "The owner came up with the Chatter Box thing. I'm not sure I like it, either. But I won the more important battle. It will *not* be on the Women's Page! It will be on the Editorial Page."

"What's wrong with the Women's Page?" Mrs. Bailey White asked innocently.

"No, no, no, I will never write for the Women's Page," Jackie said crossly. "It's all weddings and gardening tips and all that junk. No, no, no! I don't want my column to be stuck there!"

"But everyone reads the Women's Page," Mrs. Bailey White said softly.

"Men don't!" Jackie cried out. "If it's on the Women's Page it implies that my column is for women only or about women's 'concerns' and that's not what I'm going to write about."

"Well, what are you going to write about?" asked Plain Jane.

Jackie smiled, and to me it seemed a little mischievous. "The agreement is that I get to write my column about anything I want. My first column is supposed to run in two days and I couldn't decide what to write about. The editor suggested a piece about how Collier County seems to be forgotten at the statehouse in Tallahassee. But that seems deadly dull, doesn't it? Now I'm thinking I could write about Seminole Joe."

"*What?*" I asked, realizing I was at least one step behind Jackie's thinking.

"Well, what if I wrote a piece about Seminole Joe, pointing out that he haunts the area where Darryl is going to do all that construction? And maybe get everyone in Naples all scared and stirred up, so there'd be opposition to the project?"

This was either the best or worst idea I ever heard. I'd have to think on it overnight to decide which. In some respects it was brilliant. It might even work. On the other hand, it was one of those ideas that could have consequences we couldn't anticipate. Jackie had a history of getting herself, and everyone else around her, in over their head. She was good at coming up with creative ideas but her strong suit didn't include fixing up the messes that sometimes resulted.

She saw our hesitation. "Aw come on, girls! What could go wrong?"

Not the words I wanted to hear, but I admired her confidence just the same.

Twelve

If he hadn't been so overburdened with work, Ted Hart might have enjoyed the challenge to start an airline for Mr. Toomb, his boss. The fact was that he was already away from his wife and kids more than he or they had expected. Hopefully, Mr. Toomb would quickly allow him to hire an assistant.

But he was off to a bad start. He and Mr. Toomb could not even agree on a name for the airline. Ted had suggested Florida Airlines. Mr. Toomb's idea? Wild Blue Yonder Airways. Ted could see immediately that marketing would be a problem. The word "wild" could be interpreted as "reckless." And "yonder" had a connotation that was anything but sophisticated. The well-heeled Yankees they would need as customers were not going to like it. Well, Mr. Toomb was the boss, and the boss always got what he wanted. Especially if the boss was a powerful, no-nonsense man like Mr. Toomb.

Ted spent two weeks in Tallahassee to get the permits lined up. It was easy compared to the way things were done up north, Ted thought. In fact, before anyone realized what was happening, the crummy little airport landing strip in Naples was under construction. The Naples airport had been so lacking that Mr. Toomb had been forced to accept that headquarters for his new airline would be in Tampa, which was, compared to Naples, an actual city. Meanwhile, the headline in the Naples paper said the state was financing some "improvements" to the humble airstrip, but in truth it was being modernized and expanded to accommodate Mr. Toomb's vision.

One problem was going to be Ted's son, Judd, who was deeply involved with the cadet corps of the Civil Air Patrol. Making a mental note to himself, Ted vowed to be careful not to say too much around Judd, who seemed to be on friendly terms with everyone at the Naples Airport. Mr. Toomb was a secretive man, which meant Ted—if he wanted to stay employed—had to keep secrets, too. Not that Mr. Toomb was doing anything illegal, Ted quickly told himself. Mr. Toomb was an opportunist. A well-connected opportunist, the most formidable kind.

Ted sighed. This was not what he thought he was getting into, back when he was in the Army during the war and wanted to make the world a better place. Somehow that dream had been diverted, one little decision at a time, into a simpler, more *personal* goal: go to college on the G.I. Bill and become the first person in his family to wear a suit to work. It had meant leaving Boston, which he hadn't counted on. It had meant long days on the road, travel, and, needless to say, time away from Jackie and the kids. Was it worth it? On good days, the answer was yes.

Jackie's parents, owners of a well-known restaurant in downtown Boston, were not happy when Ted proposed to their only daughter. Sometimes it occurred to him that he was still trying to prove himself to them, even though he knew it could never happen. They would not even come to visit. It wasn't Florida they were opposed to; God knows they'd spent their fair share of time at the Fontainebleau in Miami Beach and the Breakers in Palm Beach. They just wouldn't come to Collier County, that's all. In their minds, Collier County was the sticks.

Of course, the way things were headed, his in-laws might change their stubborn minds about Naples. There could come a time when Naples *surpassed* the swankier places on Florida's east coast. Not likely, but possible.

As for his own parents, they didn't have the money to travel to Cape Cod for a holiday, let alone Naples. In fact he wasn't sure if his parents had ever gone on a vacation. This thought made him so sad that he found it necessary to light his pipe, a habit that calmed him.

He watched as a tiny, single-engine plane landed gracefully on the lone runway and taxied carefully around construction equipment and scores of workmen who hadn't even looked up when it landed. There were no hangars, only the terminal building which housed a weather station, a bathroom, and a so-called lobby with a half-dozen molded plastic chairs, a Coke machine, and plenty of ashtrays. He'd seen better accommodations overseas in the Army during World War Two.

He had no desire to feel nostalgic about his stint in the Army. Back in Boston, he'd had a few beers now and then at a local VFW but, unlike many other veterans, he discovered he couldn't think of his war service as his glory days. Unusual for his generation, Ted was bitter about the war. About all wars. About powerful old men, since the beginning of time, who sent young men to their deaths. More than nine thousand Allied soldiers killed or injured on D-Day alone. Ted thought about those numbers every day.

He watched another plane land then realized that his pipe

had grown cold. He leaned over to empty the bowl by tapping it against the heel of his shoe and was surprised, a moment later, to realize that he'd struck the pipe so hard that he'd broken it in two. He was glad no one was around to see this. Men like him didn't show their emotions when it came to the war.

His unit had landed at Normandy without him. He had been pulled out at the last minute and never knew why. The shame and guilt resulted in unrelenting pressure. *You should have been there,* his mind told him daily. *You'd better have a good life; you're living for all of those who didn't make it.*

Twenty years had passed but it didn't matter. And, as luck would have it, there were fresh reminders. The only suitable type of aircraft available for Mr. Toomb's airline, it turned out, were old Army transport planes affectionately known as "Gooney Birds." And the pilots? The only ones who had answered the newspaper advertisements were former World War Two pilots who had kept up their credentials in civilian life. He'd already hired two.

So far, the federal government had approved a route between Tampa and points east (Orlando) and north (Tallahassee). It was a huge accomplishment in a short period of time, but much work remained to be done. When he was younger and dreamed of the white-collar life, Ted had envisioned smoke-filled boardrooms and leisurely lunches of prime rib and bourbon. In his mind, a secretary would take care of all the mundane details at work, just as a wife would do at home. Well, fantasy did not match reality. While he was making more money than he'd ever thought possible, the truth was that he hardly had time to enjoy spending it.

At least Jackie seemed happy now. Their first year in Florida had been tumultuous. Between the book club and the radio show, she'd caused quite a ruckus. She had irritated the heck out of Mr. Toomb, but even that seemed smoothed over. The book club had mostly disbanded, and Jackie was spending most of her time helping with that baby. Yes, it was a bit unorthodox, but it was certainly worthwhile. He was relieved by the decision by Jackie and her friends to keep the baby primarily at Mrs. Bailey White's house, which was off the beaten path. It also meant that the baby's mother, Priscilla, could stay there—and not at his house—when she returned on her visits from college. Ted was not prejudiced, or at least he didn't think he was. However, a man had to protect his wife and children, and he was not going to let them be a target for some furious redneck who might throw a Molotov cocktail through the living room window.

Like Jackie, he believed that the best way to address the race problem in America was to help Negroes advance through education. In fact, one of Ted's favorite charities was the United Negro College Fund, to which he donated every year since it was founded in 1944, even when his wallet had been thin. He had met Priscilla only once, but he agreed with Jackie that the young girl was college material.

He was surprised—but kept it to himself—that Jackie seemed to be enjoying the baby as much as she did. He recalled how brittle she had been as a new mother and it was interesting to see that she was so relaxed with Priscilla's baby. Maybe, because Jackie was a little older now, and experienced. Jackie's friend, Plain Jane, seemed to be enjoying the baby, too, at least judging from Jackie's comments. He had his doubts about weird old Mrs. Bailey White, but from everything he'd heard, the old woman had paid her debt to society and was settling back into a normal life. If Jackie and Plain Jane were, in a sense, helping with Mrs. Bailey White's rehabilitation, that seemed like a good cause, too.

Obviously, this was not the life Jackie expected when she'd married him. Of course, it wasn't what he had planned on, either. If only there'd been a way to climb the corporate ladder without being on the road so much of the time, or relocating the whole family to a place that seemed as far from Boston as Timbuktu.

Thirteen

Dolores Simpson did not have a radio or television, nor did she care to. Even if owning one or both had been her heart's desire, the electric grid didn't come anywhere near her little fishing shack. She had considered buying one of those newfangled transistor radios, but it cost too much. As for a telephone, the thought was laughable. It would be "a hundred years shy of never," as the saying went, before anyone put phone lines there.

Robbie-Lee had been her grapevine to the outside world. He would come home from school—and later, from his job at Sears—and tell her the big news of the day (the Cuban Missile Crisis, for example) along with local news (who had gotten married, who had up and died) and, best of all, little tidbits from Hollywood that he heard on the radio during his lunch hour. If he had something new to tell her about Elizabeth Taylor, it made her day.

But those days were gone. She didn't miss people in general. She just missed Robbie-Lee. And with changes coming to the river, she needed the information that her son, had he still been living at home, would have provided. Walking to town was tiring, but she'd done it when necessary, for example, when she'd sent the telegram to Dora Witherspoon in Mississippi. Fortunately, her neighbors, Billy and Marco, aware that Robbie-Lee had gone away, had started dropping off the *Naples Star* at her fishing shack on their way back from—well, from somewhere. She never really knew what they were up to but followed the unofficial rule of Gun Rack Village: Don't ask questions.

The gift of a newspaper miraculously landing on her narrow dock, courtesy of Billy and Marco, didn't occur every day but it was often enough to suit her. She no longer had to keep track of the passage of days by marking a scrap of paper each morning. She didn't care that the newspaper was secondhand; there were signs, like cigarette ashes smudged into the newsprint, that the brothers had read it already. That was fine; it meant she didn't have to pay them.

On this particular day Dolores heard the truck followed by the familiar *thump* as the paper hit the dock but didn't bother to retrieve it right away. Not a thing was happening of any importance. For real news—news that mattered—she'd have to wait for Dora Witherspoon.

Only when she went outside an hour later to clean her shotgun did she remember the newspaper, saw it sitting there, and picked it up. She took the rubber band off (she saved them; they were hard to come by) and saw this announcement on the front page:

"Read Our New Column by Collier County's Very Own MISS DREAMSVILLE!" page 11

Like everyone else in Naples, Dolores flipped immediately to page eleven. Peering out at her was a little pen-and-ink sketch of a grinning, winking woman who was clearly supposed to be Jackie. Next to the drawing were the words "Chatter Box by Miss Dreamsville!"

There was a headline beneath it that read, THE LEGEND OF SEMINOLE JOE. Dolores did not take the time to sit down or go back in the house. She read it standing stock still, not even bothered by a sliver of sunlight breaking through some bad-weather clouds and shining in her eyes. Some of the words were hard for her so she read slowly and aloud:

> Residents have long spoken in hushed tones about a dangerous apparition who is said to reside near the Mangrove River and has been known to wreak havoc in our lovely community.
>
> Seminole Joe, as he is called, has killed (and, some say, eaten) at least seventeen persons since he himself was murdered by Spanish Explorers. It is believed he only attacks Caucasian men. Mr. Joe has been fairly quiet in recent years, but old-timers are concerned this will change with the proposed new real-estate development (cheekily called Dreamsville Estates by Mr. Darryl Norwood, who, it should be stated here, did not ask permission of yours truly).
>
> Since the beginning of time, one of the peculiarities of the human condition is that people can look at the exact same event, or in this case, the same place, and see entirely different things. Some look at the river and see Nature in all her glory. Others envision a river of money, created with asphalt, timber, and glass. It is not hard to

imagine which side Seminole Joe will take as it is widely known that he abhors change and wanton waste.

A model citizen who has lived in Collier County for all of her eighty years was willing to speak but not for attribution. "I'm very worried that Joe will get all stirred up again," she remarked. "Anyone working on that project, or living there after it's built, will never again have a sound night's sleep. I know I won't."

Will Neapolitans be safe from the wrath of the ghostly Indian? Will Seminole Joe rise again? Only time will tell.

Dolores crumpled the newspaper in her hands and tossed it as far as she could, only to have a wind gust pick it up and toss it straight back, mocking her. What was that crazy Boston gal up to now? Having her involved was not helpful. The woman made a mess of everything she touched. Why was she bringing up *Seminole Joe*?

Old-timers knew it wasn't wise to talk about Seminole Joe unless you absolutely had to, and then, only in quiet, funeral-parlor voices. You surely didn't write about him in the newspaper.

The fact that Darryl was planning to call his development Dreamsville Estates was a shock. A wickedly clever business idea on Darryl's part. But what kind of fool would provoke Jackie Hart and Seminole Joe at the same time?

Over the years, Dolores had occasionally heard a child being disciplined by a thoughtless parent saying, "You'd better behave or Seminole Joe will get you tonight." Well, first of all, Dolores thought that was mean. Why would anyone scare a child like that? She'd never talked to Robbie-Lee like that. Second, Seminole Joe wouldn't be bothered with some poor skeerty-cat child who hadn't done his homework or his chores. He had far more worthwhile wrongs to right. Besides, no one could summon Seminole Joe for selfish reasons. Some spirits could be conjured for specific reasons, but not Joe. He had a mind of his own.

Jackie was the type of Yankee who, no doubt, would laugh at the idea of Seminole Joe, like the woman manager who came down from Chicago to train Robbie-Lee to run the Sears catalog store. Miss High and Mighty had interrupted a conversation between Robbie-Lee and a customer by announcing, "What are you talking about?! Surely you know there is no such thing as ghosts!" And, according to Robbie-Lee, it was said in a way that made both him and the customer feel ignorant.

Dolores knew the type. What the lady manager didn't say, but might as well have, was, "I don't believe in them, therefore, they cannot possibly exist." Dolores knew differently. The truth was, if you didn't encounter spirits it was because you refused to see them—possibly, to your own detriment.

Why were Yankees so certain they understood the world better than anyone else? You'd think life was some kind of big joke, and they were the only ones smart enough to know what was funny and what was not. Folks like that weren't open to mystery or magic. They thought they had everything figured out, so their minds were closed like a steel trap. It was kind of sad, when you got right down to it.

Maybe the problem was that Yankee folks, even on vacation, were always in motion, running from one activity to the next. If they weren't swimming, they were golfing. If they weren't golfing, they were boating. That was fine—they were welcome to it—but Dolores was puzzled that people could claim to love the outdoor life and yet seem so far away from nature. They preferred houses built like bunkers with cement floors and walls, barriers to the swampland where, God forbid, bugs and other scary things lurked. Dolores imagined them in their nice houses, some with air-conditioning, all of them with plumbing. They put on shoes that looked like combat boots, just to walk to their mailboxes. She'd seen them and tried not to laugh.

Did they ever spend hours looking at the stars, as Dolores did? There was nothing quite like star watching on a clear night, or witnessing the fight for survival among the plants and critters in the swamps, to make a person remember that she was just a speck of dust.

Seminole Joe was more than a story. He was a spirit, and spirits live on, in different ways and for different reasons.

What most folks didn't seem to understand was that Seminole Joe was the spirit of injustice. He represented all the wrongs that had been done in the 'Glades. Folks were scared of Seminole Joe but in her opinion, it was Darryl they should have been skeert of. Darryl was like an overseer with a whip, a man with no soul. Darryl was a man who had choices, and he'd chosen mean over good.

From time to time, Dolores actually understood—just a little—what it must have been like to be colored or Indian. It didn't take a genius to see that white people were at the root of just about every mess you could think of, and Darryl was just the latest version. White folks had a knack for finding their way to the top of the pecking order and ruling the roost. Dolores could see this, and yet it created a problem for her because she was white, so what was wrong with her? What was she lacking? Why wasn't she rich and powerful, and sitting at the top of the henhouse looking down on everyone else? Maybe she wasn't quite mean enough. Or ambitious enough.

She uncrumpled the newspaper and reread the column. Jackie Hart's bringing up Seminole Joe was bound to complicate an already-tricky situation. Jackie seemed to thrive when she created chaos. But Dolores had lived long enough to know that a wise person didn't let a bobcat out of its cage and assume it would eat only varmints. No, sir, it might eat you instead.

She looked over at the night heron. "Let's hope Dora Witherspoon talks some sense into her man," she called out, and the bird stretched its wings in response. To herself, she added, "Otherwise, I'm afeared we be in for a wild ride."

Fourteen

What do you suppose Seminole Joe looks like?" Judd asked, wiping the sweat from his brow with the hem of his T-shirt. He had fled to my little cottage to get away from the craziness that had been going on all day, ever since the *Naples Star* landed in people's driveways or hedges. Judd said the phone had not stopped ringing with excited people wanting to talk to his mother about her column on Seminole Joe. No wonder he wanted to hide out for a while at my cottage. And I put him to work, helping me dig some new holes for the turtles to wallow around in.

"Haven't you ever seen the local Indians?" I asked, surprised.

"You mean selling baskets?" he said. "No one ever said they were Indians. I didn't know who they were. My teacher said we should stay away from them, that's all I know."

"Well, did you ever see the movie *Key Largo*?" I asked.

He looked like he was racking his brain. "No, I don't think so," he said. "That was before my time."

Judd cracked me up. Sometimes he sounded like a thirteen-year-old boy, and sometimes he sounded like a sixty-year-old man.

"Well," I said, slurping on my iced tea, "Lauren Bacall was in it. And Humphrey Bogart."

"Seminole Joe looks like . . . Humphrey Bogart?"

I tried not to laugh. "No, no, Humphrey Bogart plays a man who was in the Army in the war and visits his dead friend's father and widow who live down yon in Key Largo. There's a bunch of gangsters in the movie, too—Edward G. Robinson plays one of them."

The word "gangster" got Judd's attention. He was behaving like a thirteen-year-old again. "So what happens?" he said, completely focused. I noticed, once again, that he had Jackie's blue eyes—the exact shade. And yet he looked like his dad, Ted Hart, too.

"Well, the real star of the movie is a storm," I said. "A hurricane. But maybe I shouldn't tell you more. Sometime maybe you'll see the movie and I wouldn't want to ruin it for you."

"But—wait—what's this got to do with Seminole Joe?"

"There are characters in the movie who are supposed to be Seminole Indians," I said, "and I think some of them really are. So Joe probably looked more or less like the Indians in *Key Largo*."

Judd looked disappointed. "But how am I going to see the movie?" he said. "It could be five years before they show it on TV."

"You could go to the library and see if they have any books on the Seminoles," I said, and his face brightened. "They must at least have a book about Andrew Jackson and the Seminole Wars," I added.

Well, that was the last I saw of Judd that day. He was off

on his bicycle like Paul Revere warning folks that the British were coming, an image that fit mighty nice, considering that he'd spent the first eleven years of his life in Boston.

Judd's energy was inspiring. After fixing myself a fried bologna sandwich, half of which I fed to my turtles, I decided to go for a stroll on the beach to look for shells and clear my mind. To my surprise, every little shell or pebble seemed to hurt my bare feet. In my year away from home, it seems I'd become a tenderfoot on account of wearing shoes all the time. But the surf was gentle and soothing as bathwater, and I realized, splashing along in ankle-deep water, that I was happy. Not happy about Darryl's development plans or his remarriage to some Northern gal, of course, but happy with the general direction of my life. I had learned a great deal during my year in Mississippi—some of it hard to take—but I was more independent than I'd ever been. I was going back to Jackson, not forever, but for a little while longer. I was not going to run away from the city of my mother's birth and the story that was unfolding there about her past. *My* past.

There was still plenty of daylight, so I went home, found my old Keds, and walked slowly downtown. I told myself I was going to get a root beer float at the Rexall counter but truth be told, I wanted to see if anything was going on. Sometimes, folks would gather downtown when something important was happening. I'd be able to judge how big a reaction Jackie's story was getting by the number of people—usually at home on a hot night in Naples—milling around and looking for an excuse to talk.

Sure enough, there were people gathered by the bench in front of the post office, outside the Rexall, and by the Winn-Dixie. I recognized a few people from high school but wasn't eager to talk to them, especially Betty Jane Pomeroy, who was holding court over by the Green Stamp Redemption Center. Betty Jane had a way of inserting the topic of her happy marriage, brilliant children, and fabulous house into every conversation. Fortunately, I saw Plain Jane walking along by herself from the direction of the Dairy Queen. We saw each other at the same moment, and I was reminded, once again, how much my old book club meant to me. Before them, especially since I'd gotten divorced, I'd felt like a stranger in my own hometown.

Plain Jane and I perched on the top step of the Everglades Savings and Loan, a good location for spying on people ever since it was rebuilt at eight feet above sea level after being trounced by Hurricane Donna. "You know what they're talking about, don't you?" Plain Jane said, between bites of an ice cream cone that was melting faster than she could eat it.

"I can guess," I said.

"Someone said Darryl is going to have a press conference tomorrow," she said. "Apparently she really stirred things up. You know, people don't talk about spirits, much less Seminole Joe. Everyone around here knows the stories but no one has ever written about it in the newspaper."

This was true. Somehow, just the fact that Seminole Joe had made the pages of the *Naples Star* made a scary story seem real. Official. Or, as Mama would have said, bona fide.

Hard to say where this was headed, though. Were they upset about Seminole Joe, or mad at Jackie for writing about him? Would their fear become anger at Darryl for possibly disturbing Seminole Joe?

That night I didn't sleep well and I bet the same was true for half the population of Collier County. I couldn't decide which was worse: to sleep with the windows shut and die of the heat or leave them open and possibly be ax-murdered by Seminole Joe. When I finally fell asleep, my eyes were closed but my ears were wide open, and any little sound had me leaping out of the bed.

The next day, the *Naples Star* carried this story on the front page:

STRONG RESPONSE TO 'MISS DREAMSVILLE' DEBUT

by the Editors

Collier County residents reacted with unusual animosity yesterday to an opinion piece by our new columnist, Mrs. Jackie Hart, also known as Miss Dreamsville, after her famous radio show of that name. Our phone rang off the hook yesterday from calls by readers incensed by Miss Dreamsville's (and this newspaper's) decision to publish an account of the legend of Seminole Joe. A logbook kept by our staff showed that eighty-seven callers complained that Seminole Joe did not like attention and that Miss Dreamsville's column could cause him to rise from his ghostly grave and commit new atrocities. We find this highly unlikely, although we are flattered that so many residents assume that Seminole Joe is a faithful reader of the *Naples Star*. Collier County residents, let us remember that "Joe" is a legend! This is 1964, the Modern Age, and as such it is time we put these superstitions to rest, or at least keep them in check, or our fine community will remain stuck in the putrid fog of backward thinking. We will be running a special Letters to the Editor section on Friday to address readers' concerns. In a related development, Mr. Darryl Norwood has announced that he will hold a press conference today at 7:00 PM to answer questions about his project.

Well, I had the answer to my question. So far, at least, people were more upset with Jackie and the newspaper than they were with Darryl. As I tried to decide what to do next, Judd came by on his bicycle. He said he'd tried to call his father, who was in Tallahassee, but hadn't been able to reach him.

"Mom was on the phone with a lawyer in New York City, then she got so mad she left the house," he confided. "I tried to call Dad but the long-distance operator wouldn't make the call because I'm a kid."

Judd left, but not before agreeing to go with me to the press conference in case Jackie showed up and made a scene. I would rather have a tooth pulled without novocaine but I knew in my heart I had to go—for Judd's sake, at least.

About two o'clock in the afternoon, while I was writing a letter to Mrs. Conroy, my landlady back in Mississippi, I heard Jackie's car pull up. To my surprise, she marched right in—right past Norma Jean, Myrtle, and Castro. This was not a good sign. She was so mad she forgot to be afraid of "those dreadful things."

"That odious, reprehensible, son of a lobster boat!" she hollered, by way of a greeting. I'd never heard anyone utter that particular string of words before but, considering the circumstances, I figured this was some kind of exotic, Northern insult.

I was relieved somewhat by the realization that I was not likely the intended recipient of her anger.

She remained in the doorway, her hand still on the knob of my front door, and yelled again. "He's going to get away with it! He can *use my name!*"

"Jackie," I said, my voice shaking, "come sit down." I approached her gingerly, like she was a wild critter that had escaped from Jungle Larry's African Safari, a tourist trap on the Tamiami Trail. Carefully, I took her arm and led her to Mama's old chair, where she collapsed in a theatrical heap. I left her side long enough to retrieve a tall glass of sweet tea and carry it back to her on a little tray with a napkin. After a few sips, she was calm enough to tell me what had happened. She spoke in short, little sentences, like she was going to blow a fuse if she tried to say a whole sentence at once.

"I talked to the lawyer. On the phone. I called him long distance."

I waited. "Well," I said. "What did he say?"

She swallowed hard. "Darryl can call his development Dreamsville if he wants. He just can't use my picture on any of the advertisements. He can't say that I endorsed it, since that would be a lie. But he doesn't have to get my permission to call it Dreamsville, or Dreamsville Estates."

"I see." Actually, I didn't understand it at all.

"I don't 'own' the name Miss Dreamsville," she added, sensing my confusion. "Not in a legal sense."

"So you can't sue him?" I asked quietly.

"Well, I could sue him. But I wouldn't win."

"And that's what the lawyer told you? On the phone?"

Jackie lit a cigarette. "Yes," she said. "That's the way it is. Unfortunately."

"And this was the lawyer in New York?"

"I called two—one in New York, the other in Boston. They both said the same thing."

I let this sink in. Jackie seemed more relaxed, like she'd used up all her anger, but I was becoming madder by the second. What the heck was wrong with Darryl that he would steal my friend's name? Was this another swipe at me? I had to admit it was, in a sickening way, an ingenious move on his part. Jackie had put Naples on the map with her radio show. Even Walter Cronkite, the most trusted man in America, had done a little segment on *CBS Evening News* about Miss Dreamsville. It would be easy for Darryl to market his new development to Yankees by calling it Dreamsville Estates.

I hoped Mama wasn't listening in on my thoughts. She never had approved of cussin' in any way, shape, or form. But all I could think of was, *That odious, reprehensible, son of a lobster boat.*

Fifteen

The challenge at the press conference would be keeping Jackie from speaking her mind. Judd and I made her promise six ways to Sunday that she wouldn't say a single word, what with her talent for making bad things worse.

"Jackie, tonight we are going to be flies on the wall," I kept admonishing her as we walked downtown from my cottage.

"Yes, all we're going to do is collect intelligence," Judd added.

"Judd Hart, you've been watching too much of that spy stuff on television," Jackie scolded.

"Mom, what I'm saying is that we should lay low and observe what happens. Then we can reconvene and plan our next move."

Jackie sighed and ruffled Judd's hair. "Do you think the girls will show up?" she asked, referring to her twin daughters—Judd's older sisters.

"Not a chance," Judd said.

"Well, that's good because I wouldn't want to *embarrass* them," Jackie said. "They think I'm *embarrassing enough* already."

"They're girls, Mom," Judd said soothingly. "They're weird."

Jackie looked at Judd as if she were going to say something more but didn't. Instead, she ruffled his hair again.

"You're not going to embarrass anyone," I said firmly, trying to get back to the point. "You will be dignified, like Elizabeth Taylor in *Cleopatra*."

Jackie had insisted we go early and stand directly in front of the stage set up by the Chamber of Commerce on the grass next to City Hall. I would rather we stood in back but I soon realized what she hoped to accomplish. She wanted everyone to see her. She stood with her arms crossed, staring tragically into the distance. Judd put one hand on her shoulder protectively. I copied Jackie's stance except I planned to look eyeball-to-eyeball with Darryl once he started speaking.

Just as I began to think everyone was staying home, folks starting showing up in little groups of two and three. By the time the press conference started, five minutes late, there were close to two hundred people there, all itching to hear what Darryl had to say. Of course, this being a small Southern town, we had to be patient. First, the mayor led us in the Pledge of Allegiance followed by the Sons of the Confederate Veterans performance of "Dixie." After that, Little Miss Swamp Buggy 1964 sang "Collier County, I Love Thee" and a rousing rendition of "Yay! Rah! for Naples."

Yay! Rah! for Naples,
Yay! Rah! for Naples,
Someone in the crowd's singing,
"Yay! Rah! for Naples."
One, two, three, four,
Naples, that's us! Rah, rah, rah . . .

And then came a string of announcements: The Garden Club needed volunteers to water the flower boxes near the train station (even though most people arrived by car or bus and hardly any trains came through anymore). And someone from the Naples Players announced that the new season would start the following week with *Stop the World—I Want to Get Off*, starring Bucky Holmes from the Esso station.

By the time Darryl was about to speak, I had the embarrassing image of myself crumpling to the ground and being placed on a cot and resuscitated by the eager Boy Scouts who were manning the first-aid squad. Judd looked flushed and Jackie, a bit glassy-eyed, was having trouble maintaining her pose.

The mayor spoke briefly. "I'm sure we all know Darryl Norwood, who grew up right here in Collier County, and is making it his personal goal to bring us into a new era." I was relieved to hear grumbles in the crowd, and there was no applause when Darryl took the microphone.

"I know why you all are here, and I'm grateful for it," he began. "I'm glad for the opportunity to straighten out any misunderstandings. It's very important that you all understand that Dreamsville Estates will be the best thing that ever happened to Collier County. And I want to assure all of you that all of this needless fear about Seminole Joe is not helpful. Frankly, I'm surprised that in this day and age, y'all would get yourselves worked up into a lather over the idea that we could be disturbing a haint." He paused, and laughed dismissively. "There is no such thing as Seminole Joe. There never was."

I had to hide a grin that was creeping up the corners of my mouth. Darryl was handling this all wrong. I knew it before he did; I could feel it in the crowd.

An old-timer with skin like cowhide elbowed his way to the front and struggled up to the platform. "Don't you go talking down to us," he shouted into the microphone. "We gonna believe what we want to believe. You're a dog-gone fool. You're playing games with the devil and we aren't going to allow it!"

The crowd cheered like their team had just scored a touchdown against Punta Gorda High. Clearly, Darryl was losing. If everyone continued on this path, the people of Naples were turning their anger from Jackie and the newspaper to Darryl, where it belonged.

I peeked at Jackie and could see she was biting her lower lip. Poor gal, it was killin' her not to get into the fray.

Just when it seemed the sheriff might need to tell everyone to settle down, the mayor stood up and prevailed upon us to behave in a more Christian manner. "We are civilized people," he scolded, holding the microphone so close that it screeched and hurt our ears. "Sorry about that," he said. Then, "We must remain calm and listen to our speaker. These are the leaders of our community, and we should be respectful."

"Darryl Norwood ain't a leader!" a youthful voice called from deep within the crowd. "We never elected him to nothin'!"

The Reverend Wesley Whitmore from Sweet Savior Baptist Church took the microphone from the mayor, who didn't look at all sorry and retreated quickly to the back of the stage. "I have something I would like to say," the reverend said in a voice deep as a bullfrog's in mating season. "Talking about haints and conjuring and black magic and whatnot is not worthy of this community." He received a polite round of applause mostly, I noticed, from his parishioners.

Darryl tried to take advantage of the preacher's comments. "Thank you," he said, leaning into the microphone, still in the clutches of the preacher. "Y'all should listen to Reverend Whitmore here."

But the good reverend snapped back. "Now just a moment," he said to Darryl, "don't presume to pretend that I'm endorsing your project. I'm just saying that folks should stop this nonsense about . . . well, about an Indian spirit. And another thing," he added, "I don't think it's nice that you're planning to call the place Dreamsville Estates when Mrs. Jackie Hart doesn't approve. She's our Miss Dreamsville, and it's disrespectful to use a lady's name against her wishes, and to profit from it."

This was a surprise. Of course, Reverend Whitmore was new here. He'd never heard Jackie's at-times risqué radio show and had missed the uproar she had caused.

Defending a lady's good name was a surefire way to stir up a crowd anywhere south of the Mason-Dixon line, and it most definitely had that effect in good old Naples. The crowd applauded warmly. Jackie, seizing the moment, waved and mouthed, "Thank you."

Then another preacher stood up and the Reverend Whitmore handed over the microphone. "My name is Reverend John McDaniel," he said politely, "and I'm the new interim pastor at Airport Road Methodist. I am from North Florida and I was educated in Chicago. I am in full agreement with Reverend Whitmore here, but I'd like to add something else, if I may. Last month, as I traveled nearly the length of our great state with my family to arrive here at my new appointment, I was alarmed at the pace of development in so many places. Why is this? I asked myself. Is it *progress*, as some would say, or is it worship of that false God, *money*? And, what are the consequences? These undeveloped areas are a gift from God, my friends. Remember your scripture—we are *stewards* of God's earth."

The mayor jumped up from his seat and grabbed the microphone a little roughly from Reverend McDaniel. "Now let's get back on track here," he said. "This project is a mighty good thing for Naples. Dreamsville Estates will attract people from all over the United States. The Chamber of Commerce has already agreed to sponsor Welcome to Dreamsville signs at every entrance to Naples. Our airport needs work, and we are fortunate that one of our most eminent citizens, Mr. Toomb, has agreed to oversee some improvements there. Neapolitans, we must think of the big picture! We already have two major assets—the fishing pier and the swamp buggy races. Three of the world's great religions—Baptists, Methodists, and Presbyterians—are represented right here in our little town. We are a welcoming place and it's about time we move forward into the nineteenth century."

"What? Don't you mean twentieth century?" someone hollered from the back of the crowd, which exploded into laughter, the kind with a mean edge to it. Emboldened, the heckler added, "Just what century do you think we be livin' in, Mayor? I thought this was 1964. Are you saying this is 1864?"

The mayor looked upset and ruffled like a hen that's being bothered by a rooster. "Aw, heck, you know what I mean!" he said. Now that even the mayor had been set back on his heels, it was fair to say that Jackie, the *Naples Star*, and Seminole Joe had won the day, with Darryl the loser. So far, so good.

JUDD TOOK OFF FOR CIVIL Air Patrol, and Jackie and I, feeling a little triumphant, went to Mrs. Bailey White's house. Our good mood soured immediately, though, because, of all things, Mrs. Bailey White was peeved that Jackie had mentioned her in the newspaper column. Jackie admitted that the line about the "model citizen who has lived in Collier County for all of her eighty years" and who feared the return of Seminole Joe was indeed a reference to Mrs. Bailey White. What I didn't get—and I could see that Jackie was puzzled, too—was that Mrs. Bailey White's name had not even been mentioned.

"I do not like the whole world thinking of me as eighty years old," she said, brushing a piece of lint off her skirt.

"But no one will know it's you," Jackie said, trying to sound reassuring.

"Well, I know it's me, and that's enough," Mrs. Bailey White sulked. "A woman should never reveal her true age. Do you know what they say about a woman who will reveal her age? That she'll reveal everything else, too! And I wasn't raised like that."

Plain Jane, who had been reading the final pages of *To the Lighthouse*, set down her book. "Mrs. Bailey White, I don't see why—"

"And I'll tell you something else," Mrs. Bailey White interrupted. "A woman should only be in the paper two times in her life—when she gets married and when she dies."

"But Mrs. Bailey White," I started but stopped short. What I wanted to say was, *But you must have been in the newspapers plenty of times when you were arrested, tried, and convicted for shooting your husband back in the day.*

"Please believe me, Mrs. Bailey White, I am very, very sorry," Jackie said, as I prayed silently for an end to this uncomfortable conversation. "It was stupid of me. I should have thought of it. And it won't happen again."

"Well," Mrs. Bailey White said slowly, "I guess maybe it doesn't matter. Maybe I'm being too thin-skinned. All this talk about Seminole Joe is getting on my last good nerve. And, yes, I know it's my fault because I'm the one who brought him up—"

"Oh, no," Jackie said quickly. "This is my fault."

"No, it's not," I said, wondering why women were always quick to blame ourselves. "It's that no-good, good-for-nothin' former husband of mine. That's whose fault it is. He started all this mess and everyone's in an uproar because of it. And you know what? The louse is getting married again."

There were sighs and groans enough to fill a graveyard on Halloween. "Oh, Dora," Plain Jane said, speaking for the rest. "That's too bad. Or, at least I think it must be . . . Oh dear, how do you feel about it?"

"Not great, especially because she's a Northern gal," I said miserably.

"Why does that make you feel worse?" Jackie asked.

"Oh, I don't know. Maybe because I just assume she must be smarter and prettier than me," I said.

"She's probably meaner than a wet hen," Mrs. Bailey White said. "Where's she from?"

"Some town in New Jersey called Basking Ridge. That's what Darryl said."

"Oh!" Jackie said. We looked at her in alarm. "Basking Ridge—that's the place where Darryl's investors live! That's what Ted said."

We were puzzling through the implications of this until Plain Jane finally put it into words. "So maybe Darryl is marrying into the family that is paying for his real estate development?" she said aloud.

That was a disgusting thought. The possibility of Darryl marrying for money could mean he was even more of a low-level creep than I thought.

I hadn't even thought of bringing up the topic of Darryl and his remarriage but I was glad that I had. Sharing my distress about Darryl's remarriage reminded me that I loved my friends. I *needed* my friends. And, despite the depressing reason for my return, at this moment I was thrilled to be back. I was still a member of the Collier County Women's Literary Society, and it felt awfully good.

Sixteen

The airline business was far more complex than Ted Hart had anticipated. First of all, there were the unions, the most obstinate being the pilots' organization which made it difficult for Ted to create schedules that made any kind of sense from a financial point of view. Then there was the government (pronounced *guv-mint* up in Tallahassee, Ted's new home away from home). The state didn't have many regulations when it came to commercial airlines but at the federal level, administrators kept close tabs.

To Ted it seemed like interference until one of the pilots, who had flown so many missions during the war that it was a miracle he survived, gave him a wake-up call on the tarmac in Orlando. "All you talk about is profit margin! What do you want us to do, kill the passengers?" the pilot yelled. And for a moment, Ted thought he was about to get shoved straight into a propeller of a DC-3. Afterward, he realized the pilot had been right. He—Ted Hart, a blue-collar son of Fall River, Massachusetts—had put money ahead of people. It was one of the worst moments of his life.

He walked away from the runway and lit his new pipe, which he'd purchased after breaking the old one. He hadn't been able to give up smoking but at least he quit a cigarette habit. If only Jackie would do the same. The woman smoked like a chimney. The kids complained about it all the time. The Surgeon General's announcement earlier that year about a strong link between cigarettes and cancer had an impact on him, but not Jackie.

Maybe, Ted thought, he should throw in the towel. All he really wanted was to go home, not that Naples was "home," exactly, but that's where Jackie and the kids were living and waiting for him. Waiting, waiting, waiting. He'd done so much of that in the Army. He'd thought that once the war ended he would no longer have the feeling that the present was to be endured. The future was when life would really start. But it didn't feel that way for a New England boy living mostly in a hotel in Tallahassee, Florida.

Things were not going well for Jackie. She was upset, and he didn't blame her.

Darn that guy Darryl Norwood. Ted was furious, not so much about the possible destruction of the river but the fact that some lowlife redneck was exploiting his wife by calling the new development Dreamsville Estates. That was nerve, even by Yankee standards. So much for Southern honor! Ted had a strong desire to settle the dispute the way it was done in the Army—by presenting Darryl Norwood with a knuckle sandwich right to the jawbone.

On Jackie's behalf, Ted had swallowed his pride and talked to his boss Mr. Toomb. Unfortunately, but not surprisingly, the old geezer refused to interfere with Darryl Norwood, shrewdly pointing out that if Darryl's development was successful, the airline would be, too.

Mr. Toomb, however, agreed that Ted could use his connections and time on the job to try to find out more about Darryl's backers. So Ted figured that on his monthly trip up north, he would make the short drive from New York to this place called Basking Ridge, New Jersey, and see if he could get some background and, ideally, maybe even meet the investors—information that Jackie wanted as well.

Ted wondered what it was about Jackie that made her get in over her head. He wanted to help her, and he wanted to be on her team, but he'd come to realize that part of being married to her was coping with her impulsive side. Had she been like this in Boston? He couldn't even remember anymore. The past two years in Collier County overshadowed all the years that came before.

Meanwhile, the kids were getting older. His daughters were in a perpetual state of warfare with Jackie, and although this was worrisome Jackie assured him it was normal for teenage girls. Judd spent much of his time steering clear of his sisters and Jackie when he could, but the result was that the boy was basically raising himself. He'd joined Civil Air Patrol, and he'd been looking after Dora Witherspoon's turtles, so he was busy. But he needed a father's guidance. A father who was home.

Ted had hoped his family would adjust, and until this new problem with Darryl Norwood there'd been some progress. When they arrived in the summer of '62, he and Jackie had the worst fight they'd ever had. If only she hadn't encountered that palmetto bug sitting on the toilet seat on the very first night in their new home. After the screaming was over she'd said, "Ted, we need to talk about this *palace* you've brought us to *here* in this *cultural mecca.*"

Judd had settled in fairly quickly. But for Jackie and his

daughters, it was a struggle. At least, Ted reasoned, the girls had each other. After all, they were twins. But they were not happy; anyone could see that. As for Jackie, she'd had some spectacularly bad moments but at least she'd made some friends with that book club. And ever since she'd put Naples on the map with her *Miss Dreamsville* radio show—which, thank God she wasn't doing anymore—the local people seemed more tolerant. For a while, she'd even been something of a hero.

The fact that Ted was old Mr. Toomb's right-hand man had given the family a little extra leeway. No one in town wanted to provoke Mr. Toomb, one of the richest and most powerful men south of the Mason-Dixon line, with money invested in cotton, orange groves, tobacco, sugarcane, and—that old Southern favorite—land. Mr. Toomb would stray from Ted's carefully constructed business plan and buy a piece of land, and Ted would ask why. There was never a reason beyond, "Well, it was for sale." The last time it happened, though, Mr. Toomb put Ted in his place by saying, "I hired you to give me the know-how into the way business works in the North, not to tell me what to do."

So Ted had learned to walk a thin line. He was still trying to figure out what worked and what didn't. Up north, the best way to stay gainfully employed was to play the game. Generally speaking, this meant giving your boss all the credit publicly and then you'd be rewarded later. Ted had tried that with Mr. Toomb, and it hadn't worked. He was baffled until he began to notice that in the South an employee seemed to fall into one of two categories: You were either a servant with no rights or say whatsoever or you were "family." You didn't have to be related. In fact, you could be any color of the rainbow and possibly be referred to as "family" by a white person (although never, Ted observed, the other way around). To Ted's Northern ears, there was something patronizing about a white person referring to a black person (usually a longtime servant) as "part of the family."

Then the day came when Mr. Toomb said to him, "Ted, you're like a son to me. You're a part of the family." And Ted felt very special and very honored, until he remembered that Mr. Toomb said the same thing to his longtime, long-suffering chauffeur, who was black.

He had discussed it that night with Jackie, who was just as confused and disturbed as he was. She relayed a conversation she'd overheard two women having at the Book Nook. In loud voices they'd said, "You know, Yankees have their race problem, too. They shouldn't be coming down south telling us what to do about our Negroes." Jackie was pretty sure she was meant to overhear this remark, and was about to say something when Judd and the twins entered the store. She had planned to meet them there and buy each one a book of their choosing.

"So you didn't say anything?" Ted was surprised.

Jackie had sighed. "I'm learning to choose my battles," she'd said, "and I didn't want to embarrass the twins. But I talked to all three kids about it later at home. I asked them to think about it and I'm proud to say that all three of them had the same reaction. The phrase 'our Negroes' made them nuts."

Our Negroes. Yes, Ted had heard it many times, too. Another common saying which jarred his Yankee sensibility was "Here in the South, Negroes know their place." And the people saying it didn't seem to realize how they sounded. What was brazen and insulting to his ears was normal chitchat to them.

It was a huge relief to him that Jackie was being more careful about what she said and did. Three civil rights workers—two of them white—had been murdered three months ago in Mississippi. Even with Jackie being more prudent, he wished he was at home more, not that he could control Jackie but at least to keep a close eye on her.

Jackie complained often that she hated how much he was on the road. If she was in a particularly bad mood, he would get the "it's not easy being a woman" rant. Clearly, she was restless being a housewife and mother. Well, it wasn't so great being a man, either. That's what he wanted to say but didn't because starting a third world war was not in anyone's best interests. But was it really so bad for women? It was men who were sent off to war. It was men who died in battle or came home and had to live with what they'd seen or done. And then what? A man had to get training or an education, find a job, earn money to support a family. Sometimes he actually envied Jackie. When the kids were at school she had time on her hands. When was the last time he had that luxury? She loved that book, *The Feminine Mystique*, but he blamed it for leading to her breakdown in early '63. He would never forget how she took off in the family station wagon only to return hours later in that 1960 Buick LeSabre convertible. He understood that it was her personal declaration of independence, a way of defying the "drudgery" (her word) of her boring life as a wife and mother. What about him? What if he traded in his dull sedan for a sports car? That would be the day! Frankly he didn't feel so fulfilled, either. She wasn't the one who had to put on a suit every day and duke it out in the white-collar trenches.

Ted was surprised that the world of business felt so similar to the Army. Mr. Toomb could be as insufferable as any general, and Ted was a lowly foot soldier being sent to do the hard part, or so it seemed. And who knew the airline industry would be so awful? People thought it was glamorous, but it was like running a bus company, except these buses had wings and flew in the sky and, therefore, presented a lot more risk. The pilots were proud and stubborn, and completely unwilling to have their authority challenged. They had survived the war. Surely they didn't need "babysitting," as they called it.

But the pilots proved to be a little too casual for Ted's (and the guv-mint's) taste. They didn't worry about running low on fuel. Crash-landing? Oh, not to worry. Did that all the time during the war.

Worst of all was the shell-shocked former bomber pilot who forgot to put down the landing gear and slid to a stop—with a plane full of passengers—near the airport terminal (as these buildings were unfortunately called, in Ted's opinion) at Jacksonville. The pilot's only comment was, "Oops. Crappy landing."

Ted was beginning to think the airline wouldn't make it to the end of the year. It was now early September 1964. The incorporation papers hadn't even been signed—a "detail" (Mr. Toomb's word) that made Ted sick with anxiety. They shouldn't even have been flying. And yet Mr. Toomb was concocting ridiculous plans for expansion. To himself, Ted wondered if it was time to get his résumé ready, just in case.

Seventeen

I didn't have my phone turned back on in my cottage because I thought I'd be turning right around and heading back to Mississippi. At least, that's what I told Jackie and the rest, but the truth was a little more complicated. First, I couldn't really afford it. Second, I didn't necessarily want to be reached. It seemed to me that if people really wanted to see me, they would come and sit on my porch. People who called generally just complicated my life. They wanted something. As Mama used to say, "Sometimes a phone is more trouble than it's worth."

Still, I'd encounter folks at the Winn-Dixie. My old Sunday School teacher, Mrs. Stanley, always seemed to be in the baking aisle when I made my erratic excursions for the few necessities I needed. Maybe she just camped out there, every day for hours, so she could start a conversation with someone. Of course, being a dutiful member of Olde Cypress Methodist Church, Mrs. Stanley was a prolific baker. All Methodists love to bake. Mama used to say there wasn't a Methodist alive that didn't have a big ol' sweet tooth. At Olde Cypress, it was said there was never a meeting—and they loved meetings—without some homemade goody and a pot of coffee. Maybe Mrs. Stanley truly did need to be there in the baking aisle eleven times a week, responding to an emergency request from the preacher's wife for a pineapple upside-down cake or some Collier County cheese grits. And she would have done it, too, because Mrs. Stanley was one of those church ladies who responds when duty calls.

So there she was, moseying around the flour and sugar aisle. I made a quick dash behind a display of canned green beans but, alas, Mrs. Stanley was faster than a Chihuahua that smells a chicken bone. Mama would have been ashamed of me for trying to duck from Mrs. Stanley, but my life was messy and small talk was not my forte.

"Oh, Miss Dora!" she shrieked. "I put a note in your mailbox not more than an hour ago. We just got a new shipment of Advent calendars for the children and I need someone to open the boxes and get them ready. And it's time to plan Christmas dinner for the needy."

Advent calendars? Christmas dinner? It was mid-September. I'd been home for three weeks. To me, Christmas was far off in the distance, somewhere on the horizon. I didn't even want to think about Christmas. But to Mrs. Stanley, bless her heart, this meant she was running far behind. She was the type who started getting Easter linens out of mothballs before some folks had even taken down their Christmas lights. I spluttered, trying to buy time, but failed to come up with an excuse. I had helped her with many little tasks over the years and it seemed that in Naples, if you'd ever agreed to do something charitable, it was pretty much guaranteed that you'd be doing it for the rest of your life. You'd be in the boneyard before they let you off the hook.

These thoughts were so unkind that I felt instant remorse. I hoped Mama was busy doing something else in heaven—maybe having tea with our former neighbor, Miss Pettigrew—and not listening in on my thoughts and deeds or, sure enough, wouldn't she be ashamed of me? That was the problem with having a guardian angel sitting on your shoulder. Yes, you were protected much of the time. But it did put a certain kind of pressure on the way you behaved. To make amends to the Spirit World, I smiled at Mrs. Stanley and asked her what time I should show up.

And that is why I ended up the next day at my old Sunday School classroom, perched, with my knees halfway up to my chin, on a chair meant for a five-year-old, making lists and calculating the amount of food the church would need for Christmas donations. When I was done with that, I opened boxes filled with Advent calendars, removing them one by one from the elaborate wrapping and organizing them—as Mrs. Stanley liked—in batches of five. Mindless, yes, and yet freeing. Focusing on the simple tasks at hand, I was able to take a break from thinking about Darryl, the possibility of Dreamsville Estates, the money I would owe my landlady in Mississippi, and the important news I had discovered while I was in Jackson. News that I hadn't completely digested yet.

Going to Mississippi, all by my lonesome, had given me a new way of looking at Naples and all the folks I'd spent my life around. Sure, I'd lived in St. Petersburg when I went to junior college, and when I married Darryl we lived in Ocala. But that was all Florida. There was something about crossing the state line for the first time that made me feel like I was truly in charge of my own life. I could now say that I'd been in three states— Florida, Alabama, and Mississippi.

Now that I was home for a spell I realized that it's one thing to be stuck in your hometown and quite another to come back for a visit. It doesn't seem half as bad once you've been away. In fact, the familiarity of it—which had been suffocating—was now kind of pleasant. I mentioned this to Mrs. Stanley as we worked, side by side. She had smiled gently and said, "Sometimes you have to go away to understand the importance of what you've left behind."

After finishing my work for Mrs. Stanley, I started to head home but decided to wait an hour to hear a talk hosted by a formidable group calling itself Methodist Ladies in Action. The title was "Change Is Coming to Naples, Too!" There it was, on the bulletin board, in great big block letters.

Well, this was interesting. Living in Jackson for the past year, I was near the frontlines of the civil rights movement but I'd had the feeling since coming home that time was still passing by Naples. If there'd been protests here, they'd been small ones. The drugstore counter was still "whites only" and schools were segregated by race.

I didn't have any plans. Jackie was doing something with her kids. I had no easy way to go to Mrs. Bailey White's house and spend time with her or Plain Jane and the baby. I figured, *why not?*

The speaker was a petite lady wearing a gray suit and sensible shoes. Her hair was cropped short. No pretty bouffant and no makeup, and a smile that showed perfect teeth, a rarity in Collier County. She was introduced as a member of a church in a suburb of Cleveland with a quaint name, Shaker Heights.

She didn't waste any time getting to the point. "Let me be blunt," she said. "Your black population is not much better off than they were during the days of slavery more than a hundred years ago, and there's not much momentum here. When it comes to race relations, you're at least ten years behind Mississippi, Alabama, and Georgia."

I glanced around the room, expecting an exodus, but there was none. "You also have a migrant-worker problem inland in Immokalee," our speaker added. "Some of your seasonal farm workers are white, but many are black. And the life they are living—that includes children—is worse than anyone should be living in this country."

This was not news, especially since "Harvest of Shame," the Edwin R. Murrow special report, was broadcast by CBS the day after Thanksgiving 1960. That was nearly four years ago, and from what I'd read, the broadcast had a big impact nationally. It was a wake-up call to many Americans. Unfortunately, it was dismissed in Collier County as Northern liberal propaganda. In fact, I'd never heard anyone say anything positive about the broadcast here. What had changed in the past year was that inequality was no longer a taboo subject—at least in some circles.

The women in the audience were nodding thoughtfully. Something was happening here. I could feel it, sitting right there in the fellowship hall of the church I attended while growing up. I knew several of the women. One had been on a committee with Mama that collected funds for back-to-school clothing for poor children. With the rest, I had what was called a "nodding" acquaintance.

It was hard to know which event had broken the camel's back and galvanized these women to become something more than spectators, but if I had to guess, I'd say it was the church bombing the previous year in Birmingham, Alabama, in which four little black girls were killed. The idea that a bunch of grown men would murder children *inside a church building on a Sunday morning* would be intolerable to these women, no doubt about it.

Naples still had plenty of mean folks, including an active Klan. They were still lurking, much like Seminole Joe. The Klansmen were out there in the swamps, fields, and tidal rivers. Mama had no patience whatsoever for the Klan. As a nurse, she believed all people were the same and should be treated as such. When I was in high school, I had a long conversation with Mama about the way the world worked. "The Klan members think they're settling some kind of score from long ago," she had said. "That's just malarkey. They're just a bunch of bullies picking on colored folks for one reason: They can! They can murder colored folks, burn their churches, do what they please and no one has stopped them. That's just wrong," she said. "You remember that, Dora. It's just plain wrong. If anything, those other folks—the coloreds and the Injuns—they're the ones who ought to be settling scores, 'cause so much been done to *them* over the years. The Klan—they got it all backward."

My eyes started to tear up, as always happened when I thought about Mama. She was so wise, and I missed her so much.

"Collier County is right in the crosshairs of some of the greatest stressors in our country," the lady from Ohio was saying. That jerked me to attention. "Besides the racial problem, and the farm-worker issue, you have a new group of immigrants, the Cubans. You don't have a lot of them, mostly spillover from Miami, but they tend to find the transition to American life very difficult, especially those who were well-off in their home country and are overeducated for the jobs they can get here."

Cubans? I hadn't been aware. No one I knew had mentioned it.

"You are also perfectly positioned for explosive growth," the speaker went on. "With the growing availability of air-conditioning, you will see a large influx of people from the North."

Good Lord, I thought. *Now I'm really awake.*

"You have beautiful beaches, great fishing," she continued. "Your challenge will be managing your growth in a way that doesn't ruin what you have. And doesn't leave anyone behind."

Ha! I thought. *Ain't that the truth.*

I looked around the room again. Wouldn't it have been great if the mayor had been here? Or someone from the newspaper? I wish I'd thought to call Jackie.

"I'd like to finish by saying that I wish it weren't just women in this room," our speaker said, as if reading my mind. "For some reason, men won't come to hear a woman giving a talk," she added with a slight smile.

"Well, they don't come to nothin' that's been organized by Methodist *women*," one of the organizers said, trying to sound playful. I recognized her as the wife of one of the deputy sheriffs. "I wish they would, 'cause we talk about a lot of important topics here. When we have a special guest, we always let them know they are welcome!"

I thought to myself, *That will be the day.* This led to another thought. *And we may fix all the other problems mentioned here tonight before anyone faces the fact that women aren't taken seriously.*

"Well, we can all go home and tell our men what we learned tonight," our organizer added. "If they won't come, we can always bring it to them."

What if you don't have a man? I thought. I raised my hand. The speaker nodded, and I asked my question. "Hello," I heard myself saying. "I am divorced. If you're saying we need to go home and serve our man some newfangled ideas with his breakfast grits and eggs, how do I fit in? I mean, I am just wondering. What else can women do?"

I don't know what got into me. I'd never called attention

to the fact I was divorced, and now I was pointing it out in a very public way. In a room full of Methodist women, no less. I was horrified. Did I sound bitter? Sassy? Maybe even *sarcastic*? What was happening to me?

Lawd have mercy, I might have learned it from Jackie! Wasn't this a Yankee thing—not to speak up, necessarily, but to speak up *in a way that made others uncomfortable*? I surely hadn't learned this in Mississippi.

I realized all of the women in the room were staring at me. "I'm sorry," I said. "I was trying to be funny, I guess."

"Well, actually you raise a valid point," the speaker said soothingly. I was so grateful that she came to my aid that I nearly cried. "What women can do—married or not—is to speak up. Speak up at home, in church, in your civic groups, anywhere you have a chance. We are more powerful than we know, if only we make our feelings and wishes known."

Later, having retreated to my home and my turtles and their blessed unconditional love, I realized that I was, in fact, following the speaker's advice already. The unvarnished truth was that little Dora Witherspoon had changed. I was less worried about what others thought of me and more willing to speak my mind. Jackie may have had some influence, but so had the other members of the book club. Mama's death—and, no doubt, my divorce—played a role, too. I was not the same person I had been. Plus, having gone to Mississippi on my own, and having faced some truths there, gave me a certain cockiness. Heck, I was born in a small town, and I loved it, but it didn't define me. Not entirely. Not anymore.

JACKIE KEPT WRITING HER COLUMN, and everyone in town kept reading it. "Chatter Box" was supposed to run twice a week but

Jackie, true to her nature, found it hard to be so predictable. And she didn't want to write only about Darryl. "I don't want it to seem like a vendetta," she said, so her second column was called "Mourning President Kennedy." This was a tearjerker; even those who disliked Kennedy—and there were many in Naples—had to agree that she'd really captured our nation's lingering sadness. Then she wrote one called "Why American Schoolchildren Should Learn Foreign Languages," which got no reaction whatsoever. After that, she wrote about her beloved Buick convertible and what it meant to her, which reestablished her as a bit of a loony. (Men could wax eloquent about a cherished automobile, but it was weird for a woman to do so. The fact that it was a Buick and not a Ford or Chevy made it even more peculiar.) She told us that she wanted to write about racial hatred in the South but that her editors had asked her to wait until she was "a more seasoned columnist," which, in my estimation, was their way of saying "When hell freezes over." Finally, she got back to Darryl Norwood and Seminole Joe with a column she called "Is Dreamsville a Nightmare?"

I'd been home for almost six weeks, and while Jackie was doing some damage to Darryl, and maybe slowing him down, the sad truth was that she hadn't stopped him. Unless something totally unexpected happened, I was beginning to think that nothing could.

Eighteen

Just when you think you have enough grit in your oysters, the devil has a way of upping the ante, allowing things to happen to distract or confound us mortals. Mama used to call these incidents "diversions meant to knock you off your path of righteousness." Mama surely did have a way with words, tending toward the Biblical, of course.

First, there was a little incident involving Judd Hart. He'd been one of those kids who was infatuated with the Space Race and inspired by the astronauts who were, after all, just across the state at Cape Kennedy.

Jackie got an inkling that something was amiss courtesy of the town librarian, a middle-aged woman from Sarasota with a polished appearance who had been hired to replace Miss Lansbury, who had been so helpful with Jackie's book club. One day, the new librarian called Jackie out of the blue. "I thought you should know that your son has checked out a book on explosives," she said in a crisp, yet not accusing voice. Jackie, squelching an urge to tell her that it was no one's business what anyone checked out of a library, thanked her for the information. Jackie fretted and fumed, and when Judd walked in a half hour later, she met him at the door demanding an explanation. Judd assured her that he was working on a science experiment for school and that he was trying for an A.

Later, she said she should have known better because Judd had said, "They're just *small* rockets, not like the ones on TV." And then the time-honored red flag, *"Don't worry, Mom."*

The first calls to the sheriff came from Mr. Cuthbert "Birdie" Gertleson who thought Communists from Cuba were making a land assault on Collier County. Birdie was—thank you, Jesus—unharmed but his frantic phone call and the words "missile attack!" sent the police into combat mode. Within minutes every able-bodied man in Naples was unlocking his gun cabinet, loading a shotgun, and heading for old Birdie's modest homestead.

Instead of Commies, however, all they found was Judd Hart looking guilty as a Sunday School teacher sipping moonshine. Two other boys were hightailing it into the swamp.

Everything had gone perfectly, Judd explained, until the rocket tipped over at the last second. Instead of going up into the sky in a blaze of glory it raced horizontally across a grassy piece of tidal marsh. Incredibly, it managed to hit the only house within a half mile in any direction, the simple structure owned by Birdie Gertleson. Worse, when it hit the outside wall, it kept going. And going. Not until after it was all over did the police learn that Judd's rocket, which featured a solid brass nose cone, had careered around Birdie's living room, ripping the newspaper he was reading right out of his hands while he sat in his favorite chair, terrorizing his cat, and finally bursting through the roof.

The fact that Old Birdie wasn't dead surprised everyone, himself especially. He was so glad he wasn't dead, and that it wasn't Commies that had been attacking his humble abode, that he forgot to be angry. The cat, which is all that Birdie cared about anyway, was retrieved from its hiding place underneath Birdie's rusted 1929 Ford. Birdie's relief did not appease the sheriff, however. Judd was two inches away from being arrested.

Ted Hart had been enjoying a rare day working close to home when a Florida Highway Patrol officer, wearing the familiar Confederate pink uniform, marched into Collier County Savings & Loan where Ted and his boss Mr. Toomb were meeting with the trustees. Without time even to call Jackie, Ted was escorted to "the scene of the crime," as the officer called it, without elaboration other than somehow it involved Judd.

The sheriff was already there. Once Ted realized that no one, including Judd, had been injured, he felt a wave of relief he'd experienced only one other time in his life—when Japan surrendered and the war was finally over. He'd gotten drunk with his friends and whooped and hollered until they all passed out, exhausted.

This time, however, although he wanted to shout with joy, he hid his true feelings. He was scared of what the law would do to Judd.

So Ted did what a father was expected to do: He turned and yelled at his son. He made Judd apologize to Birdie and promise he would pay for repairs. And then he threatened to send Judd to military school, a place called Admiral Farragut Academy in St. Petersburg, which was widely believed by Judd and other boys his age to be a reform school for kids from families with financial resources.

Satisfied that Judd had been properly shamed, the trooper and the sheriff decided to let the matter rest. Justice would be served at home by the boy's father. The sheriff asked the dispatcher to send Harry Donahue from Harry's Handyman Service to secure the house and make an estimate for repairs for Ted; then he took Old Birdie and his cat to the Naples Beach Club Hotel, where they would stay, at Ted's expense, until the house was livable again. Meanwhile, the trooper agreed to drop Ted and Judd off at home.

"You are going to be mowing lawns for the rest of your life," Ted told Judd on the way home, "and every penny will pay me back for all these expenses."

"Do I really have to go to military school?" Judd asked, wide-eyed.

Aware that the trooper was listening, Ted said yes. But he knew that Jackie would never let that happen. Judd figured the same. Considering that he could have found himself in juvenile jail, Judd was rather pleased overall with the outcome of the day's events. Mowing lawns would be no problem. In fact, he already had a lawn-mowing service with more than a dozen regular customers. So what if he was essentially working for his dad for a while? He'd gotten off easy.

THE SECOND UNNERVING EVENT CAME in the form of a letter hand-delivered to Mrs. Bailey White's. Jackie had just finished telling us about Judd's "misadventure," as she phrased it. She had missed all the excitement involving the rocket fiasco, having driven the twins to voice lessons with a Mrs. Pendergast in Punta Gorda. "Here I was trying to be a good mother to my girls, and when we come home I find out my son has turned into a mad scientist!" she groaned, blotting her eyes with a tissue. "I had my children when I was too young! I am a complete catastrophe as a mother!"

"Oh, now, stop being a Miss Melodrama," Mrs. Bailey White said. "Have a Dr Pepper and calm down."

"*Ugh,*" Jackie said with disgust. "I hate that Dr Pepper stuff. Do you have any tonic water? Better yet, some gin to go with it?"

"Too early in the day," Plain Jane scolded. "With this heat you'll end up with a huge headache."

"Ted went to New Orleans and he said all the people there drink even in the late morning," Jackie said defensively.

"Honey child, this ain't no *New Orleans*," Mrs. Bailey White said, shaking her head. "That's up north compared to here. We're in the *tropics*. Besides, those folks are partygoers. They got pickle juice in their veins. But they don't live as long as we do. By the way, did you know they don't bury their people in the ground?"

"Well, what do they do with them?" Jackie asked.

"They bury 'em *above* ground. They call them 'mausoleums.'"

"Oh, yes," Jackie said. "I've seen photographs of that. I think it's because the water table there is so high."

A knock at the door made us jump nearly out of our skins. In a way I was grateful because the conversation was giving me the creepy-crawlies.

"I'll get it," I said, but by the time I reached the door I wished I'd let someone else answer it. Through the scalloped lace curtain on the windowpane beside the front door, I could see a silhouette of the distinctive hat worn by a police officer in uniform. I cracked open the door, and he thrust a letter into my hand without saying a word.

"Wait," he said, as I started to close the door. "Someone has to sign for it." This made me even more uneasy, but I did as I was told.

"Dora?" Mrs. Bailey White called out. "Who is it, dear?"

I returned to the parlor. "Oh, it's nothing, probably. Just a letter from the town."

"Mrs. Bailey White, did you pay your taxes?" Plain Jane said, alarmed.

"Course I did! Don't know what this nonsense could be. Dora, dear, you open it and read it aloud, okay?"

I was beginning to think that Jackie's gin and tonic suggestion might be a good one. "All right," I said, my voice squeaky. "Well, let's see. It's addressed to you and date-stamped today— October 10, 1964. It says":

Dear Matilda Louise Bailey White:
It has come to our attention that you have exceeded the
number of unrelated persons living in this house, and that
one of the residents is a child unrelated to any of the residents.
You are, therefore, running a rooming house and/or child care
institution without proper permit.

"What else does it say?" Jackie asked, after she recovered enough to speak. "Is there a court date? Do we pay a fine?"

"It's a warning," Plain Jane said.

"Can we ignore it?" Jackie asked. "In Boston if you get a letter like that, you just ignore it. Nine times out of ten, that's the end of it."

"I don't think we can do that," Plain Jane said. "I think we'll have to address it in some way." She thought for a moment and added, "Well, I suppose it's not surprising. They always find a way to get to you."

"Who?" Jackie asked. "You mean Darryl?"

"Yes, Darryl. And maybe his backers, too. Those people from that place in New Jersey."

Mrs. Bailey White nodded. "He's fighting dirty," she said.

"We don't know that for sure," I said, but the second the words left my lips I realized it was probably true. Plain Jane, Jackie, and Mrs. Bailey White had been looking after Dream for more than a year. There had been complaints but nothing had really come of it. This felt like retribution.

We discussed what we should do. As Mama would have said, we talked that ol' topic to death and right into the next world. Finally, we agreed to face it head-on by going to the municipal offices. The plan was that we'd go together. By now it was late in the day so we decided to meet at 8:30 sharp the next morning outside the town-owned trailer, adjacent to the police station.

The first accusation in the letter to Mrs. Bailey White turned out to be easy to disprove. Jackie, Plain Jane, and I were able to demonstrate that we were only "visitors" at the house owned by Mrs. Bailey White. For Jackie, it was as easy as handing them her driver's license with her home address on it. Plain Jane and I, who didn't drive, brought our property tax bills with us.

"But what about the girl?" The clerk, a plump gal with a beehive hairdo, posed the question as if she was sure we were hiding something.

"What girl?" Plain Jane asked.

"The colored girl," the clerk said, snapping gum in her mouth. "The one who comes to stay there. And her colored baby."

Clearly, the clerk had been apprised of every detail. "What, are you guys spying on us?" Jackie said, in her usual "anything but subtle" way.

"No one's spying on anyone," the clerk snapped. "But we have become aware that a colored girl about age twenty stays in that house from time to time. And her baby is there *all* the time. Is it their legal residence?"

The question caught us off-guard. "The girl's legal address is at her grandmother's," Mrs. Bailey White said. "And the baby's, too." Whether or not this was true, I didn't know, but it was a good answer.

The clerk sighed. "All right," she said. "Looks like you've satisfied the first part of the complaint. But not the second. If that baby isn't related to any of you, and you have no legal status in her life, then she shouldn't be living there. Unless you have a license for some kind of school or maybe a home for unwed mothers and their babies, something like that."

A smile that I recognized as mischievous suddenly appeared on Jackie's face. "Well, thank you *so very much!*" Jackie gushed to the clerk. "You've been *so very helpful!*"

Jackie practically skipped out the door.

"What are you so happy about?" Plain Jane asked warily.

"That gal in there just handed us the solution!" she said. "All we have to do is open a house for unwed mothers and babies. It's that simple! We can keep Dream and maybe help some other young women, too."

"Whoa, wait a minute," Plain Jane said.

"What do you think, Mrs. Bailey White?" Jackie asked, adding, "Of course, this is entirely up to you."

Mrs. Bailey White looked overwhelmed but smiled. "I don't know how much good I'll be to y'all," she said slowly, "but you're welcome to use my house."

"I admit that it's a fascinating idea," Plain Jane said cautiously, "but Jackie, aren't you getting ahead of yourself? You always have us rushing into things!"

"Dora, what do you think?" Jackie asked, ignoring Plain Jane.

"Well, I won't be here. I still plan to go back to Mississippi," I said. "But if y'all think you can do it, I don't see why not. Of course, there's something you're forgetting. We need to talk to Priscilla first. She should be told what's going on. She would need to be on board with this."

It was agreed. Jackie would try to reach Priscilla by telephone and report back to us the next day.

As I nodded off to sleep that night, I marveled at Jackie's enthusiasm and her ability to find answers while I was still busy mulling over the question. She was persuasive, and made things sound easier than they were—like talking me into going to Mississippi to find out about Mama and her people. Once you've known someone like Jackie, however, you can't easily go back to a life in which you're sitting on the sidelines, waiting for something to happen. Before I knew her, I thought the best way to travel through life was to take the most comforting and familiar routes. While I still longed to do this at times—it was part of my nature—I could see now that playing it too safe might mean never really living at all. From Jackie, I had learned to take the plunge into the deep end of the pond, not just stick my toe in, or wade around in the shallows.

Nineteen

As the Trailways bus rambled toward Naples, Priscilla yawned politely and stretched, taking care not to bump into the older woman sitting next to her. She reminded Priscilla a little of her grandma—tiny and hunched over, with hands swollen and disfigured from a lifetime of working in the fields.

Priscilla had been trying to read on the long bus ride from Daytona, with some success on the Sanford to Tampa stretch, but then began dozing off, tired from working late in the college laundry. One employee went home sick, so she'd been doing the job of two people but complaining was unthinkable. Working until midnight—even in a hot and humid laundry—was easy compared to what her grandma did, day after day.

The older woman suddenly elbowed her and cried out, pointing to something outside the bus window. Even wedged as they were in the far-back seat of the colored section, it was hard to miss: a brand-new, oversized billboard with lime-green lettering.

Welcome to Dreamsville! the sign hollered.

What in the world? Priscilla thought.

And then they passed another, identical to the first. This time, Priscilla got more than a glimpse. Accompanying the astonishing words was a stylized illustration of an idealized American couple. A white gal was tastefully reclined in a lounge chair with a long cigarette in one hand and a cute little mixed drink—the kind with an umbrella in it—beside her on a small table. A white fellow, presumably her husband, loomed in the foreground with an expensive-looking fishing pole in one hand and a golf club in the other, grinning so broadly it was scary. *Lord,* Priscilla thought, *you'd think God himself had just handed him the keys to the Kingdom of Heaven. Imagine going through life with that amount of self-assurance.* The couple, to Priscilla's eyes, looked vaguely Northern. For one thing, they were tan. With the exception of men who worked outdoors—a farmer with his red neck from driving a tractor, or a fisherman with deep crows'-feet wrinkles acquired from squinting at the water—local white folks protected their skin from the sun. In fact, it was said among black folks that the Caucasians of Collier County were so white that looking at them hurt your eyes. Priscilla tried not to join in when others joked like that. White folks couldn't help being white any more than she could help the fact that she was not. Besides, she'd been treated exceptionally well by white folks. Most of them, anyway.

The other indication that the folks depicted in the sign were supposed to be Yankees was, in a word, jewelry. The gal on the lounge chair had a ring on one hand that would have made Elizabeth Taylor pass out, plus ropes of gold, pearls, and who-knows-what hanging heavily around her neck. All this, and wearing a bathing suit, too. The man, who wore a polo shirt with some kind of insignia like a family crest or college logo, sported an oversized watch on one wrist.

In sociology class, Priscilla had learned that these folks were called "the Northern Leisure Class." But why would they come to Naples? Who was putting out the welcome mat?

And why were there so many? Unlike the South, where there were a handful of rich folks in every small town—with everyone else poor as dirt—there seemed to be a surplus of people with money to burn in Yankeeland. She couldn't imagine being able to afford one house, let alone one up north and a second one in Florida just for vacations. Vacations! That was a concept she couldn't grasp, either. Life was not a cakewalk for anyone, her granny used to counsel, but sometimes it sure seemed that way from the outside looking in.

When the bus passed a third, identical billboard, this time Priscilla noticed the words "Coming Soon!" on a banner that stretched across the lower right corner. Well, whatever was going on, it probably wasn't good, and Priscilla felt a cool chill move down her spine like someone had just walked over an unsettled grave.

Jackie had not said a word on the telephone about any of this. Did she not know? Or did she not care? No, Jackie would care. She would be angry, unless she was involved in it in some way. But why would she be involved? Jackie wouldn't like the idea of someone using "Dreamsville" without her permission, and Priscilla couldn't imagine Jackie accepting payment for it, or endorsing a development of some sort, either. That didn't seem like Jackie's style.

Of course, maybe Jackie hadn't mentioned it because long-distance calls cost a pretty penny. More than that, though, was a lack of privacy on Priscilla's end. With more than fifteen girls sharing one phone at the rooming house that was Priscilla's home-away-from-home at Bethune-Cookman College, someone always seemed to be lurking in the hallway awaiting her turn. Opportunities were ripe for eavesdropping. The other complication was that Priscilla, working in the laundry and attending classes, often missed Jackie's calls. It was remarkable how much information a nosy floor-mate could glean from a simple phone message, so Jackie quickly learned to avoid chitchat and to leave a message saying only that Priscilla needed to call home.

Whenever Priscilla found one of these messages stuck in the doorjamb of her little room, she felt a little faint. Without fail, she was at first convinced that something had happened to her baby. Maybe Dream was sick and desperately needed her mama. A negligent, selfish, fool-hearted mama who was clear across the state, and almost as far north as the Georgia border, studying English and sociology at a black college where no one knew her secret.

The hallway was silent, thanks to the late hour, so Priscilla dropped her book bag and purse and dashed to the phone to call Jackie back. As always she asked the long-distance operator to reverse charges, which made her feel wretched until she forced herself to remember her baby daughter. She was doing this for her child. She would do anything for her child. That was why she was away, to build a better life for herself and, in turn, for Dream.

She felt the same way the next morning when she sat in the back of the Trailways bus. She was doing that for Dream, too. Nine years after Mrs. Parks refused to move from the white section of a bus in Birmingham, the colored section was business as usual in Florida. Here it was 1964, the Civil Rights Act had just been signed by President Johnson, and the yellow line that designated the "back of the bus" was as bright and menacing as ever. There were times when Priscilla could sit wherever she wanted, especially if the bus was nearly empty. But if a bus driver was a bigot, he'd tell you to go to the back of the bus. Or, if there were mean-looking white passengers—and you could never tell, really, just from a glance—it was better to go sit in the back of the bus and live to talk about it. This stuck in Priscilla's craw and she felt that familiar flash of soul-crushing shame, but again, just like those collect calls, they could be tolerated if she was doing it for her child.

Jackie had declared that Priscilla should sit wherever she wanted when she rode the bus, but Jackie was a Northerner. More to the point, Jackie was white. What did she know of such things? It was Plain Jane, the poet who paid her bills by writing for strange magazines, who made Priscilla promise to be cautious. Plain Jane, a progressive-minded Southerner although she didn't look it with her conservative clothes and steel-gray hair that matched her eyes. "Don't listen to Jackie on this," she had told Priscilla in a hushed voice on one of her visits home. "You do what you have to."

Old Mrs. Bailey White had overheard and quickly agreed. "Get yourself through college," she counseled. "That's your job right now. Keep your focus, and don't get in no fusses."

These words of advice made all the difference. It was still hard. Hard to accept their charity for those bus tickets home and for taking care of Dream. But Priscilla was what her granny called "an old soul," meaning that from the day of her birth she seemed wise beyond her years, as if she'd lived one long life already. She didn't have all the answers, and she made mistakes, but God had given her the gift of resilience. That, and a very unyouthful tendency to be a good listener when it came to advice, made her seem much older than her nineteen-and-a-half years.

This was an odd arrangement. Unheard of, as a matter of fact, and yet it seemed to be working. There'd been a rough patch a few months earlier when Priscilla learned that her friends had endured some abusive remarks when they were out and about with Dream. At that point, Priscilla was prepared to come home for good. She would live with her grandma and do her best to raise Dream.

Plain Jane and Mrs. Bailey White had straightened out the situation, however. They understood that most Southerners would look the other way unless provoked. Privacy and minding your own business trumped speaking up and interfering. The problem was Jackie, who was in the habit of driving around town with Dream in that crazy convertible. She would take Dream with her into the Winn-Dixie and when people stared she'd say, "What's the matter, haven't your ever seen a black child with a white nanny before?" And then she'd laugh out loud.

Naturally, that got folks stirred up. And it wasn't necessary. So on one of Priscilla's trips home, the remnants of the little book club had a discussion. There was a whole lot of finger-pointing, with Plain Jane and Mrs. Bailey White taking sides against Jackie. Poor Jackie had this harebrained idea that she was somehow helping the civil rights movement. Finally, after hearing them out, Priscilla spoke her mind. It was hard to think of the right words. She prayed to God to help her find them.

"Jackie," she began slowly. Having been in the book club together, they all knew what it meant when Priscilla spoke cautiously. It meant she was trying to think of a way to say something powerful without hurting too many feelings. "Jackie," she began again, "you know I love you and that I am indebted to you for making it possible for me to go to college. And I know that your heart is in the right place when it comes to helping my people. But you are endangering my child."

There it was, like a bomb had gone off. *You are endangering my child.* Those were words harsh but true.

Of course, Jackie had reacted like someone had dumped a bucket of wet collard greens over her head. Priscilla couldn't even bear to look at her. But she had said what needed to be said.

Plain Jane, who quarreled with Jackie on a fairly regular basis, could not resist adding her two cents. "I told you so," she said to Jackie. "You were flaunting that baby around like that, just to make a point—"

"Ladies, please," Mrs. Bailey White interrupted. "Let's all calm down and remember we are friends. We are all in this together. Jackie didn't mean any harm. She just don't understand sometimes, that's all."

Jackie said nothing for the next hour, maybe longer, and avoided eye contact with all of them. Priscilla, meanwhile, had been consumed with despair, thinking she had been rude and ungrateful, and had pushed too far.

Plain Jane and Mrs. Bailey White talked about the baby, how much she had grown, about her sleep habits, and how cute she was, in far more depth than was necessary. Finally, Plain Jane addressed Jackie. "Didn't you say that Dream was the smartest little thing you ever saw?" she prompted.

Jackie cleared her throat. "Yes, I think she is very advanced. And since I'm the only one here—other than Priscilla, of course—who is a mother, I do think I know what I'm talking about."

"Of course you do," Priscilla had said quickly.

"No one is questioning your instincts or experience," Plain Jane said. "It's just that you're a foreigner here, you don't understand how to behave—"

"A foreigner! Why, excuse me, but I thought we were all citizens of the United States of America. I didn't realize I needed a *passport* to live in the Confederate State of Florida."

This was getting nasty but at least it signaled to Priscilla that Jackie was not upset or angry with her. Just the entire South.

No one, even Jackie, wanted to take this conversation any further. "Priscilla," she said bluntly, "I will reign in my boorish Yankee *behavior* but I will do it for your sake, and for Dream's. Not for any other reason. And not because I'm wrong."

Six or seven months had passed and Jackie had held to her promise. No more driving around town with Dream. The baby was transported, and taken out in public, only when necessary. And, no more comments about being a white nanny. As Plain Jane and Mrs. Bailey White predicted, the rumor mill ground to a halt. People didn't really care as long as they didn't have their noses rubbed in it. Their attention was focused elsewhere, on some other unlucky target.

But now the problem had suddenly flared up again. That was the gist of the conversation when Jackie made the latest phone call. When Priscilla got the message and called back, Jackie seemed to be waiting by the telephone. "There is a new problem with us taking care of Dream," she whispered into the phone. Specifically, she said, that the baby was "residing" at Mrs. Bailey White's house.

And so Priscilla had asked the college's dean of women students for an emergency leave. Eyebrows were raised, but Priscilla managed to convey in the vaguest of terms that there was a family emergency without providing details that would get her expelled.

As the bus pulled away from Daytona Beach, Priscilla said her silent good-bye to the little city on the Atlantic coast where people drove cars on the beach, and to the college where all the students looked like her, and no one thought it delusional to dream of becoming an English teacher or anthropologist. Each time she left, she wrestled with the feeling that perhaps she might never be back.

Twenty

Blast those old war pilots, Ted Hart thought with disgust. He knew it was wrong to think that way about his fellow veterans, but they were still making it awfully hard to bring civilization to Florida.

He was beginning to suspect that some of them enjoyed rough landings. More than once, he'd heard them laughing and boasting about cutting things a little close.

"This is a *business* and these are *passengers*," Ted implored after another complaint.

The pilots responded in nearly identical ways. "Well, that's the way we flew in the war and we survived, so don't tell us how to fly," they'd say. "Especially since you were a foot soldier, fella. Your kind doesn't know the first thing about flying."

The latter part was true. Ted didn't even know how to fly a kite. But he was in charge and he figured these guys should listen to him. He'd have fired them all but they were the only qualified pilots who had applied. A few crop dusters had answered the ads and while they didn't make the grade, Ted secretly wondered if they might not have done a better job from a customer-service perspective.

On one particularly awful day, a pilot failed to secure the nose hatch on a plane flying south from Tampa. Unfortunately, the hatch sprang open in midflight, sending airbags belonging to the U.S. Postal Service straight into the right engine propeller. The result was a shower of shredded mail dispersed over Fort Myers, followed by an engine fire which resulted in a noteworthy emergency landing on a golf course.

Meanwhile, Mr. Toomb was starting to lean harder on Ted. None of the routes, which now crisscrossed the state, were making a profit and were not likely to for months. Most of the airports were not up to par, and several lacked hangar space for planes bigger than a two-seater Beechcraft. Ted needed to persuade local officials that Wild Blue Yonder Airways would be a boon to their communities. He traveled the state with mixed results. At times, officials wouldn't even meet with him unless Mr. Toomb called first on his behalf. Finally, Ted found his niche. When the mayor of Daytona Beach mentioned he was going on a fishing trip to Crescent City, the "Bass Capital," Ted remarked that he'd spent several summers on a fishing boat out of Gloucester, Massachusetts. Next thing Ted knew, he was invited not only to fish for bass by the Daytona Beach mayor but to go deep-sea fishing with the mayor of Fort Lauderdale. As word got out that Ted not only liked to fish but was quite good at it, he found doors opening to his sales pitch. His wardrobe of navy blue suits was pushed to the back of the closet.

Jackie wasn't thrilled with this development. In fact, she was furious. "Oh, Ted, where are you going this week?" she would ask on Sunday nights. "Shall we pack your new Brooks Brothers suit, or would you prefer your *fishing regalia*?"

Try as he might, he wasn't able to convince her that he was, in fact, working. "This is the way I have to do business here," he would say. But she would give him what he thought of as "the look," a sideways glance of her suddenly chilly blue eyes. What he hesitated to tell her was that he ought to be working on his golf game, too.

He tried to interest Jackie with stories from his time on the road. Sometimes she was so resentful of his being away that she didn't want to hear them. But there were other times—the best times—when he and Jackie talked late into the night about this surprising place called Florida. The biggest shock had been learning that the state was, in fact, a part of the South.

From a Bostonian's point of view, America consisted of Northern and Southern states, the Great Plains and the West Coast. Of course, there were subcategories: New England was one, but also border states (people who could not make up their mind which side of the Civil War they were on), the Deep South (a place where cotton was grown and people walked barefoot all the time), Texas (cowboys, the Alamo, oil rigs), the Rockies (extremely tall mountains), Chicago (a notable area of civilization in the vast and confusingly laid-out Midwest), California (Hollywood people), and Seattle (so far away that it was exotic). Hawaii? That was a honeymoon destination for the well-heeled. And Alaska? A place that got more snow than Boston and had an unusual variety of wild animals.

That pretty much left Florida, a place that didn't fit into any category except its own. More than thirteen hundred miles of coastline gave the impression that the whole state was a tropical paradise. Many inland communities, however, were afflicted by the type of Deep South poverty Ted had thought existed only in states such as Alabama or Mississippi, or in the Appalachian Mountains of Kentucky. This inland poverty affected both whites and blacks. It was the one thing the two races had in common.

Ted felt badly for blacks living in Florida—especially those living inland. They often had a sort of downcast look, like they were trapped and knew it was hopeless. The sorrow in their eyes reminded him of the displaced persons he had seen in Europe, civilians who had lost everything in the war and had nowhere to go.

At least the black people seemed to be living in reality, Ted thought. He was not so sure about the whites. Like an episode of the TV show *The Twilight Zone*, many white people acted as if someone had set their clocks back a hundred years and they hadn't noticed. Again and again, Ted would be told that Union troops had "invaded" the South, ending a perfectly decent way of life, and that colored folks were "happier in the old days." Ted concluded that white Southerners, generally speaking, were looking backward, clinging to the past with increasing desperation at the very same time that Northerners were fixated on the future. In April, New York City had opened the 1964 World's Fair with a hopeful theme called "Peace Through Understanding." From what Ted had read in *Time* magazine, the fair focused on marvelous inventions that would make life better. But what good was any of it, he thought, if we didn't fix the big problems first, like race and poverty?

In the last year, he noted that it seemed to have become more difficult being a Yankee, unless you were a typical beach tourist. Comments were made. Looks were exchanged. Previously, his Boston accent had been tolerated or even met with friendly curiosity; now it seemed an invitation to be harassed. There was, for example, the restaurant owner in Hardee County who sat down uninvited opposite Ted and grinned menacingly. All Ted had wanted was a lousy cup of coffee and a doughnut but instead he was treated to a disgusting lecture about "the inferiority of the Negro race" and how Yankees needed to mind their own business. Ted had not taken the bait. He was expected, he knew, to get up and walk out or throw a punch but he did neither. While the old redneck droned on and on, Ted had simply pulled out a recent copy of the *Wall Street Journal* and began to read it. He munched slowly on the doughnut and, after he finished his coffee, he left.

In his free time he visited libraries and historical societies, especially when work took him to larger cities. The territory of Florida, Ted learned, had been in Spanish hands, then English, and back to Spanish again, until Spain ceded the territory to the United States in 1821. Slavery of blacks (and also Indians) was fully entrenched long before Florida became a state in 1845. When Southern slave states began to secede from the Union, starting with South Carolina in December 1860, Florida was third in line. More than 15,000 Florida troops fought for the Confederacy.

Now, this was the part Ted really wanted to know about: What happened after the Civil War? To his surprise, he found that black Floridians endured decades of intimidation and violence by whites that rivaled—*and even surpassed*—other Southern states. Ted was appalled that in one particularly heinous act, an NAACP leader named Harry T. Moore and his wife were murdered on Christmas Day 1951 in their home in the small town of Mims in Brevard County.

One thing Ted was trying to figure out was whether he should use the term colored, Negro, Afro-American, or black.

After thinking it through, he started habitually using the latter since it seemed to have been the term preferred by the Massachusetts-born Dr. W. E. B. Du Bois, a black scholar and one of the founders of the NAACP who had died the previous year.

Anger and anxiety was not about race only, Ted was discovering. Longtime Floridians both black and white were increasingly at odds with the tourist industry. How could Old Florida hang onto its proud past as part of the Confederacy and remain a place that tolerated the KKK while attracting Northern tourists? By downplaying the true identity of the state and painting a lovely portrait of endless beaches, golf, and fishing. That was the truth that Ted was beginning to understand.

Meanwhile, his children, most unfortunately, were starting to speak like the local rednecks. This was worrisome. How would they ever get ahead in life? The twins insisted that if they spoke in their native tongue—that is, a Northern dialect—they would never be accepted, never get a date, and simply die of boredom. They picked up the far-south accent almost immediately, probably, Ted thought, because they were so young. Judd, too, sounded like he belonged on that TV show *The Beverly Hillbillies*. But Judd and the twins could turn it on and off with a natural ease, depending on who they were talking to. To Ted, it was the darndest thing. He couldn't even say "y'all" without the word sounding like a chicken bone were stuck in his throat.

On one hurtful day, all three kids announced that they felt humiliated by their parents, who sounded like the Kennedys. Those Boston accents, the kids insisted, had become grating to their ears. The kids pointed out that Jackie, when she'd had her radio show, had learned from the station manager that by speaking very slowly, and dragging out the syllables, she could hide it. She was aghast that they would ask her to try to adapt her radio technique to everyday speech. No way, she said. As for Ted, he was a hopeless case. He didn't seem to be able to drop the accent even when he tried.

Jackie ended the family quarrel with a linguistic triumph: A Boston accent, she noted, was not that dissimilar from a Charleston accent. "And, heck," she said, "Charleston is in *South Carolina*, which, by anyone's definition, is a Rebel state." ("Tell *that* to your friends next time they make fun of the way your mother talks," she added.)

These were the issues Ted hadn't foreseen when they moved here. When he was in the Army twenty years earlier, there was some teasing about accents but mostly it was good-natured. Then again, it was wartime and they were all facing a common enemy. It didn't matter if you were the son of a factory worker from Massachusetts or the son of a wealthy landowner from Tennessee. You could be a ranch hand from Texas or a college boy from Milwaukee, but when each of you was wearing a U.S. Army uniform fighting side by side against the Axis forces, you were American, that's all.

Now, for the first time in his life, Ted was self-conscious about his Northern background. In the tight smile of a waitress or the cool, perfunctory nod of a gas station attendant, he felt a wall descend the second he spoke. Sometimes he wondered if he was reliving the exact dynamics of the Civil War era, a deeply troubling thought for a man who had lived with the assumption that he would always be welcome anywhere in the USA. He had noticed more and more people calling him "Yankee," and not in a playful way. Someone leaving a bar in Tallahassee had even called him "carpetbagger," which shocked him. He trudged back to his hotel, thinking, *They'd rather live in the past and be left behind.* But he was an interloper, a harbinger of change in the same way that a mackerel sky indicates rain. If there was one thing that Southerners found disturbing, it was change. Especially, Ted had learned, when it wasn't their idea.

Twenty-One

"You know, you and me, we got a lot in common," Dolores said in the direction of the heron's nest. "Say, are you even in there? Can't see you."

A small tuft of yellow feathers slowly rose into view.

"Oh, now I see you there," Dolores said. "Out late last night, huh? I used to be like that, too."

The small head slowly sank back out of sight.

"So what I was saying," Dolores continued, "was that we have a lot in common. For one thing, I don't believe you have the slightest idea what you're doing. You shoulda had them babies earlier in the year, not now. *Hmmm*, maybe it's a second clutch of eggs. Or maybe you're just out of kilter with everyone else.

"But I have to tell you, girl," Dolores added. "I ain't seen no man around your nest. Where'd he go? Saw him here for the first few days, when y'all were building it, but he's gone scarce on you now. Ha! What did I tell you! I never had no luck with men, neither! Ha!

"I hope you don't mind, but I've decided to call you Peggy Sue. You know why? Because it reminds me of a song my son used to sing when he'd come home from school. Yes, that son. Robbie-Lee. The one who up and left me. Went to New York City and all. Well, when he was a teenager there was this song, and it was sung by a fella named Buddy Holly. Poor Buddy Holly got hisself killed in a plane crash. Anyway, he had this song called 'Peggy Sue,' and my son loved to sing it. I'd hear him coming down the path singing that song. It was kind of a silly song but awful fun to sing. Anyway, that right there is the best memory of my life. The one I turn to when I'm feeling bad. Robbie-Lee, singing that song. Always made me laugh.

"I'll tell you what, if you'd told me twenty years ago that I'd be sitting here talking to a night heron, I wouldn't have believed you. No sir. I only wish you could talk back. I'd be mighty curious to hear what you had to say."

Peggy Sue stretched her wings either by coincidence or in response. "You sure put up with a lot from me." Dolores laughed. "Crazy old woman, worn out by the world, talking to a bird. Ain't that something. And I'd swear on a stack of Bibles that you are listening to me.

"I hate to be the one to tell you this, but we have something else in common besides men who love us and leave us," Dolores said. "You and me, we be average. That's right, average. I ain't nothin' special and neither are you. I was nice lookin' in my day but never spectacular. Girl, if you don't mind me saying so, you got the same problem. You're not one of them special birds, like a spoonbill. Nope, ain't nobody gonna come down here from the Audubon Society and try to take yer picture. Mine, neither. Fact is, we're just average folk in a world that don't care none for average. This world only cares about special. But you just go on sittin' on your eggs. Do your job. I surely hope things work out better for you than they has for me."

Twenty-Two

Six weeks had passed since I left Mississippi and I was now so broke that I considered raiding my childhood piggy bank that still sat on a bookshelf in my old room at the cottage.

I guess I could have asked for a loan from Mrs. Bailey White, who was independently wealthy; Jackie, who was married to a man who had a good salary; or Plain Jane, whose work as a writer probably didn't pay especially well but she seemed to be a good saver. I knew they were helping Priscilla, however, so I was very reluctant to ask. I wanted them to keep their focus on her and the baby. Somehow, I'd manage.

But it did make me nervous. Money was always an issue for me. The hardest part of going to Mississippi had been taking my hard-time money out of the bank. It just about killed me to do it. The way I was raised, spending your savings was a guaranteed way to provoke the devil. If you wasted your emergency funds on something frivolous then something terrible was bound to happen. Appendicitis, for example. That's what happened to Miss Caraway, who wanted a better handheld mixer than she could buy in Naples, so she took money out of her savings and went up to Fort Myers to buy a special edition General Electric four-speed deluxe cake mixer. Next thing we knew, her appendix burst—right there in the appliance store in Fort Myers! She survived, but she had to have a big operation, and after that, all of us who knew her story were afraid to spend any money at all.

Jackie, being a Yankee, did not believe in any of that stuff. She called this "swamp logic." She gave me a pep talk about how I should be "living my life to the fullest" and that I was "limiting myself" with my various fears and superstitions. I told her, heck, that was easy for her to say. She grew up in Massachusetts, a place that is tidy and civilized. I grew up in a place where one minute you could be washed away by a hurricane and the next you could be eaten by swamp critters.

I was managing pretty well in Mississippi, but the unexpected trip home to Naples was costing me. I couldn't imagine leaving now, but what could I do? I needed to get back to my job shelving books at the Jackson Library. It was now mid-October. I'd written several letters to my landlady, the ever-anxious Mrs. Conroy, and the head librarian, a woman named Geneva LaCroix who was kind of like the Mother Superior of the library. Both were quite gracious considering that I didn't provide any details, only that there had been a family emergency in Naples that needed my attention. There's a point, though, when even nice people grow weary, and I sensed that day was close. I had maybe two or three weeks left, and that was definitely pushing my luck.

I tried to settle my restlessness by digging a new pond to give my turtles a little change of scenery. I was up to my thighs in "mush," the word Mama used to describe the wet, sandy Collier County soil that comprised our yard, when Judd appeared on his bicycle at my backyard fence, hauling another melon he had absconded from his mother's kitchen to feed Norma Jean and the others.

"Whatcha doing, Miss Witherspoon?" he called to me, a little alarmed. Judd had grown a little proprietary about my yard and my turtles. I couldn't blame him. That can happen when you leave someone in charge.

"I'm just digging a new place for them to play," I said, adding, "You want to help?"

Now he was all smiles, and I noticed the gap between his front teeth had grown larger. Jackie had said something about Judd getting braces but it hadn't happened yet.

"Before I forget, Mom said to tell you that Priscilla's bus came in last night," he said cheerfully.

This was a surprise. Priscilla surely had come home in a hurry.

"The bus came in around seven o'clock," Judd continued, "and she—Mom, I mean—is going to pick you up later to take you over to Mrs. Bailey White's to see her. To see Priscilla, I mean."

Judd had a way of talking that made it seem like he thought he had to translate himself. Not being accustomed to boys his age, I wasn't sure if they all did that or if it was just Judd's habit.

"What did she mean by 'later'?" I asked, looking down at my crud-encrusted clothes. At least I had remembered to wear work gloves so my hands would clean up easy.

"Well, she didn't say," Judd said, frowning. "But I know she has to take my sisters somewhere really stupid, maybe the beauty parlor. And then they were going to take some old books and drop them off at the library for the book sale. And then they're supposed to go to Winn-Dixie. But I betcha they have a fight at the beauty parlor and Mom will end up taking them directly home. And then Mom will have one of her headaches, so she won't end up going to the library or Winn-Dixie, either. Which means she'll probably be here in about an hour."

I tried not to smile. I never could get a short answer out of that boy, but his reasoning was sound.

An hour was just enough time for me to get cleaned up. Judd happily took over the digging project while I went inside. I had never gone through Mama's closet and I took a peek in there, thinking it would be nice to wear one of her dresses. But I wasn't ready to do that yet.

Maybe I never would be.

PRISCILLA WAS SITTING OUTSIDE ON Mrs. Bailey White's porch swing with Dream sitting on her lap, waiting for me.

She hopped up and gave me a one-armed hug with the baby being sort of squashed between us. I was afraid that maybe Dream would cry, or at least protest, but she giggled instead.

"Dream doesn't know me too well," I said, stepping back a little.

"She doesn't know me that well, either," Priscilla remarked.

"Aw, now, I can see that ain't true!" I said with all the cheerfulness I could muster, trying to soothe the heaviness in my heart and hers. Priscilla was one of my favorite persons in the world. I really wanted her to be happy.

Jackie was unloading bags from the trunk of the Buick. She left the car radio on and "Do Wah Diddy Diddy" drifted cheerfully through the air. "Hey, doesn't Priscilla look good?" she called out.

"She always looks good! She is the cat's meow," I hollered

back. I sounded like a hillbilly, even to myself. Conversing with Jackie was the only time I noticed how country I sounded.

Priscilla smiled modestly. She looked so prim in her light-blue dress. I wondered if she'd made it herself and was about to ask when she said, "There's a sewing machine at my rooming house. We take turns using it. Took me two months to make this because of all the pleats. And 'cause I didn't want to hog the machine. Jackie, do you need help with your packages?"

"No, I'm fine," Jackie said. "I just picked up a few things at Winn-Dixie before I picked up Dora, nothing terribly perishable. You know what?" she said, as she passed by us and went into the house. "I keep buying melons and they just seem to disappear. It's the strangest thing."

I pretended to be distracted. Thankfully, Plain Jane poked her head out the door. "Y'all come on in! Mrs. Bailey White and I been busy making Boston Coolers. And we've got some talking to do."

There was nothing quite like ginger ale in a tall glass with a scoop of vanilla ice cream to make gathering at a table for a difficult conversation a tad easier. While the unfortunately named (from a Southern perspective) Boston Cooler had been the rage in the Victorian era even in the South, the drink had fallen from favor in recent years. In fact, it was considered a relic from days gone by. But Mrs. Bailey White, who hailed from way-back-when herself, always seemed to have the ingredients on hand.

Priscilla spooned a little out of her glass and let Dream taste it.

"Ha ha ha, look at that," Mrs. Bailey White shrieked. "She loves it!"

"She should not be getting so many sweets," announced

Plain Jane. "Of course, her mama can give her whatever she wants. And today is a special day. I'm just saying that in general she shouldn't have them." Plain Jane turned and glowered at Mrs. Bailey White.

"Uh-oh, here we go again," Jackie said. "Priscilla, we need to review Dream's diet with you while you're here. We were going to ask your grandma but now that you're here, you can set us straight. There have been some—shall we say—*disagreements*. Especially now that Plain Jane has become an expert."

"What?" Plain Jane said, setting down her spoon. "What is that supposed to mean?"

"I didn't mean for that to sound as mean as it did," Jackie said. "It was supposed to be a joke."

"A joke?" Plain Jane looked like she'd been stabbed with a fork.

"Well, now that you've given up writing for *Sexy Secretary* magazine and started contributing to *Perfect Mother Weekly*, you've started to believe you actually are an expert. And it's kind of funny. And charming."

"It's not *Perfect Mother Weekly*." Plain Jane almost spat the words out. "It's *Pious Mother Weekly* and you know it."

"Whatever you say, dear," Jackie said. "I just miss the days when I had a friend writing incognito for sexy magazines, that's all."

Plain Jane relaxed a bit. It was a trait I'd always liked about her. She could laugh at herself. "Well, that's true," she said. "Those were the days!"

"Have you given up writing poetry?" I asked, and immediately regretted the question.

"Of course not," Plain Jane said. "My first volume will be

published next year. It seems to be taking forever but that's the way academic publishers work, or so I'm told. In the meantime, I'm paying the bills with stories about babies and child rearing." She blushed. "I admit it's become something of an obsession to me."

"It's my fault," Jackie said with a wink. "Ever since I loaned you my copy of Dr. Spock, you turned into an authority."

I peered at Priscilla out of the corner of my eye, wondering what effect this conversation was having on her. She looked like she was trying to suppress a smile. When she saw me looking at her, she spoke up. "I appreciate how much y'all care about my baby," she said.

"You probably didn't think they would go off the deep end, though," I said teasingly.

"No," Priscilla said, "I surely did not. But I'm awfully glad they have. I know Dream is in good hands. And I do appreciate you calling me when there is a problem or a question," she added, looking directly at Jackie. "Now, what was it that we needed to talk about?"

"Oh," Jackie said. "Oh yes, *that*." She sighed heavily. "Well, you know I've been living up to my promise of staying under the radar with Dream. We all have. But out of the blue, Mrs. Bailey White received a letter. Seems they thought we were breaking some kind of rule that limits the number of unrelated people living in one house. Well, we were able to show them that for Plain Jane, Dora, and me, Mrs. Bailey White's house is not our legal residence. But they also raised a question about one of the residents being a child who is unrelated to any of the residents. They concluded that we need a permit for running a home or school for children."

"Who's *they*?" Priscilla asked quietly.

"Well, the letter came from the zoning department. We went down there to talk to them and at least we straightened out the first part. But, they don't want Dream living here. And they mentioned you, too."

Priscilla jerked back in her chair. "Me? They mentioned me?"

"Well, not by name. But they knew you stay here occasionally."

"I see," Priscilla said softly. "So they've been watching us."

"Apparently," Mrs. Bailey White said.

"But y'all have been looking after Dream for more than a year. We had that trouble last spring and it died down. Why this? Why now?"

"We think it has something to do with Darryl's plans," Plain Jane said, looking at me.

Priscilla turned to me. "Darryl?" she asked. "You mean your former husband?"

I felt red, the color of shame, move up my cheeks like a brushfire. "Well, I'm not married to him anymore," I said, exasperated. Why was I always having to explain Darryl? "Look, to make a long story short, he's raisin' Cain around here with plans to fill in the swamp and the river and build a development—a golf course, houses, and shops."

"He wants to call it Dreamsville," Jackie added. "If you can imagine the nerve."

"Oh!" Priscilla said. "I saw the billboards on my way into town."

"What billboards?" Jackie asked, sitting straight up.

"They said, Coming Soon—Welcome to Dreamsville, or something like that."

Jackie, inhaling her cigarette, began to cough.

"Good Lord. They must have just put those up," Plain Jane

muttered. "Priscilla, they didn't have a photo of Jackie on them, did they?"

"No," she replied. "Not the ones I saw."

"Well, that's good news, at least," Jackie said, choking through her words. "But nothing would surprise me at this point. Can you believe it? He can call it Dreamsville Estates and the lawyers say I can't stop him."

"This is terrible," Priscilla said. "But what does it have to do with me or Dream staying here at Mrs. Bailey White's home? I don't understand."

There was a noticeable pause. Finally, Jackie spoke. "We think it's retaliation," she said. "We've been fighting Darryl to try to stop him. His plans are outrageous. He wants to tear down Dolores Simpson's house and—oh, Priscilla!—it looks like his development might include where your grandma lives."

Priscilla looked like someone had slapped her. "At the settlement?" she cried out. "I wonder if they know! Probably not. They'd probably be the last ones to find out."

"They might not know," Plain Jane agreed. "It had been hush-hush for a while, and it's happening very quickly."

"Is there anything we can do?" Priscilla said, her voice rising.

"We're working on it," Mrs. Bailey White said grimly. "But by fighting Darryl, we've stirred up a hornet's nest. That's what Jackie meant by retaliation. We think it's the reason the town is suddenly asking questions about you and Dream. Darryl has the backing of the mayor and all the other bigwigs in town. It wouldn't take but one phone call from Darryl to get the town to start harassing us."

"I suppose it could be a complete coincidence," Jackie added. "We can't rule that out. Either way we have to deal with it."

"There ain't no such thing as coincidence when it comes to

something like this," Mrs. Bailey White scoffed. "Just follow the trail and it leads to one place: money."

Priscilla began chewing her nails, something I'd never seen her do before. "Oh, sweet Jesus, what a mess we have here," she said, her voice low, like her sorrow was between her and the Lord himself, or maybe it was "graveyard talk," the things you say to a loved one who has crossed to the Other Side.

"I told them that your legal address, and the baby's, too, is at your grandmother's house," Mrs. Bailey White said to Priscilla. "I hope I did right."

"Why, of course you did right," Priscilla said. "You've all done right. *More* than right. But I don't know what we should do now."

"Well, before you get any more upset, let me tell you about my idea!" Jackie said. She didn't quite grasp that her ideas were not always joyfully met, but we were desperate for any kind of hope, so we latched onto it. "The clerk said that Dream shouldn't be living here, right? But she also said, 'unless you have a license for a school or a home for unwed mothers and their babies,' or something along those lines. So you see, that's the solution!"

"What's the solution?" Priscilla said.

"We open a house for unwed mothers and their babies!" Jackie said triumphantly. "See, we can go through the state and circumvent those idiots downtown. I've already had Ted look into it while he's in Tallahassee. He said it shouldn't be a problem. That way it would be okay for Dream to stay here and for you to visit! And maybe we could expand—"

"Imagine that," Mrs. Bailey White interrupted. "My old house, empty for so long, and it could be a place full of life. We could call it the Collier County Home for Unwed Mothers." I could see that Mrs. Bailey White was hooked.

"What do you say, Priscilla?" Jackie asked, anxiously. "This way we can keep Dream and maybe, at some point, help some other young women, too."

Priscilla smiled. "Jackie, I admire your faith," she said slowly. "If you all want to try to make this happen, I won't stand in your way. It sounds like the Lord's work to me."

"I'm on board," Plain Jane said. "It may not work out, though. It might make things worse, at least in the short term—"

"Then we'll deal with that if it happens," Jackie said, cutting her off. The rest of us exchanged glances, and I guessed that we were all on the same page. There weren't no use in arguing. As Mama used to say, "You can't reason with crazy."

Twenty-Three

Priscilla stayed for only one more day; Jackie drove her to see her grandma for a brief visit. Jackie waited in the car, as she usually did to give Priscilla some privacy, but she asked Priscilla ahead of time to check with her grandma to see if she was aware that Darryl's plans might include paving over the Negro settlement.

Well, they didn't know, or at least that's what they said. Maybe they knew more than they were saying but didn't want to become a target. Sad to say, but it wouldn't help if they got involved. It wouldn't bring any sympathy to our side of the fight.

Meanwhile, Jackie was momentarily distracted by something that occurred on the home front. Judd was busy making amends with his lawn-mowing business and got the bright idea that the family could really use a new mower. The one they brought down from Boston was hard to push through South Florida grass. Judd had the blades sharpened but that wasn't enough. He figured he'd make a deal with his dad: Maybe they could go in on a new mower fifty-fifty.

Before he had the chance to make his case with Ted, he tried a trial run with Jackie. One thing that Jackie did not want to spend money on was a lawn mower. She insisted on demonstrating that the current mower was adequate. The problem was that Jackie had never pushed a lawn mower in her life. She pretended it was easy, all the while struggling to make progress, while Judd stood to the side sulking and drinking a Coke.

At this exact moment, Judd's classmates rode by on their bicycles. The image of Mrs. Jackie Hart mowing her own lawn in a muumuu and tennis shoes while her able-bodied son stood to the side caused them to stop, stare—and laugh. They took off before Judd could say anything, but the damage was done. At school the next day, Judd was teased mercilessly.

A particularly nasty boy, Calvin Treadwell, saw his opportunity to take Judd down a peg or two. Judd was a star in Civil Air Patrol; this was the root of the jealousy that now expressed itself openly. "Is that what y'all do up north?" Calvin hissed. "You let your *mama* mow the lawn for you?"

"That's not what happened; my mom was just trying to prove a point," Judd had replied, but no one wanted to hear the truth when Calvin's version was so much better.

Calvin used the opportunity to remind everyone in earshot that Judd was the same "dumb Yankee kid" who ate fried chicken and watermelon with a knife and fork. "He thinks he's better than us," Calvin sneered.

It was a cruel reminder to Judd that he was still very much an outsider. "Why does it matter?" he asked me wistfully. Judd had absconded with another melon from home and was helping me slice it for the turtles. "I mean, it was kind of funny, I guess, but why do they always bring up the fact about my being Northern?"

"I guess it's just 'cause you're different. I'm different, too."

"How are you different? You mean because of the turtles?"

I thought for a minute. "Well, the turtles, yes," I said slowly. "But also, because I'm divorced. Or, *especially* because I'm divorced."

"Oh," Judd said. "So there are some things that are okay. Being the Turtle Lady is fine. Being divorced isn't. Like being from up north."

"Yes, I guess some sins are worse than others," I said, meaning it as a joke but it fell flat. "Look, Judd, they're just picking on you, that's all. There's always folks who will do that. Not just kids. Through your whole life there will be people who try to make you look small, any way they can, just to make themselves feel big. It's pathetic, really. But you can decide if they're going to make you unhappy or not. Ignore it. Laugh about it. You'll see—it will pass. They'll move on to something else."

Sure enough, something did happen. Someone vandalized the Welcome to Dreamsville billboards. On each one, a crude-looking tomahawk had been painted over the head of the smiling man in the illustration. This was so exciting that no one, even Judd's mean classmates, could talk of anything else.

Of course, speculation began immediately. There were all kinds of theories but the most popular notion was that Seminole Joe had done it himself. It was a warning from the ol' haint that we were playing with fire.

As for myself, I didn't know what to believe. In the light of day it was easy to dismiss the idea. Late at night, alone in my cottage, was another story.

Jackie's reaction was predictable. "Oh, here we go again," she said. "News flash! It's *not* Seminole Joe. There *is* no Seminole Joe. It's someone who is taking advantage of the situation. Or maybe it was just some kids being foolish—after all, it's getting close to Halloween."

"Is it you?" Mrs. Bailey White asked.

"Of course not! Don't be ridiculous. Those billboards are set back at least fifteen feet from the edge of the road. Do you really think I would walk back there? And then what—climb up the billboard? With a can of paint and a brush?"

She had a point.

"Well, then, who did it?" Mrs. Bailey White persisted.

"It wasn't me," I said, surprised at how defensive I sounded. "Do you think it could have been Judd?"

"What?!" Jackie snapped. "He would never do that. Besides, I asked him this morning, and he said he didn't."

"I'm telling you, it's not nice to make fun of the people around here," Plain Jane said to Jackie. "They have their ways. You have yours."

Jackie sniffed.

"You don't understand it here and maybe you never will," Mrs. Bailey White said, sounding more than a little cranky. "People have a right to be spooked around here. All kinds of nasty things happen."

"Like what?" Jackie was nothing if not curious.

"Well, did you know that a corpse turns to bones in twelve hours?"

"*Ew!*"

"I mean, the whole cycle of life—and death—is sped up here. You got to understand that, Jackie. That's why it's so easy for folks to believe in Seminole Joe. Things are different than they seem. This is not a place where folks get second chances. You get lost in the swamp, you're dead. You get bit by a snake, you're dead. You go out fishing in the Gulf, get caught in a storm, you're dead."

"How cheery."

"Sarcasm is hardly helpful, Jackie," Plain Jane said.

"Dora, dear, are you going to pick on me, too?" Jackie said to me, but I could tell she didn't really expect an answer. She looked away and, with surprising force, ground her cigarette into an ashtray.

Twenty-Four

Two days later, Jackie was in a far better mood. The billboard vandalism had upset folks in a way that nothing else had. Jackie reported a flurry of letters to the editor coming into the newspaper's office. Not all of them were printed, but Jackie, on the sly, had been reading each one and was keeping a secret tally—for, against, and why. The billboard vandalism was a big boost in our favor.

Ultimately, she hoped to go to Tallahassee with a petition asking the state to intervene with Darryl's plans. With enough opposition from local citizens, she hoped Dreamsville Estates might be dropped altogether. Still, Jackie admitted that it was unclear if we could turn back the tide.

Meanwhile, Ted had returned from a business trip up north that included a day trip to check out Darryl's investors. "Ted did some exploring for us," Jackie said. "Well, actually, of course, he was doing this on Mr. Toomb's behalf, but he rented a car and drove to Basking Ridge."

My heart lurched.

"What did he find out?" Mrs. Bailey White asked impatiently.

"He actually got to meet the main investor," Jackie replied. Then she turned to me. "Dora, I don't know how to tell you this except just say it straight out. The young woman Darryl is marrying—just as we suspected—is the daughter of the man who owns the investing firm. Her name is Celeste."

"I bet she's ugly as sin," Mrs. Bailey White said with conviction.

"Well, Ted didn't actually meet the daughter," Jackie said quickly. "He met with her father and his colleagues for drinks at a country club. It was all very collegial. And Ted said it was a very quaint town, Basking Ridge, and just an hour from Manhattan. Wouldn't that be lovely? Anyway, that's all I know right now."

I realized they were looking at me. "Can we change the subject?" I asked, a bit abruptly.

"I'm sorry, Dora, but I had to tell you," Jackie said.

"Well, now what do we do?" Plain Jane asked. "That doesn't sound very promising in terms of using it against Darryl. I mean since his investors seem on the up-and-up."

"Well, it would be great if it turns out they're corrupt in some way," Jackie said cheerfully, "but it almost doesn't matter."

"How can it not matter?" Plain Jane asked uneasily.

"Because I'm going to use it against them anyway." She refused to say anything further but her column the next week provided an answer.

YANKEE CASH TO PAY FOR
DREAMSVILLE DEVELOPMENT?

Neapolitans, sources suggest that Mr. Darryl Norwood's real-estate development is being quietly funded by a wealthy investor who resides far north of the Mason-Dixon line—in New Jersey, in fact. While the investor and his colleagues appear to be aboveboard, should it not raise the question about the future of our beloved Naples?

This angle was both shameless—since, after all, Jackie was a Yankee herself, through and through—and brilliant. If there was one thing you could count on, it was folks' distrust of rich Northerners.

"Now I see how they won the war," Mrs. Bailey White said, with grudging admiration, to Plain Jane and me. "Yankees will throw their own kind off a cliff to get what they want."

The column raised alarm bells and sparked the ire of the Collier County Sons of the Confederacy, one more important group now squarely in our back pocket. Jackie's new estimate of letters to the editor was 50 percent in favor of the development compared to close to 90 percent just two months before.

While I was pleased with Jackie's progress, it was anyone's guess if her plans would actually work or how long they would take. The fact was I needed to get back to Mississippi or I'd have no job at the library and no rented room at Mrs. Conroy's. It was late October 1964. It was time to fish or cut bait, or, in other words, stop postponing.

Jackie and the others knew I had to leave. But someone—and, unfortunately, that person was me—needed to inform Dolores Simpson. I could have gone away without saying good-bye to her, I suppose, but I knew I'd never be able to live with myself. She deserved to hear that even if I hadn't been successful, I had tried. Sometimes, that had to be enough. And, surely, it counted for something.

But I sure wasn't looking forward to saying that to Dolores. I'd stood up to her and survived but I wasn't sure my luck would hold a second time. To be honest, I was still scared to death of her.

I decided I should bring a present—an apology of sorts—so I spent hours making Mama's homemade biscuits. I took a basket that I'd used for picking flowers and filled it with the biscuits and a small ham I bought at the Winn-Dixie. Even though I was sure that her son, Robbie-Lee, must be sending her money when he could, she was not likely to spend it on luxuries like meat.

When I arrived and she saw the basket, she knew it was either a celebration or a farewell gift. A glance at the guilty look on my face, and she knew which one it was.

"So, you weren't able to stop him," she said gruffly. I watched her hands as she worked with a tool the size of a nail file on a flat piece of pine. It took me a moment to realize that she was making a sign.

"I didn't know you were such an expert woodworker," I said.

"Oh, girl, there's a whole lot of things you don't know about me," she said, without looking up.

"What's your new sign say?" I asked.

She turned it around and held it up for me to see. It read Trespassers Will Be Shot, except one letter was out of place so it actually said "Trepsassers."

"Well, now," I said, "that's what I call a mighty friendly sign." I said nothing about the error.

"Just want to warn folks off, fair and square, if they come snoopin' around here. Like your Darryl, for example. I'm half expectin' him to show up at any time—"

"Like I told you and everyone else, he's not *my* Darryl!" I said. "Not anymore."

"Well if he comes 'round here he's likely to get his head blowed off," she said with a sniff.

"Look, Dolores, I'm here to say I'm sorry," I said wearily. "I'm going back to Mississippi. But I wanted you to know that I tried. I really did." I set my present of ham and biscuits down beside her.

"Thank you," she said. "For that there present. And—thank you for trying."

"Well, I'm a-gonna go now," I said. "Next time I'm back, I hope to get to see Robbie-Lee. I hope he comes home to Collier County by then."

She shrugged. "Don't know if we'll ever see that day."

"I'm going to write to him to let him know what's going on," I said. "He would be here helping you if you told him the truth."

I expected her to say, "Don't you dare." But instead she muttered, "Suit yourself."

I turned to look at the night heron and for some reason tears filled my eyes. "I wish there was more I could do," I said sadly. "About Darryl, I mean. I wish I'd never married him." She didn't say anything so I added, "Well, good-bye, Dolores," and I turned and walked away.

I'd gone ten or fifteen yards away when she called out to me. "He don't own the land."

I stopped in my tracks.

"He don't own the land," Dolores repeated. "He didn't buy it fair and square."

I turned around warily. Was this a ploy to keep me from giving up? Did she want me to postpone my trip back to Mississippi, stay here, and continue the fight against Darryl?

"What do you mean?" I called back. "Darryl told the newspaper that he bought it from some folks in Kentucky who have been hanging onto it for years."

Dolores drew in a sharp breath. "That's a lie," she shouted. "He didn't buy it. He must have made that up, because I'm the one from Kentucky. I mean my people were from Kentucky. I own it. The land. The river. The whole thing, lock, stock, and barrel."

I couldn't have been more surprised if the night heron had started singing "How Great Thou Art." I thought, *Surely I didn't hear that right.* But if it was true, or partly true, it could change everything. And something about the expression on Dolores's face made me realize it wasn't a lie. She looked frightened. Vulnerable.

"Well," I said slowly. "What in the name of our sweet Savior would you be talking about?"

"Come inside and I'll show you."

"Show me what?"

"Like I said, you'll have to come inside."

"Why are you telling me about this *now*? I've been home two months. *Why did you wait?*"

She hesitated. "I was hoping it could be handled some other way," she said.

We had a standoff for about three or four minutes, which in the swamp heat of far South Florida feels more like three or four hours. Finally, I gave in, but I tried to look tough as I did so, although I didn't feel it.

She directed me to the small table I remembered from my previous visit. "Now, sit down and close your eyes," she said.

This seemed like a stupid thing to do but I did it anyway. For all I knew I was about to get a hatchet over the top of my head. But again, there was something new in the tone of her voice. There was no edge to it, no bitterness, as if she'd set down a burden too heavy to carry anymore. Her voice actually sounded younger, like the woman she might have been years before. She walked away from me in the dim, indoor light. "Are they closed?" she called.

"Oh, all right," I said impatiently. "Yes, they're closed. But they won't be for long."

I heard a board creaking, followed by what seemed to be her shuffling around. Then I heard what sounded like the top of a large jar or container being unscrewed. More shuffling around. Then the top being screwed back on again. I heard a scraping noise, followed by a latch clicking into place.

"Dolores, I am not going to sit here forever with my eyes closed," I said, trying to sound angry and impatient when in fact I was terrified. There's a fine line between bravery and stupidity, and I think I'd crossed it.

I heard her footsteps as she moved closer to me. I held my breath. "Okay," she said, "you can open your eyes now."

She stood less than three feet from me, on the opposite side of the table, holding several pieces of paper in her hands.

"What in the world?" I asked.

She didn't reply. She set them on the table in front of me. I picked them up carefully, but there wasn't enough light in the fishing shack to read them. I squinted but still couldn't decipher the words. We'd left the door ajar, creating a shaft of light, and without thinking I stood up and walked toward it.

"You ain't leaving here with them papers!" Dolores shouted.

"I'm not leaving!" I said quickly. "I just need some light so I can read them, that's all." I stayed stock-still until she was re-assured. A long minute passed, and I slowly handed the papers back toward her. "Here," I said, "take them back. I don't want you to be upset."

I thought she might grab them and—woe is me!—I would never get to read them. Maybe, the papers were nothing important at all. Or maybe they could change my life and hers, and a whole lot of other people who loved the river. Instead of taking them from me, though, she moved closer to me and took my arm, a gesture which took ten years off my life. Yet all she did was gently steer me closer to the ray of light by the door.

"My eyes are not as good as they used to be," she said. "And the ink has faded. I haven't looked at them in a long time. Now, you read them to me."

I began to read the first one. Instantly, I realized it was a deed of some sort. The language came from a lawyer, I had no doubt. Lawyers had a peculiar way of making the English language seem a lot more convoluted than it actually was. There were lots of "herebys" and other highfalutin words until I finally got to the good part: the name of the person who owned the property and the date, "the Third Day of April 1877."

I recognized the name: General John Stuart Williams, a United States Senator from Kentucky who had been a Confederate general. Williams was generally credited as the founder of Naples.

As for the property, I knew it immediately. It described the exact spot where I was standing, and all the way past the Negro village.

In other words, it was almost exactly the same parcel that included the river and surrounding land where Darryl was planning to build his Dreamsville.

AN HOUR LATER I HIKED back to the main road carrying the precious deed, along with a few other miscellaneous pieces of paper that might or might not have had anything to do with the deed.

Dolores had gently rolled the documents into a scroll which she covered with a layer of spatterdock lilies and tied with Florida bear grass. All this, to keep the elements from attacking our precious documents during my walk back to town. Still, I prayed it wouldn't rain. The skies had been threatening all day.

I say "our" documents because that is what they had become. Once they left their secret hiding place inside Dolores's fishing shack, they were mine, too. Mine to protect, and mine to share. It wasn't that Dolores trusted me. I was simply her best hope and last chance.

I went directly home and put the papers into Mama's old trunk. Then I went back out, locking the door behind me, which, I realized, was only the third or fourth time in my life I had bothered. I was so energized by my exciting secret that I commenced to walking all the way to Jackie's house.

One of Jackie's twins opened the door a crack, announced that her mother was not home, and shut the door. Never mind that Jackie's car was in the driveway. I knocked again, and waited an embarrassingly long time. When Judd swung open the door,

I was happy as a Cheshire cat with a new container of Py-co-pay Tooth Powder.

"Come on in, Mom's in the kitchen," he said. "Sorry about my sister."

Jackie was trying one of Mrs. Bailey White's recipes, Died and Gone to Heaven Cake. She was five minutes away from taking it out of the oven. She took one look at me—I had hardly ever walked all the way to her house—and knew I had big news. The problem was the twin daughters were lurking about, and I didn't trust them one bit. Even Judd—I wasn't sure he should be in on this, either. He had gone out to the carport to work on one of his science experiments.

Finally the cake was done, and Jackie set it out to cool. "Girls," she shouted, almost knocking out my eardrum. "I'm going out with Miss Witherspoon. The meatloaf is still in the fridge—just take it out when you're ready for dinner. And be sure to leave some for your brother, would you please? Don't be greedy! And—*are you listening to me?* Don't any of you touch this cake until I get back." To me, she said, "My girls hate me. I wish I knew why."

She started demanding answers before we even got to the car. The convertible top was up; Jackie was anticipating that it was going to rain. "What's going on?" she asked. "Where are we going?"

"I guess to Mrs. Bailey White's," I said with a shrug. The old Victorian murder house was, more than ever, a refuge for the remaining members of our old book club.

"Are you going to tell me what this is about?" Jackie pleaded.

"I have something to show you," I said. "Some old papers."

"Old papers?"

"Yes, but I didn't bring them with me because it looks like

rain." In fact, the wind was picking up and a deluge was increasingly likely—one of those tropical rains that comes down so hard that it feels like someone in heaven opened a spigot.

"Dora, please tell me what's going on," she said.

"Well," I said breathlessly, "you are not going to believe it. I almost don't know how to say it."

"Oh for Pete's sake, Dora, just spit it out, would you?"

I frowned. Yankees could be so rude. What an expression—"spit it out." Mercy.

"All right, all right," I said. "I think there may be a way to stop Darryl." I paused, then blurted out, "Dolores gave me some old papers. One of them looks like a deed."

"*What?* A deed? You mean a land deed?"

"Yes. And it *appears* to be a large piece of land that includes the river," I said. "But I didn't look at it all that long."

"So you don't have it with you—this deed?"

"No, it's hidden in a safe place, along with the other papers."

"Where?"

"My house."

Jackie hit the brakes and did one of her famously sloppy three-point turns, right there in the middle of the Tamiami Trail with me screaming the whole time. How I wished I had my own car.

"Where we going?" I howled.

"Back to your house, to see those papers, of course!" Jackie yelled. The woman was crazy. Plumb jack crazy.

"Now wait just a minute!" I shouted, surprising myself as much as Jackie. "I'm the one who has been entrusted with the papers, and I think I should have some say in what we're going to do!"

Jackie surrendered. "Okay," she said, pulling to the side of the road. "You tell me what you want to do."

"We can get the papers but I'm not showing them to you until we're at Mrs. Bailey White's house where we can all look at them at the same time."

Jackie started to protest but I held my ground. "Stop your fussing, Jackie, and drive the car." And to my surprise, she did.

Twenty-Five

I may need my smelling salts," Mrs. Bailey White announced. "Do y'all realize what this is?"

None of us being lawyers, we weren't sure what we were looking at, but Mrs. Bailey White recognized the name on the deed, just as I had.

"This could be our saving grace, gals," she said, fanning herself with her hand. "One is definitely a land deed, but I don't know about the rest."

The only legal papers I'd ever set eyes on were Mama's hand-written will and my divorce papers. Jackie was at a loss, too. But Plain Jane had more worldly experience. She had worked for a land surveyor during the war, and later, for an insurance company. This was long before her current career as a magazine writer, but she remembered the earlier jobs well.

"I can't say for certain, but I think this second piece of paper is a trust document," Plain Jane said. "And this third piece of paper—it looks like a birth certificate, filled out by a midwife for a home birth. For a newborn by the name of Bunny Ann McIntyre."

"Who in the world is that?" Jackie said.

"Well, whoever it is, she comes from royalty," Plain Jane said. "Not Queen Elizabeth kind of royalty. More like Collier County royalty. That is, if she's a direct descendant—and maybe the heir—of the old general. Now, this last document doesn't look as authentic. It just seems like a crude family tree that somebody has drawn up. But again, if you look carefully," she added, studying the paper, "you'll see the name Bunny Ann McIntyre on there."

I cleared my throat. "I know who she is. Dolores Simpson told me that's her real name. She says she's Bunny Ann McIntyre."

"Are you kidding me?" Jackie shrieked, almost dropping a lit cigarette.

"Ha, ha, ha, ain't that something?" Mrs. Bailey White said, clapping her hands together.

"Do you think Robbie-Lee knows?" Plain Jane asked.

"I don't think he knows any of this," I said. "I don't think she ever wanted him to know. At least, as long as she was alive."

"Well, how do we know any of it's true?" Jackie said, bringing us back to earth. "This may be a bunch of donkey excrement."

"What?" Plain Jane said, frowning. "What kind of saying is that?"

"Oh, something I used to hear up north," Jackie said. "It's just a polite way to say—"

"Never mind," I interrupted. "How are we going to find out if it's true? What if we can use this to stop Darryl?"

We were lost in our own thoughts. "Who would name their daughter Bunny Ann?" Jackie said suddenly, with a snort.

"Well, you named your daughters Bronwyn and Halcyon," Plain Jane said. "No wonder they're mad at you all the time."

"But those are family names," Jackie said defensively.

"Maybe Bunny Ann is a family name." Plain Jane had a point.

"Ladies! Ladies! Please," cried Mrs. Bailey White. "We have more important fish to fry."

"Agreed," I said hastily. "What we need is a lawyer. Jackie, what about those lawyers you talked to on the telephone in New York and Boston? The ones who gave you advice about Darryl using your name—"

"No, no, no," Mrs. Bailey White interrupted. "We don't need some highfalutin Yankee lawyer! What we need is a local boy."

Naples was a small town and between us we quickly came up with a list of every lawyer in town. They all had ties, however, to the most powerful folks in town. Finally, we agreed that several of us should make a day trip up to Fort Myers in search of a lawyer. Whether one could be found—indeed, whether one existed—who would meet with all of our approval, and who was willing to look into our situation, would remain to be seen. But as Mama used to say, "You've got to get out there and try. Sitting at home and doing nothing but frettin' will never get you anywhere."

I DID NOT HAVE A dime to contribute and felt badly for it, but between Jackie, Mrs. Bailey White, and Plain Jane, there was enough to pay for a lawyer.

They returned from Fort Myers feeling triumphant, having managed to find "a nice young man who is not connected," as Jackie explained. This made me a little uneasy. "Young" could be good; passion and energy might trump experience. "Unconnected" to Jackie and the others meant "uncontaminated," but I wondered if it might translate as powerless.

The lawyer's name was John Ed Yonce. He was very interested in the case but said he'd have to meet Dolores first. This, of course, was a problem. How would we get Dolores to go to Fort Myers? Even if Jackie offered to drive her up there, we didn't think she would go.

Somehow, Jackie had persuaded poor Mr. Yonce to come to Collier County and meet Dolores at her home. I say *poor* Mr. Yonce because that fella was in over his head. I don't think there was anything he learned in law school that could have prepared him for Dolores. Or Jackie, for that matter.

Jackie offered to transport Mr. Yonce from Fort Myers to Naples if necessary but announced that she would not drive him to Dolores's fishing shack. "It's horrible for my car," she declared. "I really don't want to drive back there again." And who could blame her?

Neither Mrs. Bailey White nor Plain Jane were in a position to help. That left me to figure out what to do. I could escort him by foot or canoe. Mr. Yonce chose the latter.

The next morning, I waited at the public boat launch as agreed. The day started badly. When I tried to pay the fee to rent the canoe with a Kennedy fifty-cent piece, the man in charge refused to accept the coin on account of the fact that he was a Kennedy hater. Now, I found this disgusting for a variety of reasons. Number one, Kennedy was dead—assassinated!—and the way I was raised, "of the dead say nothing evil." Secondly, he had been our president and therefore deserved our respect whether you agreed with him or not. Last but not least, the coin was issued by our government and was therefore as legitimate as a twenty-dollar bill or anything else.

Well, I won that battle based on the last point. He took my

fifty-cent piece, but I was left with a sick feeling in my stomach and an angry headache.

I was relieved when Jackie finally pulled up. A man I presumed to be Mr. Yonce sat beside her in the front seat. Was it some kind of mistake? He didn't look much older than Judd. As he climbed out of the car, my heart sank even further when I saw that he was wearing a suit and wing-tip shoes.

Jackie took off with a wave of the hand, leaving us to our own introductions.

"My, isn't she something?!" he said. "Mrs. Hart, I mean. She told me all about her radio show, how she gave that up, and now she's writing a newspaper column."

"Oh, she's something else all right," I said with a smile. Men of all ages were always impressed with Jackie. What I didn't say was, *Oh boy, if you think Jackie is something else, just wait until you meet Miss Bunny Ann McIntyre, aka Dolores Simpson.*

"Thank you for taking me today," he said.

"Mr. Yonce, um, why are you wearing . . . *those clothes?*" I asked.

"Because I'm meeting a client!" he said as if it was the most obvious thing in the world.

He put on a lifesaving vest—few of us locals wore them, even though they were made available at the dock—and climbed daintily in the canoe. I could see I had a long day ahead of me.

"Aren't you going to help me paddle?" I asked.

"I don't know how," he said.

"I'll show you how," I replied. "Get in the front."

Despite my instructions, Mr. Yonce was not much help, especially after a ten-foot gator splashed into the water from a riverbank not ten feet from us. Mr. Yonce proceeded to do exactly the wrong thing: He panicked and stood up.

"Sit down, Mr. Yonce! You'll flip us over!" I yelled.

He did as he was told, but after that he didn't try to paddle at all. After a few minutes he asked my permission to turn around and face me. I don't think he even wanted to look at the water the rest of the trip.

"Where the heck did you grow up?" I asked.

"Atlanta," he said. "Downtown. Near Peachtree Street."

Well, that explained a few things. "Whatcha doing in Florida?"

"Wanted to start somewhere new," he said. "But I didn't know it was going to be like this," he added hastily.

I started to feel sorry for him. This was always my downfall. I could not stay mad at someone I felt sorry for.

"See those trees there?" I asked, trying to distract him. "Those are called mangroves. They are incredibly adaptive—"

"What is that over there?" he asked nervously. "That thing near the mangroves."

I saw the back of a manatee bobbing in the water. "Oh, that's just a sea cow," I said reassuringly. "Don't worry, they don't eat people. They only eat vegetation. They are the gentlest creatures on earth."

"Oh," he said with a weak smile. "Glad to hear it."

With me paddling alone it took a good forty-five minutes to arrive at Dolores's dock, and, as luck would have it, she wasn't there. I tossed a rope around one of the posts and secured the canoe, not that it was going anywhere. The tide and the current were gently pushing us against the dock for now. At least something was going in our favor.

"Do we have to get out?" my passenger asked somberly.

"What? Out of the canoe? Why, yes, of course we do."

"I'd rather not," he said, looking around.

"Who's there?" Dolores bellowed from the vicinity of the outhouse. "What do y'all want?"

"Dolores," I called out, "it's me, Dora Witherspoon, and I've brought a . . . friend. He wants to meet you."

"Well, I don't want to meet *him*," she shouted. But she was walking toward us, craning her neck to get a look at him. Another moment and she was on the dock, looming over us. Then she burst out laughing. "What's he wearing? A suit and tie? Have you lost your mind, Mr.—?"

"—Yonce," he said automatically. "Pleased to meet you." He was still sitting in the canoe, gripping the sides.

"Mr. Yonce is an attorney," I said. "A lawyer. He's here to help us."

"I know what an attorney is," Dolores said. "You must think I'm dumb as this post here," she said, shoving a calloused hand against one of the wood pilings, which shook slightly. The whole structure, shack and all, could come crashing down into the water for all I knew. And yet it had survived many storms, even Hurricane Donna, so perhaps the underpinnings were sturdier than they appeared.

"I do not think you're dumb and you know it," I said, a little surprised at myself for sounding so fresh. "Mr. Yonce came quite a distance to talk to you. So please hear what he has to say."

"Are y'all going to get out of this here canoe?" Dolores asked, putting her hands on her hips.

"I'm quite comfortable here," Mr. Yonce said, "but thank you so much."

Dolores stifled a chuckle. "You mean you don't want to come inside and maybe sit in my, er, *parlor?*" She laughed heartily at her own joke, which startled Peggy Sue, the night heron, who made an unhappy squawk.

"Uh-oh," I said, "now we've upset Peggy Sue."

"Peggy Sue is a bird," Dolores said to Mr. Yonce by way of explanation. "Over yon, up in a tree. She be sitting on her eggs like a good mama."

Mr. Yonce looked from Dolores to me and back again. "Yes, um, okay," he said, clearing his throat. He began talking very fast, explaining that if Dolores agreed, he could file papers that would stop Darryl from proceeding with construction until a judge could review the rightful ownership of the land.

"I have done some preliminary work," he said, "and did some research on the documents that, I understand, belong to you."

Dolores, still standing on the dock, nodded. I wondered how many lawyers had met with a client like this, sitting in a canoe and wearing a life vest.

"What I learned is that your main document is a deed put in trust, with a large amount of cash, many years ago," he said. "It's called a perpetual trust, and it was set up by General John Stuart Williams—your ancestor. The taxes have been paid automatically through the trust. Very clever idea—maybe the old general was concerned about carpetbaggers trying to grab property when the owners were late paying their taxes. Now, in your case, this was set up at a bank in Pensacola. There weren't many banks in Florida in those days, and fortunately, the one the general chose was bought up by other banks over the years and is still in existence."

"So the bank in Pensacola has been taking money from the trust to pay the taxes all these years?" I asked.

"Yes," the young lawyer said. He paused for a moment to wipe his forehead with a monogrammed handkerchief. "I believe the deed in Mr. Darryl Norwood's custody must be a fake," he added. "I'm not sure where he got it, and I'm not sure it matters to us. If it's fabricated and he knows it, he could face criminal charges, but that's beyond what I think we should be focused on here."

"Well, then, what are we focused on here?" Dolores asked suspiciously.

"Producing your deed in court and stopping Darryl Norwood's development in its tracks."

Dolores grinned. "Ain't you some young whippersnapper?" she asked, causing him to blush flamingo pink from the base of his neck to his forehead. "Well," she added, "that's what I want. It's only right. The way I was raised, land is the greatest wealth a person can have, other than family. There's just one problem."

"What's that?" Mr. Yonce asked nervously.

"I can't pay you for all this work you're doing," she said. "I'm land rich but cash poor. Unless I can get my hands on some of that money in the trust. But something tells me that money's tied up in a neat little knot. Or else it wouldn't be there no more."

"You are correct," Mr. Yonce said. "We can look into it but I rather doubt you have access to it. The money is there to pay the taxes year after year, just to be sure it stays in the family."

"Dolores," I interrupted, "your friends are going to pay Mr. Yonce."

"What friends?"

"Dolores, I thought I told you before. If we needed to hire a lawyer, Mrs. Bailey White, Plain Jane, and Jackie Hart are going to pay for it. If I had any money, I would chip in, too."

"What about your son?" Mr. Yonce asked Dolores. He shuffled through his notes. "Robbie-Lee Simpson, lives in New York City. Works as an usher at a theater."

"What about him?" Dolores said icily.

"Can he help you? I mean financially? Have you spoken to him?"

Dolores sighed. "I get letters from him. He's been gone over a year now, but I don't want him to think I need him."

"But Dolores," I said gently, "the fact is you do need him."

"He needs to be brought into the picture if for no other reason than he is your heir," Mr. Yonce said.

"I hadn't thought of it like that," Dolores said so softly I barely heard her. "Go ahead," she added. "Just do what you got to do."

Mr. Yonce asked a few other questions. Had she ever had a driver's license? A Social Security card? Was there a birth certificate, other than the one filled out by a midwife?

She said no to the remainder of his questions, but I had a feeling that her mind was now far away.

Twenty-Six

Our young lawyer, bless his city-born heart, was turning out to be a real go-getter. He called Jackie the following afternoon with big news: He had persuaded a Collier County judge to sign a stop-work order on Darryl's project until a hearing could be held.

The only downside was that the judge wanted the hearing to take place the following Wednesday, which did not give us much time, Jackie said.

Time for what? I wondered to myself. I'd left Mississippi during the last week of August. It was now early November. From my way of thinking, the sooner this whole thing was over, the better. But there were several details that Mr. Yonce needed to nail down.

Jackie explained it to us over tea sandwiches prepared by Mrs. Bailey White. "He said he has to hire a genealogist to verify that Dolores—er, Bunny—is in fact a descendant of the general," she said. "He knows a professional who could do the work pronto."

"What if there are other descendants?" Plain Jane asked.

"Good question!" Jackie said. "Actually, even if there are others it only takes one descendant to step forward and file a stop-work order and have a chance to prove that Darryl is not the owner of the property. If there are other descendants, well, they can sort out what they want to do—or not do—with the property later. It's not relevant now."

"Jackie, you are starting to sound like a lawyer," Plain Jane teased.

"Well, I talked to Mr. Yonce on the phone for an hour, and he was pretty good about explaining things to me. You know, I always wanted to be a lawyer. I mean, if I had a profession, that's what I—"

"What else did he say?" I interrupted.

"Oh," Jackie said, flustered. "Let's see. There is a copy of the deed at the bank in Pensacola. The fact that Dolores—uh, *Bunny*—has the original deed is very important. Possession is nine-tenths of the law."

"There's something I'm wondering about," I said. Even I could hear the anxiety in my voice. "I hate to say this, but even if the genealogist shows that Bunny Ann McIntyre is a direct descendant of the general, how do we know for sure that she is, in fact, the real Bunny Ann McIntyre?"

"I thought of that, too," Plain Jane said, speaking quickly. "She says she's Bunny Ann McIntyre but she's been using the name Dolores Simpson for a long time. Darryl's lawyers could claim she's not the real Bunny. We need some additional proof. Do we have it?"

We all started talking at once, just like in our old book club days. "Girls, girls, one at a time!" Mrs. Bailey White said. "Dora, you first."

"Well, when I took Mr. Yonce to meet with her, he asked if

she'd ever had a driver's license or a Social Security card and she said no. He also asked if she had a copy of her birth certificate other than the one we've all seen already—the one written up by a midwife. Again—no."

"What about a family Bible?" Mrs. Bailey White asked.

"Yes," I said, "she said there was one and her name was written in it, but she doesn't know where it is now."

"Excuse me, could I get a word in edgewise here?" Jackie asked crossly. She pushed a dangling lock of hair out of her eyes. "I already talked to Mr. Yonce about all this!"

"And what did he say?" Plain Jane said.

"He said this was all fine and good, but that it would be very helpful if we could prove she'd ever used the name Bunny Ann McIntyre."

"How are we going to do that?" Mrs. Bailey White said, dejected.

"Well, ideally, if we had some sort of identification from her younger days, especially if there was a photograph or, even better, fingerprints. Mr. Yonce said she could be fingerprinted again today and if it were a match, then there would be no question."

"Good Lord," Mrs. Bailey White said. "We better hope she was arrested somewhere along the line."

Jackie smiled in a wry sort of way. "Funny," she said, "that's exactly what our lawyer said."

"Maybe it's time we checked in with Robbie-Lee," Plain Jane said. "He might know."

"I wonder how he's doing way up thar in New York City," Mrs. Bailey White said, making it sound as if he were on a dangerous expedition to the North Pole. "I mean, I wonder if he's got himself any friends."

"He sounds pretty good in his letters," I said.

"Yes, but do you think he has a *special friend*?" Jackie asked hopefully. Robbie-Lee was what my mama's generation called "a doll"—handsome, charming, debonair, and absolutely useless in the romance department. He wasn't interested in women in the Biblical sense, but he was kind and respectful, and awfully fun to have around.

"I have no idea," I said. "I just hope he isn't lonely."

THAT EVENING, WITH OUR BLESSINGS, Jackie began trying to reach Robbie-Lee by telephone. I wish we had included him sooner. After all, this whole mess concerned his mother. But now our lawyer, Mr. Yonce, said it couldn't wait.

Jackie had some trouble reaching Robbie-Lee. The long-distance operator said there was no telephone at the address of the apartment where he lived—not too surprising, since having a phone was expensive and Robbie-Lee was pinching pennies. Jackie finally called the Booth Theatre on Broadway where Robbie-Lee worked as an usher and, after persuading one of the box-office ladies that this was a family emergency, a message was left for Robbie-Lee to call her collect on his break.

He called back within an hour, Jackie said, and was completely frantic. Jackie explained what was going on, as rapidly as she could. He was relieved, she told us, that nothing terrible had happened to his mother—he was sure that's why Jackie had called—but he was furious about Darryl's plans, the first he'd heard of them.

When Jackie told him about the deed, she couldn't judge his reaction. If he was surprised, it wasn't obvious. Then she told him the court date—just one week away—and asked if there was any chance he could come.

"By the way," she asked before they got off the phone, "would you happen to know if, well, if your mother has ever been arrested? It would take too long to explain right now but it would help us prove her case."

There was a long pause, Jackie said, and then he replied, "Yes, I think she was. A long time ago, before I was born. When she was working as a, um, dancer in Tampa." Then he added, "Listen, Jackie, I have to get back to work now."

She said it was hard to tell if that were really true.

Twenty-Seven

While Mr. Yonce scoured the arrest records up in Hillsborough County, we tried to keep our minds occupied. We tried various things to distract us, including a picnic on the beach, an excursion to the library, and then a cookout where we got a little tipsy on account of Mrs. Bailey White making Jell-O wine.

Then Plain Jane got this idea that we should revive our book club, just for the time being. I was eager to participate. Working at the library in Jackson meant I'd been reading all the latest books as they came in. I read anything and everything. I was impatiently awaiting Hemingway's latest, *A Moveable Feast*, which was coming in December, and I'd just finished an unusual autobiographical novel by a young woman with schizophrenia called *I Never Promised You a Rose Garden*.

"What books have you read lately?" I asked breathlessly.

"Ha! Funny you should ask," Plain Jane replied. I noticed everyone turned to look at Jackie.

"What?" Jackie asked. "Oh, I know what you mean. That

book, *Tropic of Cancer*. Are you familiar with it, Dora? A novel, written by Henry Miller and published in France in the '30s. Apparently, considered too vulgar for Americans."

"That's because it *is* vulgar!" Mrs. Bailey White almost shouted.

"Well, let's just say that some of it is not in good taste," Plain Jane said. By way of explanation to me, she added, "It was finally published in the U.S. a few years ago and then the courts said it was obscene. I think it's available again now. Anyway, Jackie got her hands on a copy. Jackie, how did you get it, anyway?"

Jackie lit a cigarette. "I didn't buy it at the Book Nook, that's for sure."

"We read passages of it aloud, and it was shocking!" Mrs. Bailey White howled.

"Oh, I was just trying to get us out of the rut we were in."

"What rut was that?" Plain Jane asked.

"Reading books that were too safe."

"What else did you read?" I asked.

"Well, just before you came home we'd been discussing *Cross Creek* by Marjorie Kinnan Rawlings," Plain Jane said.

"Oh, I read that in high school and liked it very much," I said, thrilled that we were now on safer ground. If only Priscilla, Robbie-Lee, and the librarian, Miss Lansbury, were here, it might feel like old times.

"I don't know why we read that," Jackie grumbled. "I really didn't care for it that much."

"She's the same author who wrote *The Yearling*," Plain Jane replied testily, "and we all loved that."

"I liked that it was by a *woman* author and it's about Florida," said Mrs. Bailey White.

"I remember it as a pioneer story," I said, "except that instead of out west it was set in north-central Florida. It's a memoir, right? And she's very independent and endures all kinds of hardships—"

"Hardships?! She was out of her mind!" Jackie interrupted. "Poison ivy? Snakes? I could hardly read it. Why put yourself through something like that?"

"Oh, Jackie, you're missing the point!" Plain Jane said crossly, having stood and retrieved the book from Mrs. Bailey White's shelf. "Listen to this passage: 'It is more important to live the life one wishes to live, and to go down with it if necessary, quite contentedly, than to live more profitably but less happily.'"

"I agree, that is a beautiful sentiment," Jackie said snippily, "but I have never really understood this type of adventure memoir— you know, where some naïve person goes out into the wilderness and goes through all kinds of hell of their own making and somehow supposedly emerges as a better, fuller human being. *Ugh*!"

"Jackie, you have no spirit of adventure!" cried Plain Jane.

"How can you say that?" Jackie blew a stream of cigarette smoke toward the ceiling. "I live here, don't I? I came all the way from Boston to Collier County, doesn't that count for something? Why do we always end up talking about me, anyway? Let's talk about something else." She turned to me and, without blinking an eye, said, "Dora, speaking of *adventure*, when are you going to tell us what happened in Mississippi?"

Now if there is one thing I hate, it's being ambushed. I had been planning on telling them in my own good time.

"Jackie, must you always put Dora on the spot?" Plain Jane scolded.

"Oh, it's all right," I said, sighing. "I guess now's as good a time as any. Especially since—as I keep telling y'all—I have to go back soon."

"Well, maybe you could start by telling us what Jackson, Mississippi, is like," Jackie prompted. "They certainly have been in the national news, lately—"

"Yes," I said, "that poor man, Medgar Evers! That was two months before I arrived in Jackson. The Klan is crazy there. I mean, killing a leader of the NAACP! In his own front yard. Right out in the open!"

"Did you see any protests, or altercations, or anything of that sort?" Plain Jane asked.

"You can't help but encounter some of it," I replied.

"But what's it like to be there—in the city, I mean?" Jackie persisted.

"Well, it's hard to describe, but there's a feeling like there's not enough air to breathe," I said, struggling to find the right words. "I guess it's like—well, like when a big summer storm is rolling in from the Gulf and you can see the lightning strikes on the horizon. The air is so ripe with electricity and humidity that it makes you shiver even though it's hot. Well, that's what Jackson feels like to me these days. Especially since those three civil rights workers were murdered in June in that little city over in Neshoba County."

"You mean the city they call Philadelphia, of all things," Jackie said.

"Yes," I said.

"Well, I guess that's the difference between Mississippi and here," Plain Jane said. "Florida is still waking up."

"Actually, I think we are in the land of *Rip Van Winkle*," Jackie said sarcastically. "In twenty years' time we'll wake up and discover that the civil rights movement has arrived here."

"Maybe not!" I said. "I mean, maybe sooner than that. I can't believe I forgot to tell you about the speaker I heard over at the

Methodist church. I wish you all had been there. She was from some place in Ohio. An activist, I guess. She said we were ten years behind Mississippi, Alabama, and Georgia."

"No surprise there," Jackie said.

"But don't you see?" I asked. "A year ago that lady activist from Ohio wouldn't have been invited to speak here. *She was right here in Naples at one of the Methodist churches.* Isn't that progress?"

"Yes, I suppose it is," said Jackie. I must have looked skeptical because she added, "I mean it seriously. I agree with you, Dora."

"I think Florida is more genteel," Mrs. Bailey White said. "Yes, we have the Klan, but they're just a bunch of idiots running around in the bushes setting churches on fire. Things like the Medgar Evers assassination—that doesn't happen in Florida."

"Oh, yes it does!" Jackie said. "What about that man, Harry Moore, and his wife? The Klan put dynamite under their house and killed them on Christmas Day back in 1951 in some little town in Brevard County."

"Why, Jackie, you've been doing your homework," Plain Jane said admiringly.

"Well, there is some information at the library," Jackie said. "But Ted's been doing research when he's been traveling around the state. He even went to the NAACP office in Tampa and picked up some pamphlets there."

"Y'all are going to get yourselves shot!" Mrs. Bailey White said. "Mercy!"

"Well, Ted and I feel that we should try to understand what is happening, and the only way you can know that is to study the situation," Jackie said.

"Oh boy," Plain Jane remarked under her breath.

"What is that supposed to mean, Jane?" Jackie seemed surprised.

"It means that you're a typical Yankee," Mrs. Bailey White said. "You think you can solve every problem by studying it to death and asking questions. *Ha, ha, ha.*"

"Let's get back to Dora and her stay in Mississippi," Jackie snapped. "Did you ever feel like you were in danger?"

"In danger of what?" I asked, taken aback. "It's the black people who are in danger. Plus, the few white people who are trying to help them."

"So you didn't try to help the black people?" Jackie asked. She seemed disappointed.

"How?" I asked. "I'm from Florida. I don't understand Mississippi. I don't think I should presume to tell them how to fix their problems. I might have made things worse."

"But you might have made things *better*," Jackie said softly.

Mrs. Bailey White spoke up again. "Now, don't admonish Dora. That's not why she went to Mississippi. She is still grieving her mama's death and went there to look for her people. She did her part. Besides, it ain't Dora's job to fix the world!"

"Well!" Jackie said furiously. "That's so . . . *Southern*! Mind your own business, pass the buck . . ."

"Jackie," I said grimly, "I'm doing my part in my own way. For instance, every Tuesday my landlady Mrs. Conroy and I cook dinner for the black leaders."

"What?" Jackie said. "What do you mean?"

I wondered how much I should share with them, even though they were my closest friends. I remembered that old World War Two saying "Loose lips sink ships." "Well," I began slowly, "y'all have to promise me that this doesn't go beyond this room. But there is concern that someone may try to, er, harm the leaders, like the Rev. Martin Luther King when he comes to town."

Jackie quickly put two and two together. "You mean *poison?*" she asked, aghast.

"Sure," I said, "among other ways. I don't know what they have in place to protect him from being shot or anything like that. I'm sure there must be bodyguards. But somebody figured out that the food he and the other leaders eat could be tampered with. So the way it works is there's a very small group of people like me and Mrs. Conroy who volunteer to cook at home using ingredients we buy or grow. This is all very hush-hush, of course. We prepare the food and pretend we're taking it to Mrs. Conroy's church for potluck night. But instead the food is picked up by a Negro janitor at Mrs. Conroy's church. He gives it that same day to his colored preacher, who takes it directly to the colored side of town himself."

"My goodness!" Jackie said, "who dreamed this up?"

"I have no idea," I replied.

"Wait—Mrs. Conroy is involved? Isn't that the same lady you said was nervous as a rat terrier?" Plain Jane asked.

"Well, she is," I said, blushing a little at my unkind characterization. "She also has a heart of gold. And she belongs to one of the white churches that is trying to help the Negroes."

"Never mind all that, have you actually met Dr. King?" Jackie asked, wide-eyed.

"No," I said. "But I know I helped feed him whenever he was in Jackson."

"Oh, Dora, I am so proud of you," Mrs. Bailey White gushed.

"What else did you do?" Plain Jane asked.

I paused and thought about it. "I noticed in Jackson that I hadn't seen any groups like our book club—you know, white people who welcomed a black person to join," I said. "I don't see that kind of socializing go on between the races there at all. So every time I meet a new person in Jackson, I find a way to tell them all about our Priscilla and how smart she is, that we were in a book club together and now she's studying at Bethune-Cookman College."

"How is that supposed to change things?" Jackie asked.

"Are you kidding? That's the best way to make change happen!" Plain Jane cried. "By pointing out that she is friends with a black person, and that the black person is someone she likes and admires!"

"Oh, brother," Jackie said. "If that's progress, it'll only take a hundred years."

THERE WAS ENOUGH TENSION IN the air to fry a rabbit so we went to our separate corners. Mrs. Bailey White made some kind of excuse and disappeared into her kitchen, where she puttered about doing this and that; Plain Jane attended to the baby (we could hear her cooing, her voice echoing in high pitches down the staircase); Jackie went outside to clean the windshield of her car and have a smoke; and I went into Mrs. Bailey White's paneled library. Studying her books, taking them down one by one, was soothing. What is it about books? They are like old friends.

About an hour later, Mrs. Bailey White rounded us up like she was Mother Goose and we, her little goslings. She asked that we return to the parlor. Once there, she announced, "Now, girls, let's focus on Dora, and what she learned about her family, if anything, on her trip." To me, she said kindly, "Take your time, dear."

I cleared my throat. "Well," I began slowly, "as you know, I always wondered why I was named after a well-known writer from Mississippi, and figured Mama may have been friends with Eudora Welty, or maybe even kinfolk. Or maybe Mama had just been an admirer. But I realized that the first thing I should do is read all of her books. Miss Welty's, I mean. I read *The Robber Bridegroom* on the bus on the way to Mississippi. Once I got settled I read everything I could get my hands on. And frankly it made me a little uneasy. Because Miss Welty's writing is a little off-putting at times. Intimidating."

"Well, that one is especially eerie," Plain Jane interjected. "Sorry. I didn't mean to interrupt."

"So anyway I read them all," I continued, "just because I thought it would be rude not to. I mean, who goes to visit a famous writer and hasn't read her books? I wasn't even sure I would get to talk to her, but it seemed respectful to be prepared.

"All this time I was working up my nerve. Finally, I decided that I was being a ninny. What was the worst thing that could happen? That she would turn me away? Everyone in town knew where she lived, so I went over there on the bus and walked back and forth on the sidewalk trying to work up my nerve. Then I realized Mama would not approve of me, a complete stranger, just knocking on Miss Welty's door. So I went back to Mrs. Conroy's and wrote a letter. I told Miss Welty that I was living in town temporarily to find out more about my late mother, whose name was Callie Francine Atwater of the Jackson Atwaters, and that Callie had married a man named Montgomery Witherspoon, known to all as Monty, and that I was their only child. And that I wouldn't be bothering her—with her being an important writer and all—except I believed she may have known my mother at one time, and that in fact my name is Eudora Welty Witherspoon and while it could be a coincidence it seems highly unlikely in my most humble opinion. So I wrote this in a letter. And I mailed it.

"Of course, I hoped (and truth be told, prayed) that I would hear back from her if for no other reason than to clear up the mystery of my name. Three days later I received a letter. When I came home from my job at the library, Mrs. Conroy was standing on the porch waiting for me. The mailman had just been there. I'm still amazed Mrs. Conroy didn't steam it open because she can be nosy as a raccoon and not half as subtle, bless her heart.

"I went upstairs to open it. It was an invitation from Miss Welty to visit her at her home the following Sunday afternoon at three o'clock. That was all. Just a handwritten note, one sentence long.

"I was relieved and happy that she'd replied but as the days passed—slow as molasses, it seemed to me—I started dreading what she might tell me. I'm not sure why. I was prepared for her to say almost anything.

"Finally, Sunday arrived, and after church and Sunday dinner with Mrs. Conroy, it was time to go. I was so scared I'd be late that I got to Miss Welty's neighborhood a half-hour early. At five minutes till three, I knocked on her door. She answered herself. She's a plain little thing, but the type of person who has presence.

"'Do you mind if we sit in the garden?' she asked me. 'My mother is upstairs and feeling very poorly today.'

"And of course I said I was sorry to hear that, but the garden would be fine. So we sat in her garden—oh, what a garden!—and—"

"Wait—she has a lovely garden?" Mrs. Bailey White interrupted. Mrs. Bailey White had what Mama used to call "garden envy." Some folks have kitchen envy, some have porch envy. Mrs. Bailey White salivated over lush flower gardens.

"Let's not talk about that now—" Jackie said.

"Does she have climbing roses?" Mrs. Bailey White persisted. "I just love climbing roses."

"Why, yes, Mrs. Bailey White, she does! She has Lady Banks, American Beauty, Mermaid, and some others I didn't recognize."

"Oh, I wish I could see it!" Mrs. Bailey White said plaintively.

"Mrs. Bailey White, we all love gardens," Plain Jane said gently, "but let's let Dora get back to her story."

"Well," I continued, "we talked about her books until finally she broached the subject by saying, 'I was sad to learn from your letter that your mother has died.'

"Well, it all came tumbling out of her—this story from before I was born. Mama and Miss Welty had been friends in school, with both pledging they would remain independent, unmarried and childless, and pursue careers as writers.

"I never saw Mama write anything more than a grocery list. But Miss Welty said Mama had been a 'grand writer' with 'a lot of promise.' Then she said with a smile that Mama had been a 'great beauty' who 'had everything a person could dream of.'

"She went on to say that Mama was 'the belle of the ball,' from a rich family, and then one day she turned everything upside-down: She ran away on the day of her wedding in 1931."

"She *what*?" Mrs. Bailey White shrieked.

"She left her betrothed at the altar. And she took off with my daddy instead." It was hard to push those words out of my mouth. But I did.

"How exciting!" Jackie declared, and lit another cigarette.

"Good heavens, Dora," Plain Jane said sympathetically. "That's a lot to think about."

"Well, I had no idea that Mama was ever engaged to someone other than Daddy. She always seemed like such a sensible person. I couldn't imagine her leaving a man at the altar, abandoning her family and friends, and disappearing. That's not the woman I knew my whole life."

"I'm sorry, Dora," Jackie said, furrowing her brow. "I didn't mean to make light of it."

"Did Miss Welty tell you anything else?" Plain Jane asked gently.

"Well, I asked if she was there when Mama . . . well, when all that happened at the church, and she said, no, she missed the whole drama on account of it happened at the same time her daddy took sick and died from leukemia."

"Oh, that's sad," Mrs. Bailey White said. "What else did she say?"

"Well, I asked her, 'Are Mama's parents still living?' and 'Did Mama have any brothers or sisters?'

"Her answer, to both, was no. And I have to tell you, I was very disappointed. Somehow I had pictured Mama having a brother or sister. I would have loved having an aunt or uncle, or cousins. And another thing—Miss Welty was surprised to hear that Mama remained a nurse. She said, 'I thought she was doing that just because her parents told her not to. I didn't realize she stayed with it. Maybe it was her true calling.' And then Miss Welty looked straight at me and with no warning at all, she said, 'Well, Miss Witherspoon, what is *your* calling?'

"And that's when I told her about you—the Book Club, I mean—and how y'all have told me that you think I have a knack for storytelling. And while I didn't know if I had what it takes to make a living as a writer, I had been trying my hand at it."

"Did she read anything you wrote?" Jackie interrupted.

"Why, yes, she did," I said. "She asked me to come back a week later and bring something I'd written."

"Wow," Jackie said, "and then what happened?"

"Oh, let Dora tell the story!" Plain Jane said.

"That's right," Mrs. Bailey White said. "Just let her tell it."

They all stared at me with excitement.

"Well," I said slowly, "I brought her a short story and she read it."

"But what did she *say*?" Jackie persisted.

"Do you want the truth?" I asked.

"Of course we want the truth," Jackie said uneasily.

I thought it best to blurt it out. "She said it wasn't authentic."

"Authentic?!" Mrs. Bailey White cried out. "What is that supposed to mean?"

My friends looked wounded, as indeed I had been at the time, until I admitted a simple truth to myself: Miss Welty was right.

"What it means is that I was trying too hard to write about something I didn't know anything about."

"Well, what did you write about?" Plain Jane asked.

"A short story about a girl who has a love affair in Paris," I replied.

"But you've never been to Paris," Jackie said, stating the obvious.

"Miss Welty said the same thing," I said. "She said it's possible to write about a place you've never been but you shouldn't 'undervalue' your own experiences. She said something about Paris being overdone."

"I don't see how Paris could ever be *overdone*," Jackie said.

"I think she meant, *written about too often*, when there are other places that no one ever seems to write about," I said. "She said that if I wrote about a love affair in Paris, maybe, at least, one of the characters could be visiting from Collier County, just to make it fresh."

"Ah, I see," Plain Jane said approvingly.

"This will sound funny," I added. "On my way back to my landlady's house a phrase kept popping into my head. I don't know where it came from. Maybe from Mama in the Spirit World. It was, *Listen to your own stories*."

"Oh," Jackie said. "I like that!"

"So you're going to keep writing, right, Dora?" Plain Jane asked. "Because we think you should, don't we?" Jackie and Mrs. Bailey White nodded in agreement.

"I'll tell you what, Dora, the part about your mother running off with another man on her wedding day—*ooooWEE*, that must have been something," Mrs. Bailey White said.

"Now there's a story for you to tell," Jackie added.

I felt something closing around my heart, like a protective shield, much like a turtle, I thought, as it withdraws into its shell. There was more to say but I was not ready to tell the rest.

Twenty-Eight

This is what I kept to myself.

After my two meetings with Miss Welty, I did some research on my lunch hour at the library. I looked through old copies of the *Clarion-Ledger*, looking for stories about Mama.

I could have done this when I first came to Jackson, but I didn't. I guess I just wasn't ready then.

I worked my way through each massive index of the newspaper for the time frame Mama lived in Jackson, checking for her name year after year until I found three separate news stories in which she was said to be mentioned. I filled out a microfilm request, trying to look nonchalant while the staff at the research desk went to look for them. The rolls of microfilm, once they were retrieved, had to be threaded into a machine in order to read them, a difficult task when your hands are trembling.

I scrolled too fast and had to back up the machine to see the first news story. Suddenly there she was, Miss Callie Francine Atwater, along with Miss Eudora Welty, in a news photograph of the two of them sharing a prize for a spelling bee. Miss Welty hadn't mentioned that. Perhaps it wasn't important.

More shocking was seeing Mama in the social pages as a debutante at a cotillion, looking fancy in a special gown ordered from a store in New York City called Bergdorf Goodman's, according to the article. I stared at the photograph. No question about it. This was my mama. The same person who never spent money on clothes and hadn't seemed to care about fashion one bit.

Then I found the wedding announcement. MISS ATWATER TO MARRY MR. JENKINS TODAY IN GREENWOOD, said the headline. I could scarcely breathe as I read the story. "Miss Callie Francine Atwater, daughter of local bank president James T. Atwater and his wife, Jane, is to be married at 11 o'clock today to Mr. Harold Jenkins of Lake Charles, Louisiana . . ." How strange to be reading the announcement of a wedding that never came to be. The article went on to describe her dress and mentioned a bridesmaid, Miss Alice B. Johnson.

I felt someone's presence behind me, a little shadow over my right shoulder. It was the head librarian, Mrs. LaCroix. "I see you're digging up the past," she said, trying, but failing, to sound lighthearted. She spoke in a soft, hushed tone out of respect for the silence-only rule which librarians alone were allowed to break, and only in the quietest murmurs. "I wondered how long before you'd start looking in these old newspapers. Ah," she added, "I see you've found the society pages."

"Did you know my mother?" I asked pointedly—and a little too loud. When I'd been interviewed for my job, I'd mentioned that Mama grew up in Jackson. When I said Mama's name at the time, several of the librarians—including Mrs. LaCroix—had acted a little funny but I wasn't sure if it meant anything.

"Everyone knew your mother, dear," she whispered. "She was the star of her generation around here."

"And do you know what happened to her?"

Mrs. LaCroix looked at me, surprised. "Don't you?"

"I only know that she didn't marry this man," I said, trying to keep my voice low and pointing to the microfilm page with the account of the wedding. "On that same day she married my daddy, whose name was Montgomery Witherspoon, and they went to Florida, where Daddy was from, and they had me." My mind was spinning like a little wind-up toy Mama had given me as a child and which I still had, despite the fact that it was broken. "What has happened to Mr. Harold Jenkins?" I asked. "Do you know?"

Mrs. LaCroix pulled up a chair and sat next to me. "He died in the war," she said. "After what happened—with your mama and all—he had a broken heart and went back to Louisiana. That's what I've heard for years. And even though he was a little old to serve in World War Two, he enlisted. And he was killed. I'm not sure when or where. We could look that up if you want to. Or I could write to the librarian in Lake Charles . . . "

"It seems like everyone is dead," I said sadly. "Everyone who could give me real answers, anyway."

"Not everyone has passed away," Mrs. LaCroix said. "The bridesmaid. She's sitting right over there."

I jerked my head in the direction Mrs. LaCroix was pointing. A gray-haired lady sat half hidden behind a broadsheet newspaper. I had noticed her before. She was what we called a "regular."

The next thing I knew I was being introduced, in library-appropriate hushed tones, to my mother's long-ago bridesmaid. While I could not have been more surprised, she seemed to have been expecting this moment to occur. Perhaps, I realized, even waiting for the right moment to speak to me, these last several months.

MISS ALICE B. JOHNSON WAS a lifelong Jackson resident from a neighborhood I recognized as a poor white part of town. She had never married, she said, and still lived at home with her mother. To support herself, she worked nights as a telephone operator.

"Call me Miss Alice," she said warmly. Aware that we were creating a small disruption, and that we had definitely abused the silence-only rule, we agreed to duck outside for a little stroll. My lunch hour had elapsed, but Mrs. LaCroix nodded her approval and smiled encouragingly.

The sidewalk was sun dappled and welcoming but too crowded with children walking home from school to hold a private conversation. I did not want to miss a word. Miss Alice gestured to a side street that was blessedly empty of activity except for a small dog sniffing at the base of a magnolia tree. We found a little bench where we could talk quietly.

"Your mama wanted to be just like us," Miss Alice said.

"Like who?" I asked.

Miss Alice surprised me by chuckling. "Like down-to-earth folks. Ordinary people who didn't put on airs. She and I met over at the Salvation Army. The only difference was, she was a volunteer and I was a client. But we were the same age and we became friends. She confided in me. When she asked me to be her only bridesmaid, I didn't know what to do. I couldn't afford the dress. But she said, 'Don't worry about it, I'll pay for it.' Then I started worrying that maybe her parents wouldn't want me in the wedding. It was during the Depression, but your grandpa was still a wealthy man or at least that's the impression he gave. And your grandma was active in the Episcopal Church, which is for upper-class folk, you know. But your mama said, 'Oh, don't worry. It's my wedding, and I want you in it.'"

"Did you know that Mama was going to run off with someone else?" The words were painful to say.

"I knew she was in love with someone else but I wasn't privy to her plans," Miss Alice said tactfully. "Or maybe there were no plans. Maybe she just up and did it."

I was having a hard time picturing Mama being so impulsive, and Miss Alice read my mind. "She was young," she said. "We were all very young. People do things they'd never do when they're older. And sometimes it's impossible to look back and understand.

"What your mama really wanted," she added, "was to be just plain folk. She didn't want nothin' to do with the highfalutin family she was born into. She even learned to talk like me. And she surely didn't want to marry that fellow from Louisiana. That wasn't her dream. Her dream was to be a nurse among the downtrodden. She was going to give up all her fancy airs. And then somehow—maybe at the Salvation Army—she ran into your daddy, Montgomery Witherspoon. Oh, he was a bad boy. Had been in jail and everything. But I think she saw in him a way for all of her dreams to come true: A simple life. Helping others." She thought for a moment and added, "He was her way out."

"Daddy had been in *jail*?" I choked on the word.

"Yes'm, but I don't know what for. Nothing too terrible or I'd remember that. Where is he, do you know?"

"No," I said, "I don't know what happened to him. All I know is Mama said there was a big fuss when I was a baby, and Daddy up and left. I believe he's dead. When I was growing up, Mama gave folks the impression she was a widow but come to think of it, I never actually heard her use that word. Maybe implying that he was dead was her way of keeping up appearances. It's a lot easier to be a widow than a divorcée in this world, that's for sure. Anyway, whatever happened between them didn't end well. I always had the feeling she was embarrassed by him, or something he'd done."

"Maybe he was prone to drinkin'," Miss Alice said sympathetically. "Lots of menfolk are."

"Miss Alice," I said, desperate to put more pieces together. "Have you been watching me? Or is it a coincidence that you come to the library all the time? How did you know who I am?"

She smiled a little mischievously. "A little bird told me that a gal calling herself Eudora Welty Witherspoon was in town, and that her mama had been Miss Callie Atwater. And I thought, *Now that's mighty peculiar.* I thought maybe the Lord hisself wants me to find out what this is all about. Maybe to help you in some way since your mama and I were friends back in the day."

"But how—"

"Child, Jackson may seem like a big city to you but it's a small town at heart. My mother took a Bible study class with your landlady, Mrs. Conroy. And one day Mrs. Conroy mentioned she had a gal staying with her, and she said your name and that you were working at the library. My mother told me, and that's all I needed to know."

"Well, I am grateful to you," I said. "I thank you for telling me what you know."

It was the wrong thing to say. She looked away, and a deep uneasiness swept through me.

"There's something else," she said finally. When she glanced back at me, her smile was gone and her face sagged, making her look much older. "What your mama really wanted most was a child, but I was pretty sure she couldn't have one." She looked at me closely, as if studying my features, then said, "Maybe I shouldn't be telling you all this, but it seems wrong that you don't know. The fact is your mama had some kind of fever that almost killed her when she was, oh, maybe sixteen. And after that, she was told she'd never be able to have children."

"So you're saying I was a surprise?" I said, but the second the words left my lips I realized she meant something else entirely. "Do you think . . . ? Are you saying—?"

"—that you might have been adopted?" Miss Alice said softly. "Could be." She paused a moment, then added, "Then again, maybe you're some kind of miracle baby." She tried her best to smile brightly, but I don't think she was convinced. And neither was I.

Finding out that you might be adopted is one thing. Finding out at the age of thirty-two, and from a person you've known for exactly ten minutes, is a tough row to hoe.

"Mama always said I was born in Naples, at home," I said quietly. "I suppose that might not be true."

"Well, what does your birth certificate say?"

"I don't have one."

"Everyone has one."

"No, Mama said she never got around to registering me. I found that out when I got married. Before we could get the marriage license, Mama had to swear in an affidavit that she was my mama and that I was born at home in Naples."

"I see," Miss Alice said.

What she could see, and so could I, was that it might all have been lies. And the worst part was not being able to ask Mama because she was dead. Just ask her; that's all I wanted. I would have accepted the idea of being adopted, if only she had told me herself.

I told Miss Alice a little about my life, what Naples was like, and about my failed marriage to Darryl. She asked what had led me to come to Jackson to find out about Mama, and I told her about the Collier County Women's Literary Society and how the founder, a newcomer to Naples named Jackie Hart, had encouraged me to get out in the world, ask questions, and experience life. I had known immediately that I should go to Jackson, if for no other reason than to see where Mama had come from. And then I told Miss Alice what Mama's life had been like in Naples, and how she'd gotten sick. And how she died.

Miss Alice listened carefully. "Well," she said finally, "I'm just glad she had you with her when she got sick." Then she turned directly to face me. There were tears in her eyes, but she smiled as she added, "I hope you realize that you must have meant the *world* to her, Dora. She was truly blessed. And so are you."

Twenty-Nine

We had four days until the hearing at the Collier County Courthouse, and Mrs. Bailey White was beginning to fret. "I do believe that we should provide some new clothes and, um, a little *assistance* with Bunny's appearance for the court date," she said. "I know from my own experience, during my murder trial, that it's important to look your best."

I'm sure I flinched and I have little doubt the others did, too. I'd never been able to come to terms with Mrs. Bailey White's past—not fully anyway—but at the same time I was happy for the diversion. Any topic was preferable to the possibility that they would ask more questions about my discoveries in Mississippi.

"As a matter of fact, I'm glad you brought this up, Mrs. Bailey White," Jackie said, interrupting my thoughts. "I've been sitting here trying to figure out how we're going to get her into town for fingerprinting. Mr. Yonce said it was imperative. And I agree. We need to fix her up for court, if she lets us. Maybe we should, um, *retrieve* her from the, er, *swamp,* get these things done, then keep her in town—maybe just for one night—so that we can be sure she gets to court."

"She could stay here the night before," Mrs. Bailey White said thoughtfully. "I mean, if she's willing to."

"I have some clothes that might fit," Plain Jane interjected from across the room. "Or, at least, we can alter them. Maybe we should all ransack our closets and see what we can come up with."

And so it was agreed, at least by everyone except, of course, Bunny. Jackie even offered to pay for a trip to the hair salon and said she would escort Bunny there if I promised to go along for moral support. But someone had to get Bunny out of Gun Rack Village and into Naples. Jackie still refused to drive in Gun Rack Village, citing wear and tear on the convertible, and I balked at canoeing again. My hands were still sore from paddling Mr. Yonce over there and back. And I didn't feel like going on foot again, either.

I took a chance and left a note for her at the Esso station. I knew that Billy and Marco, the pair of brothers who lived somewhere along the river, were in the habit of stopping by the Esso station almost daily. Bucky, who owned the gas station, was pretty reliable and agreed to give my note to them. Hopefully, the brothers would then deliver it to her.

The note was hard to write. How do you tell someone that she needs to get gussied up for court? That her hair and clothes won't do? That she needed to be fingerprinted at the police department? That we wanted her to stay the night before court at Mrs. Bailey White's house because we didn't want to take any chances that she wouldn't show up?

I kept the note very short. This was one of those "the less

said, the better" moments. If it didn't work, I'd have to hike back there and persuade her to return with me.

TO MY SURPRISE, AT PRECISELY two o'clock the day before court, Bunny arrived at the Edge of Everglades House of Beauty, just as I'd hoped. Marco and Billy had not only retrieved my note from Bucky and delivered it to her, they had saved her the long hike into town by giving her a ride.

This seemed like a minor miracle to Jackie and me. We'd been nervously waiting at the beauty parlor, flipping randomly through magazines devoted to the latest hairstyles, none of which, to be honest, would look good on anyone we knew. The beauty salon's owner kept a radio tuned to WNOG, "Wonderful Naples on the Gulf." At one point Jackie turned to me and said, "Oh, for Pete's sake. If I hear that Beatles song 'I Want to Hold Your Hand' one more time, I might have a stroke and die. My kids play it day and night and I hear it everywhere I go."

"I like the Beatles," I said lamely.

"Do you know what Judd said?" Jackie asked. "He said the school principal at the junior high held an assembly and said just two words into the microphone—'The Beatles'—and two girls screamed."

"Well, aren't girls everywhere screaming over the Beatles?" I asked.

"That's the point! It means that the cultural phenomenon known as the Beatles has even reached the end of the earth— that is, Naples."

We didn't even realize that Bunny was standing right in front of us, listening. She must have slipped through the door while we were having our Beatlemania discussion, which, judging by the look on her face, was all news to her. She sort of nodded and grunted something that might have been "hello."

The sight of Bunny sent a shock wave through the salon. The other women in the salon stopped talking abruptly. Their heads swiveled in unison. Even the ladies trapped under hair dryers were trying to get a good look.

Jackie was gracious. "So glad you could join us!" Her words of welcome were scarcely said when the owner of the beauty parlor scurried up to us. "What have we here?" she asked, with alarm.

"Of course you meant *whom* do we have here?" Jackie said sweetly. "This is the woman I was telling you about. As I mentioned before, it's my treat."

The hairdresser looked doubtful.

"I was thinking maybe a bouffant of some sort, though maybe she needs some color first," Jackie said, taking Bunny's arm and escorting her to the nearest washbasin.

Bunny actually half smiled at the other customers. "I would like a manicure, too," she announced, and, in one of those peculiar moments of perfect timing, a new Roy Orbison song called "Oh, Pretty Woman" started playing on the radio. To some people, it might have seemed like irony, but to me it was like a little message of love or tip of the hat, meant just for her.

"Oh, I forgot to make introductions!" Jackie cried out. "Miss Bunny Sanders, please meet Miss Dolores Simpson. Actually, Dolores's name is Bunny, too, but I keep forgetting to call her that. Shame on me—"

"Bunny?!" The proprietor took a step back. "*Bunny?*" she repeated. "Her name cannot be Bunny. Apparently you have forgotten, Mrs. Hart, that *I am Bunny*."

Jackie looked confused. "Oh," she said quickly, "two Bunnies! How cute! You know, I never knew anyone in Boston named Bunny but now I know *two* Bunnies."

Poor Jackie. She had failed to comprehend that here in the South it is a well-known fact that trouble can ensue when two gals in a small town have the same first name. Southern women are like a bee colony. They just can't tolerate two queens in one hive.

I cupped my hand and whispered a quick explanation into Jackie's ear. She looked at me like I had lost my mind. "What are you talking about?" she said a little too loud. "Why can't there be two Bunnies?"

You could fault men for all kinds of things, but no man, I felt sure, would have a problem with having the same first name as another. Why, I bet you could have a whole room full of Bobs and they'd probably just call themselves Bob 1, Bob 2, Bob 3, and so on. Or they'd just call each other by their last names. But you couldn't have two Bunnies in the little town of Naples.

For a moment I thought the hairdresser was going to ask us to leave. I could see she was mulling it over, but professional pride or Christian charity got the better of her. "We've got us some work to do!" she announced, in what was undoubtedly the understatement of the year. With remarkable speed she shampooed our Bunny's hair, slapped some goop on it, and led our Bunny to the only available hair dryer, which happened to be right smack in the middle of the row of all the others.

Bunny enjoyed being treated like a pampered swan. She even asked for a copy of *Screen Idol* magazine. *No doubt*, I thought, *to look for photos of Elizabeth Taylor*. Only when the manicurist was ready to do her nails—Bunny chose Petunia Pink—did she let go of the magazine.

As soon as the dryer was finished, Bunny the hairdresser re-washed our Bunny's hair, cut, and styled it. Jackie started to say something but did not; she was disappointed, I could tell, that her opinion on what she referred to as the *coiffure* was clearly unwelcome. This was not going as planned but it would have to be good enough. I was thankful when Jackie paid the bill and we could leave.

Bunny's new hairdo was a stunner: a mile-high tower of teased tresses reminiscent of cotton candy. Holding her hands so that her new manicure would finish drying, our Bunny did something I'm pretty sure she hadn't done in years: She smiled the type of full-faced grin that reminded me of a teenage girl getting ready for prom.

As we left the shop, however, reality returned. "Bunny," I said, "I hate to ruin this Kodak moment, because we're having great fun here. Not to shanghai you or anything but there is something you need to know."

The smile vanished. "Go on," she said, jutting out her chin. Jackie, meanwhile, pretended to rummage in her purse for her car keys; by prearrangement, she was to stay silent during this part.

"Well, uh, it looks like it's got to come out in court that you were, um, arrested a long time ago," I said. "And it's actually a *good* thing because it means we have your fingerprints from when you were using the name Bunny Ann McIntyre. Now we can compare them and prove that you are the same person. And Mr. Yonce says this will be necessary." I said this so rapidly even I wasn't sure what I'd just said.

Bunny simply shrugged. "Okay," she said. "But doesn't that mean we need to get some fresh fingerprints? We'd better get to it."

Here I had worried myself sick about this pending conversation, and yet Bunny had taken it in stride. She was definitely a more complex person than I had thought.

We walked to the sheriff's department, where our attorney Mr. Yonce was waiting for us. It was half past three on the day before court. We were cutting things very close.

With a desk scrgeant acting as a witness, a deputy sheriff fingerprinted Bunny. Her only concern was that it had messed up her manicure.

As soon as the prints were dry, Mr. Yonce said they would be examined that night by a fingerprint expert. Our young lawyer certainly seemed to have everything under control, but before we left he whispered to me, "We better hope these are a perfect match. We might win anyway, but this would seal the deal."

THERE WAS ONE MORE TASK: figuring out what Bunny was going to wear in court.

Once again, Bunny proved to be a surprisingly good sport. At Mrs. Bailey White's house we laid out all the possible outfits and let her choose. Jackie had brought a few things from her closet. Plain Jane had purchased some items at a church rummage sale, including gloves and a hat. Mrs. Bailey White offered costume jewelry and shoes. And my contribution was a small makeup kit I bought for half-price during a sale at the Rexall.

There was a risk of offending Bunny, of course, but there was another problem as well. None of us wanted to address the fact that Bunny's artificially enhanced bustline made her figure completely out of proportion.

Thankfully, Jackie anticipated the problem by creating what one might call a modified muumuu (although she described it as "reminiscent of what Liz Taylor might wear when she is entertaining at home"). Essentially, she had taken one of her own housecoats, added a little elastic here and there, altered the sleeves, and added a patent leather belt. The result was passably good. Bunny tried it on and seemed very pleased.

I had been worried about Bunny's reaction to the baby but when Plain Jane brought Dream into the room, Bunny sort of half smiled and nodded in Dream's direction in the way women do when they see a beautiful baby, even one that was the "wrong" color. For all I knew, Bunny might have balked at staying even one night under the same roof with a colored child, but she said nothing. The only thing left was for Bunny to have a good meal, a long hot soak in a bathtub (heaven only knows how long it had been), and a decent night's sleep in one of the guest rooms of Mrs. Bailey White's house.

Once Bunny was settled for the night, and Dream had drifted off to sleep, the rest of us convened for a nightcap of rose wine in the parlor. We talked over our plans for the next day when suddenly I blurted out that I had more to tell them about my visit to Jackson "if," I said, "y'all are in the mood to hear it."

"Of course we are in the mood to hear it," Jackie said. "If you feel like telling us now, by all means go ahead."

"Should I get us some warm milk?" Mrs. Bailey White asked.

"Forget the warm milk," Jackie said.

"Agreed," Plain Jane said, adding, "But thank you anyway."

"Can I just get this over with?" I said. I was tired and my nerves too raggedy to be as polite as I should have been. I took a deep breath while they focused their attention on me. "You know how I told you that I learned from Miss Welty that Mama had run off with Daddy on the day she was to marry someone else?" I said. "Well, there's more."

"Be brave, dear, what is it?" Plain Jane asked gently.

"I learned that I was almost certainly adopted," I said in a whisper, "and I doubt I'll ever find out what happened."

"What'd you say?" asked Mrs. Bailey White. "I can't hear you."

"She said she found out she was *adopted*," Plain Jane said loudly.

"Oh!" Mrs. Bailey White said. "I'm sorry I didn't hear you, please go on."

And so I told them the rest of the story, starting with what Miss Welty had said; about my research at the library; the newspaper stories on Mama; and meeting Miss Alice, Mama's long-ago bridesmaid. I explained how at first I felt like someone had died. I was in shock and grieving like when there's a tragedy. After that I was angry for a long while. I was so prickly I could have lost my job except my boss, the head librarian, felt sorry for me. For the first time in my life, I cussed often and over the littlest things, like dropping a nickel on the sidewalk and having to bend down to get it. That would just infuriate me. Everything seemed too much, like the world was out to get me in big ways and small. But I also laughed a lot, not because anything was funny but because of the irony of it. I had gone to Jackson to find out about Mama and, oh boy, I'd gotten a lot more information than I had bargained for.

Jackie, Plain Jane, and Mrs. Bailey White were listening carefully. After it was clear I was all talked out, Plain Jane spoke up. "You seem to be doing pretty well with this," she said gently.

"Well," I said, "I've had a few months to get used to the idea."

"Dora," Jackie said sympathetically. "If there's anything any of us can do—"

"Jackie, you make it sound like someone died," Plain Jane interrupted.

"Well, Dora herself said it felt like someone died," Jackie protested. "Oh, Dora, this really is terribly unfair, isn't it? I hope we will all see the day when people don't feel they have to be so secretive about adoption. It seems so much worse not to tell a child! I think if I had adopted any of my children I would have told them from the beginning."

"Well, that's not what the experts say," Plain Jane said solemnly. "I was just reading an article about it. It's better to wait until they're old enough to understand—or maybe never tell them at all. That's what it said."

"That's crazy," Jackie snapped. "Look at poor Dora here. I think the way she found out is the worst part."

"Ladies!" Mrs. Bailey White said. "Let us be thoughtful!" She gestured to me. I was sinking further and deeper into the seat cushions of the ancient sofa.

Plain Jane and Jackie rushed to apologize while Mrs. Bailey White poured me a teeny-tiny brandy and made me drink it. "Now, you listen to me, Miss Dora Witherspoon," she said firmly. "First, I want to say that you mustn't spend your life trying to find out more about the past. Some things are just meant to remain a mystery. Second, I don't know much about adoption but the woman you called 'Mama' loved you. She must have, because she raised you right. She's your real mother. The woman that's buried over yon in the Cemetery of Hope and Salvation. But since she won't have a chance to tell her side of this story— well, not until you meet her again in the Spirit World—I think we shouldn't judge her."

I reached over and squeezed Mrs. Bailey White's hand, grateful for her wisdom.

Thirty

The day of the court hearing dawned early for all of us. As agreed, Jackie picked me up at my cottage at six o'clock and we drove straight to Mrs. Bailey White's.

Jackie was nervous. She was dressed to the nines—still in mourning black but with a few extra flourishes like a heavy gold brooch and matching earrings that I'd never seen before.

"My mother's," she said, tugging gently on her earlobes when she saw me staring. "I want to look like I'm richer than I am," she added with a laugh. "We need to impress the judge."

I was wearing a light-gray suit with a lavender blouse. At least I had found some shoe polish and improved the appearance of my loafers. Well, if I could never pull off looking glamorous, at least I looked neat and presentable, but I made a silent promise that if I ever had any money to spare I would ask Jackie to take me shopping. Maybe even go to Miami or Palm Beach, though that was *really* dreaming on my part.

We arrived at the old house to find Mrs. Bailey White fluttering around like a bird that is trapped and trying to find its way out. Upstairs in her crib, Dream was hollering in a certain shrill, hysterical way which meant she wasn't calming down anytime soon. Plain Jane came down the stairs more quickly than I'd ever seen her move.

Bunny, Plain Jane said, was not in her room. Nor was she in the bathroom, the parlor, the kitchen . . .

It was Jackie who found Bunny sound asleep in a hammock on a screened-in porch on the north side of the house which no one ever used. Bunny woke up when she sensed that we were staring at her.

"What y'all lookin' at?" she barked. "And what's all that racket? Oh . . . the baby. Forgot where I was for a moment." She stretched. "Nice hammock," she said to Mrs. Bailey White, who collapsed into an ancient wicker chair.

"Oh, I see," Bunny said, dragging herself out of the hammock. "Y'all thought I ran off. Thought I let you down, huh." I heard a twinge of resentment in her voice.

"Well, we didn't know what to think," said Mrs. Bailey White.

I went upstairs to comfort the baby while Jackie looked after Mrs. Bailey White, who looked a little peaked from all the excitement. Plain Jane, who believed in the adage "If all else fails, there's always food," announced that she was going to make pancakes for everyone.

And, of course, it worked. There are times when pancakes are not just pancakes, they are problem solvers. Sitting down together to share a meal is part of it. The other, as Mama used to say, is that a full belly solves most of the troubles of the world.

Plain Jane dearly wanted to go with us to the courthouse but agreed that she would stay home and take care of the baby. That way, Mrs. Bailey White could go. This was a deliberate strategy on our part: Mrs. Bailey White represented old money. People knew who she was—for better or worse—and that her father had been a big somebody way back when.

The new courthouse in East Naples was a short ride away, but Jackie wanted us to be the first to arrive. I'd never been inside and was curious. Until Hurricane Donna clobbered Collier County in 1960, the county seat was in the town of Everglades City, not Naples. Going to court (or conducting any county business) meant a long drive to the south. The courthouse in Everglades City was one of the few buildings that survived, and as the only two-story building in town, many folks rode out the storm there. However, it was badly damaged, the town was a shambles (even more so than Naples), and the powers that be relocated the whole kit and caboodle. We now had a newly constructed county government building on the Tamiami Trail that was—hang onto your hat—air conditioned.

Silently, I wished Priscilla was with us but that was a foolish thought. Even if she'd been home from college, she could hardly have gone with us to the courthouse. She wouldn't be allowed to sit with us, on account of her being Negro. *Ironic*, I thought, *that they could build a courthouse with all of the modern amenities but the attitudes about race were still a hundred years out of date.*

Besides—and this made me flush with shame to think it—having Priscilla with us would hurt our case, despite her talent for making a good impression. There were judges who would rule against us simply because we were seen with a black person.

And so it was just the four of us—Jackie, Mrs. Bailey White, me, and also, of course, Bunny. Our attorney, Mr. Yonce, was to meet us there; he had borrowed a car and was staying at the Naples Beach Club Hotel.

As for Robbie-Lee, we had no idea where he was. Maybe he would arrive on the Trailways bus in time to get himself over to the courthouse. If not, he would miss all the fireworks. *But*, I thought privately, *at least he will be here to help pick up the pieces if we lose.*

When we arrived at the courthouse we discovered the building wasn't open. Fortunately, it wasn't hideously hot yet. Jackie kept the convertible top up for shade or we would have roasted even at that early hour of the day.

Mrs. Bailey White broke the silence. "I know this is a modern building and all, but frankly I'm nostalgic for the old days when the courthouse was down in Everglades City," she announced. "Now *that* was a grand old building, with the columns and all up front. I have many memories—"

"It's still there," I interrupted, hoping to derail her from talking about her trial. I'd always wanted to hear all the details, but this was not the time. "They're going to fix it up and turn it into offices or some kind of museum, I think."

"Well, that's good, because that place is *filled* with rich history," Mrs. Bailey White said. "Including my trial. Or, I might say, *especially* my trial. I was the most famous defendant they ever had, you know. Oh, those were the days."

Jackie and I glanced at each other. We were sitting up front, with Mrs. Bailey White and Bunny sharing the backseat.

"Oh, yeah," Bunny said to Mrs. Bailey White cheerfully, as if they were exchanging a recipe for fried catfish. "I do remember hearing about that . . . mess. Back when I was a child."

"Oh, indeed, a mess it was! I can still hear the jury foreman saying, 'Guilty on one count of murder.' They sent me off to Lowell. Never mind that my lawyer said we had a good chance of proving self-defense. But not in Florida, not in my day. Not for a woman."

"No surprise there," Bunny said sympathetically. "It was a man's world. Still is."

"Yes-siree," Mrs. Bailey White said.

"Can I ask you a question?" Bunny asked. "How come they didn't hang you?"

"I suspect it was on account of my coming from an affluent family," Mrs. Bailey White said. "But I don't honestly know."

"Why'd they let you out early?" Bunny persisted.

"Good behavior," Mrs. Bailey White said.

"This is fascinating, ladies, but I'm a nervous wreck at the moment," Jackie said irritably. "Let's focus on *today*, please. I want to go over the particulars again. Now, remember, this is a hearing. If we're lucky, we won't have to go to trial. I mean, if the judge decides in our favor."

"I sure hope I don't have to talk," Bunny said.

"I don't think we're supposed to say anything," Jackie said. "Last night Ted called me long distance from Tallahassee to wish us luck, and he said, 'Let your lawyer do the talking,' and I think he's right. It fits with what Mr. Yonce advised, too. He said that's what we're paying him for."

"Okay," Bunny said. "We let the lawyer do the talking. How do I look?"

"You look as good as Mrs. Astor's pet mule!" Mrs. Bailey White said, and at first I thought it was an insult.

"Why, thank you!" Bunny replied playfully.

Jackie and I exchanged glances. Neither of us knew what

they were talking about. "Would anyone mind if I put the radio on?" Jackie asked suddenly. Without waiting for an answer, she switched it on. The wailing sound of Eric Burdon singing the Animals' rendition of "The House of the Rising Sun" wafted through the air.

"Gee!" Jackie exclaimed. "What a depressing song! How did that get to be a hit?"

"Oh, I know that song!" Bunny said, surprising us. "It's a folk song. Heard it a long time ago."

"Me, too," said Mrs. Bailey White.

The song finished and the next up was "Everybody Loves Somebody," a Dean Martin hit that Jackie seemed to find more palatable. "Now that's more like it," she said. "At least that man can *sing*."

"That's for sure," Mrs. Bailey White said. "Sounds kind of sexy."

"What we need around here is another radio station," I said, trying to be pleasant and conversational.

"You are *not kidding*!" Jackie snapped. "Even a country radio station would be better than having just old WNOG!"

"Why, Jackie, you are a Yankee snob," I said, trying to joke.

"What—just because I don't love country music? I like some of it," she said defensively. "I like Loretta Lynn and Johnny Cash."

"Maybe you should go back to doing your own show on WNOG and then you can pick your own music again," Mrs. Bailey White said, trying to be helpful.

"I've told you, it wasn't as much fun once everyone found out who I am," Jackie said. "The fun part was doing it incognito." She started to say more but the next song distracted her. "Oh, there's that song my daughters were talking about! 'You Don't Own Me.'"

"That's Lesley Gore," I said.

We listened to the words. "Sounds like that gal is standing up for herself," Bunny said approvingly. "Tellin' her man to back off."

"Now this is the message young girls need to hear!" Jackie exclaimed. "Your boyfriend or husband doesn't 'own' you! You are free to make your own choices!"

A deputy sheriff pulled into the parking lot, ending our conversation. He opened his car door with a swift, furious kick of his left foot, treating us to a flash of spit-polished cowboy boot reflected in the morning sun. Whether this was intended to impress or intimidate, I had no idea. Or maybe he was a show-off all the time. My nerves were so jittery I was probably reading into it.

Without looking at us, he sauntered to the courthouse door and unlocked it. Just when I thought he was avoiding eye contact with us, he turned and grinned menacingly and made a mock bow of welcome. Then he went inside.

"What in the world was that all about," Jackie complained.

"I don't know," I said, "but let's get out of this heat and go into the courthouse."

Jackie agreed. "Yes, and it would *behoove* us to figure out where we're supposed to sit," she said.

"And locate the ladies' room," Mrs. Bailey White added.

Jackie smiled despite herself. "Yes," she said, "and that, too."

"I wish Mr. Yonce was here already," I said, my voice bordering on whiny. I could no longer disguise my anxiety. Unlike Jackie and the others, I also had to contend with the fact that

Darryl was likely to be attending. He might even be testifying. Of course, he might just send his attorneys on his behalf. But I had no way of knowing in advance.

THE COURTROOM WAS DIVIDED IN half by an aisle, a bit like a church. Jackie insisted we settle into the first row on the left side. Darryl and his lawyers could sit on the front row on the right. "That's the way they do it on *Perry Mason,*" she said.

"Well, where are the lawyers going to sit?" I asked, confused.

"I think they'll be standing," Jackie replied. "There's no defendant, per se, and no jury. So they'll be arguing before the judge."

About twenty minutes later, Mr. Yonce arrived, nervously mopping his brow with a handkerchief despite the arctic blast coming from the central air conditioner. But when he saw us, he grinned and gave us a thumbs-up. He darted over to us and whispered, "Everything is under control." Hopefully this meant the fingerprints had been a match. Then he and Jackie discussed the seating arrangements. "I need to sit on the aisle," he said, "and y'all can sit right here. But save a seat or two."

Save a seat or two? I wondered why. The courtroom was empty except for us. As if reading my mind Mr. Yonce said, "A huge crowd has started gathering outside. They're making them wait to come in until after the judge arrives."

My heart fluttered. *A huge crowd.* This was surprising, considering that there had been little in the newspaper—despite Jackie's best efforts—about the hearing. But I had underestimated the power of the grapevine and the determination of both sides.

This wasn't a fight about one development. It was a fight

over dreams. Darryl and his supporters longed for buildings and roads, for new jobs, and fat bank accounts. People like me wanted just the opposite; our dream was for the land and river to stay the same, the way God made it. As for Bunny, she was protecting something she had fought for her entire life: a place where she could be left alone, which was the only dream she'd ever had.

At least Bunny and I were on the same side. To us, it had always been Dreamsville.

Thirty-One

The judge was an old-timer named Henry "Hang 'Em Harry" Prentiss, a dignified no-nonsense kind of fellow who looked remarkably like Confederate General Robert E. Lee in the classic Civil War portrait that held a place of honor in many Florida homes.

Darryl and his three lawyers walked in at the last second, just before Judge Prentiss called the courtroom to order. I was expecting to get the evil eye from Darryl, but he didn't even glance at our side. Mrs. Bailey White snuck a peek behind us, just to ascertain if there was indeed a full house, and whispered a little too loudly that it was a "gallows crowd," meaning a lot of people, many of them spittin' mad.

Had Darryl filled the place with folks hungry for jobs? Or were they on our side, eager to see the development halted in its tracks?

Judge Prentiss began the proceedings by banging the gavel and complaining heartily about the microphone and the air-conditioning. After we were treated to his tirade on new-fangled machinery, he made the following statement:

"I have been brought out of retirement to adjudicate this case, and frankly I would rather be fishing, but I am here and I will fulfill my duties to the court. Both of the justices normally serving this court have a conflict of interest in the case and have recused themselves. Justice Donald D. Battle owns land adjacent to the disputed property. Justice John Ed Jones has made a financial investment in Mr. Darryl Norwood's company.

"Remember, this is a preliminary hearing," he continued. "I have read the supporting materials but I have not made a decision. I wish to hear what the attorneys representing each side have to say."

Darryl's lead lawyer and our Mr. Yonce stood up and approached the bench. Like two awkward dancers at a cotillion, they faced each other uneasily.

Darryl's lawyer spoke first. "Your honor, my client is being prevented from his right to develop the property," he said, his tone indignant. "This frivolous claim is causing needless delay. It is causing financial harm to my client, and it is detrimental to the community. Hundreds of jobs are at stake."

Now it was Mr. Yonce's turn. "Your honor, this case has nothing whatsoever to do with the creation of new jobs, or what may—or may not—be good for the community," he said. "It is, quite simply, a dispute over the ownership of land which we can settle here easily today. My client, Miss Bunny Ann McIntyre, owns the land. Mr. Darryl Norwood *claims* to own the land, having purchased it from someone other than Miss McIntyre. The fact that he was misled or defrauded is not our concern. The fact is he does *not* own the property. It's the oldest story in the world, when one human being covets that which belongs to another, essentially saying, *I want what you have.* The deed belongs to Miss McIntyre, the eldest living direct descendant of the original property owner, and the papers have been authenticated."

"And how have they been authenticated?" the judge asked. "I have most of the papers here in front of me but I want it said aloud for the gallery."

"Well, the first document is the deed in trust," Mr. Yonce said. "It has been authenticated by a bank in Pensacola. The bank is in possession of a copy, and it is from that bank that the trust has been administered since its inception.

"Secondly," Mr. Yonce continued, "we have hired a genealogist who has proven that Miss McIntyre is the eldest living direct descendant of Confederate General John Stuart Williams and that, under the trust which he created long ago, she is the rightful owner of the land."

Darryl's lawyer burst out laughing and covered his mouth in a way that seemed rehearsed. "Your honor, excuse me!" he said. "The fact is we don't know if this woman"—he turned and pointed at Bunny—"is in fact Bunny Ann McIntyre. She has been calling herself Dolores Simpson for at least the last twenty-four years, according to our research. It seems rather convenient that she has begun calling herself Bunny Ann McIntyre just in time to claim an inheritance under that name. How do we know who she is?"

"Your honor," Mr. Yonce countered, "we have a court record from 1939 that proves she is Bunny Ann McIntyre. The document includes her name, photograph, and—most significantly, your honor—her fingerprints. Those fingerprints match those of the woman you see sitting here today. Here is a report, officially prepared by the fingerprint expert, retired Sarasota detective Dexter W. Stone." With a flourish, Mr. Yonce set the report before the judge.

Darryl's lawyer scoffed. "What is that court record, counselor? Let's be honest here! It's for *disorderly conduct*. The arrest took place outside a so-called nightclub featuring nude dancers in Tampa, where she worked as a stripper. Are we supposed to believe anything this woman says?"

Bunny jumped angrily to her feet. "I was not a stripper! I was a *fan dancer*!"

"Sit down, please," the judge scolded. Bunny complied.

"Well, the record shows you were a stripper, or exotic dancer," Darryl's lawyer replied, looking remarkably unfazed by the outburst.

"Fan dancer!" she hollered.

"Silence in the court!" the judge bellowed.

Mr. Yonce waited a beat, then said pleadingly, "Your honor, this is character assassination. My client is not on trial here. The only thing that matters is ownership of the land. *She owns it.* What she may have done in her past has no relevance."

"But it does have relevance, your honor!" Darryl's attorney said. "This woman has a history. She is not an upstanding citizen. With all due respect, I believe we need to examine this issue."

Judge Prentiss took a long sip of water, then set the glass down a little too hard right next to the microphone. "Let me think about this, boys," he said. He then removed his glasses, spit on the lenses, and used the long sleeve of his robe to clean them.

Suddenly, Jackie raised her hand and began waving it like a schoolgirl. "Your honor, may I say something?" she asked. Before he could answer she had leapt to her feet.

He squinted at her. "And you are . . . ?"

"Mrs. Jacqueline Hart," she said.

"And you wish to speak because . . . ?"

"I wish to be a character witness for Miss McIntyre."

The judge peered at Jackie. "Aren't you Miss Dreamsville? The lady who had that radio show?"

"Yes, your honor," Jackie said sweetly.

"Well, I have no objection. Since Mr. Norwood's attorney has led us down this path, I will hear what you have to say. Come up here and speak from the witness stand, though. And keep it short."

Jackie sashayed to the chair adjacent to the judge's bench. "Shouldn't I swear on a Bible?" she asked.

The judge nodded. A deputy sauntered over, held the Bible, and made Jackie repeat the oath: "I do solemnly swear . . ." Jackie was in her glory. I wouldn't have been surprised if she'd been waiting her whole life for a chance to testify in a court of law. Meanwhile, Mrs. Bailey White and I glanced at each other, and I noticed Mr. Yonce biting his lip.

"I would just like to say that I think it is entirely unfair for this man here"—she pointed theatrically at Darryl's lawyer—"to attack Miss McIntyre and attempt to embarrass her. Since the beginning of time, women such as Miss McIntyre have been used and abused, and treated with scorn. She has had a difficult life, was cast out by her parents in her youth, and treated with utter disregard by unscrupulous men. It is unconscionable, in a civilized society, to make her pay again and again—"

Darryl's attorney coughed conspicuously and rolled his eyes. Jackie noticed and took a different tack.

"*Excuse me*, but don't most of us here—probably all of us—consider ourselves to be Christians?" she cried out. "Miss Mc-

Intyre has made mistakes, but haven't we all? Who among us dares to cast the first stone? I thought we weren't supposed to judge others! And what about forgiveness? Miss McIntyre left that life of temptation and wickedness. She is an honorable person. She raised a son, who is an upstanding citizen . . ." Jackie's voice trailed off and she dabbed real tears from her eyes.

Mrs. Bailey White and I were openmouthed. For a moment our Jackie sounded like a born-and-bred Southern lady. "Why, Mrs. Hart, I am greatly moved," the judge said. "Where is this son? I would like to hear from him, if he is present."

A voice from the far back of the room called out, "I'm here!" The crowd rumbled with anticipation. Robbie-Lee, carrying a suitcase, made his way to the front. I was so happy to see him I almost cried.

"Silence in the court!" the judge bellowed. He used the gavel three times to emphasize his point.

Robbie-Lee looked just the same except maybe a little thinner. He'd always been a good-looking guy and a swell dresser. As he took Jackie's place on the witness stand and was sworn in, he seemed out of breath. The judge coaxed him to speak.

"Well," Robbie-Lee said, "she has always been a *wonderful* mother. I could not ask for a better mom. She took such good care of me. I'll never forget the time I had the chicken pox and she—"

"All right, I think we get the picture," the judge said.

"Sir, I would just like to add that I don't think it's at all nice that these highfalutin lawyers"—he gestured at Darryl's attorney—"are saying such evil things about my dear mama."

At his emotional pronouncement, hankies were removed from purses and vest pockets throughout the courtroom, most conspicuously along the left front row. Jackie, who had returned to her seat next to me; Mrs. Bailey White, on my other side; myself, and even Bunny, were crying loudly.

"And there's something else I would like to say, your honor," Robbie-Lee said. "I recall as a child visiting my mother's parents, who died a long time ago. And they had a family Bible—I surely wish we knew where it is now—but it had the names of people written into it, each time somebody was born. My mama pointed out her name—Bunny Ann McIntyre—to me, and we wrote my name just below it. And while I don't know what happened to that Bible, I swear that this is the truth."

Robbie-Lee stepped down and headed for an empty seat on our row, pausing to kiss his mama on the cheek.

Mr. Yonce looked a little shell-shocked by the unexpected testimony of Jackie and Robbie-Lee, but Darryl's lawyer saw an opportunity. "Your honor," he said, "this is a pretty scene but I believe we are getting off track here! These sorts of theatrics do not help us get to the truth. Especially coming from Mrs. Hart, who is a notorious local personality, a newspaper columnist, and previously, the host of a scandalous radio show."

The judge grabbed his gavel and slammed it twice. "Good heavens, man, can't you see that Miss Dreamsville, er, Mrs. Hart is in *mourning clothes*?" he scolded. "Have we reached that time and place where we have abandoned all decency? Were you not raised better than this?"

"Thank you, your honor," Jackie said, standing briefly. "Sir, you are a true gentleman."

The judge blushed. Mr. Yonce looked so lost he reminded me of a fish that had leapt out of water and found itself belly-up on dry land. Our poor young lawyer had completely lost control of his case.

"Is there anyone else who would like to speak?" the judge asked finally.

A laborer named Jim Beam, just like the liquor, spoke about the need for jobs. "We need this project," he declared. "How am I supposed to feed my family?"

Then one of the brothers from Gun Rack Village—Billy, I think—also chose to speak, directing his question to Mr. Beam. "Does your need for a job mean you've got to destroy what we have?" he asked. "It may not seem like much to you but it's our entire way of life."

I was waiting for someone to bring up Seminole Joe but before that could happen, the proceedings came to an end. "I've heard enough," the judge said. "I've had as much botheration as I can stand. There's no need to go further. The rightful owner is Miss Bunny Ann McIntyre. All other arguments are moot."

He brought down the gavel and left the courtroom. If he hurried, he'd be back to his favorite fishing spot by midday.

Thiry-Two

And so Bunny Ann McIntyre had won fair and square. She was now the official heir to the river. In fact, she was the largest heiress in Collier County.

Dora was thrilled, naturally. Jackie Hart rushed off to write a special column for the newspaper. Robbie-Lee was relieved and more than a little surprised that his mother had turned out to be wealthy—well, land-rich, at least. Billy and Marco had raced off in their pickup to share the news.

Before the sun reached its highest point, word had spread sure and steady like a smoldering swamp fire in dry season.

The last to hear the good news were the Negroes who would have lost their settlement. Among them there was said to be as much shock as joy, because there had been justice. They weren't used to it.

No one, of course, should have been happier than Bunny. She had insisted on walking back to her fishing shack alone. Everyone else, including her son, had gone off to celebrate.

"Oh, don't get me wrong," she told Peggy Sue, who was

snuggled in her nest and upon hearing Bunny's familiar voice, opened one eye. "I'm tickled to death that I won. But now there's one more job I have to do, and Lord knows I don't feel like doing it."

Bunny sat down on the edge of the dock and let her feet dangle over the side. She'd already taken off the strange shoes she'd borrowed for court. "What do you think I should do, Peggy Sue?" she continued. "I'm stuck between a rock and a hard place."

The fact was that one secret remained: the one she feared most.

"How am I going to tell her?" Bunny said, and the night heron responded with a peculiar squeak. "Oh, am I annoying you? I beg your pardon!" Bunny added, and laughed. "But seriously, Peggy Sue, the look on her face is going to be awful. And who can blame her? How would you like to find out your real mother was an exotic dancer turned alligator hunter?"

For years, she'd watched from a distance without her having a clue. *Dora*. Bunny liked the name they had chosen for her.

But when Bunny realized Dora was in the same book club as Robbie-Lee, she nearly passed out from fear that Dora would figure it out, or he would. The thought of the two of them, half sister and brother, sitting side by side talking about books was so painful it seemed like the devil was laughing in her face.

Then Dora went to Mississippi, and Bunny got really scared. She didn't believe Dora had any idea she was adopted, but she might figure it out if she started poking around there. And sure enough, Bunny overheard the book club ladies—Jackie, Plain Jane, and Mrs. Bailey White—talking downstairs when she stayed overnight at the old gal's house before they went to court. They were discussing Dora, how she had learned she was adopted but was dealing with it pretty well. Seems she'd found out a few months earlier so she'd had some time to get used to the idea.

But Dora still didn't know who her mother was. And likely never would.

Bunny knew in her heart that Dora deserved to hear the truth, even if she might be disappointed. She had gotten to know Dora, which made it mighty hard to keep up the lie. Dora was, also, a rightful heir to Bunny's land. She and Robbie-Lee would share it someday.

She was so desperate to save the river that she'd gambled by asking Dora for help. She knew when she sent that telegram that she might be starting something that would be hard to stop. Fact is, the State of Florida did not take her baby girl when she was fifteen and had run off to Tampa. The truth was there was a nurse, a sweet gal from Mississippi, who told Bunny that she knew she couldn't have children. The nurse's name was Callie and she was staying in Tampa, just for a while, because she needed a job and it was the only place she could find work. Her husband—she said they'd been married about a year—was from Collier County, and she would join him as soon as she could get a job there.

Bunny had a feeling there was more to this story but since she was so young and had a world of troubles of her own, she didn't ask. Then one night when Bunny couldn't sleep, the young nurse told her how she'd left her man at the altar and run off with someone else. Up and left her fiancé, her parents, her whole life, and had no regrets. The same day she was supposed to marry one fella, she married the other. She and her new man drove straight from Mississippi to Alabama and finally, just after crossing the Florida state line, got married that night in the parlor of a Methodist preacher's parsonage in some small town Bunny had never heard of.

To Bunny this was an impressive tale. Unlike Bunny, the young nurse named Callie knew what she wanted in life. She had stood up for herself. Plus, she was a trained nurse. She was educated. When Bunny found out that Callie couldn't have a child but really wanted one, she knew at that moment that she was meant to give her baby girl to Callie. It hurt less to give the baby to someone she chose. Besides, the nurse's husband was from Collier County and that's where they were going to live. Bunny felt like a part of her would stay with the baby by having her grow up where she did. Although, of course, in a better home.

When Bunny had Robbie-Lee seven years later at the same hospital in Tampa, something told her it was time to go home to Collier County. She wanted to be near Dora. She wanted to watch her grow up.

And so Bunny Ann McIntyre picked her new name—Dolores Simpson—not just because she saw it in a magazine left on a southbound bus to Naples but because Dolores sounded, to her, a lot like Dora. Just another little secret, a way to keep her close without anyone knowing.

"Peggy Sue," she called over to her avian friend, "wish me luck."

SHE DECIDED TO TELL ROBBIE-LEE first. That was only fair. The next morning she walked to Mrs. Bailey White's house. People were coming and going, and she began to despair of having a moment alone with her son. Finally, she asked him to help pack up the belongings she'd left when she'd spent the night before going to court. It was a lovely little room on the second floor, and Bunny knew she would miss it. They were taking a break;

he was sitting in a chair that was too small for him and she was perched on the side of the bed. He was talking about how he needed to go back to New York, that he wasn't on official leave from his job.

Now was the time.

"Dora Witherspoon is your sister," she blurted out. They were the most powerful and difficult words she'd ever said aloud, and to her they seemed to take over the room like a swarm of furious bees. The sting of those words mocked her and hung in the air until she noticed something odd. Robbie-Lee was strangely calm.

"Why do you think I joined the book club?" he asked.

"Huh?"

"I joined the book club because Dora was in it. I wanted to get to know her better. I knew who she was, but we weren't in school at the same time, so that was my chance."

She felt like she had a crawfish stuck in her throat. "But how did you *know*?" she asked.

"Mom, you forget, you talk in your sleep," he said bluntly, almost impatiently, adding, "Especially when you've been drinking."

"Well, did you ever say anything to her about it?"

"No, of course not. That's your story to tell, Mom. Not mine."

"Since when do you call me Mom?"

"Well, I can't call you Dolores anymore. You're not Dolores. And, frankly, I don't want to call you Bunny. All my life I've wanted to call you Mom. I never liked the way you made me call you by your first name."

"Well, I didn't feel worthy of being a mom, that's why," she said, her voice breaking.

"Aw, now, you mustn't think like that," Robbie-Lee said, adding lightly, "I turned out pretty good, didn't I?"

"Don't tease, this is a *terrible* situation. I can't tell Dora. You have to do it. I just can't."

"Yes, you can."

"No, I can't. Maybe if I was, you know, purty and . . . normal. Someone she could be proud of. That's why it would be better coming from you. You could tell her you are her brother. She'll like that. That will be good news, because she likes you as a friend. It might even be a happy surprise, for all I know."

Robbie-Lee sighed. "This is an awful thing to ask someone to do for you."

"Well, what if she upchucked when I told her?" she asked. "What if she laughed at me? What if she said something so horrible to me that I won't want to go on living?"

"Oh, Mom, please," Robbie-Lee said. But she could see that he finally agreed.

It all was happening so quickly. Not more than ten minutes later, Bunny stood at the upstairs window half-hidden by an old lace curtain, and watched her son tell her daughter that they were kin.

They sat opposite each other on wrought-iron furniture that must have been as old as Mrs. Bailey White. Someone had been making an effort to trim the grass and plants in what must have been a lovely flower garden at one time.

She wished she'd thought to open the window. It was too late now. They'd hear her open it for sure. But at least she could see their lips moving. And she could see their faces.

He leaned forward, his hands on his knees, and Bunny thought, *Oh, doesn't he look like a grown man, so serious and strong.* He said something that must have been meant to prepare Dora for important news because she reacted by folding her arms across her chest, crossing her legs at the ankle, and tilting her head. Then he said something that might have been the word "sister." Dora pulled back, surprised. Then her shoulders sagged, and she covered her face with her hands.

Just as Bunny had feared.

Dora stood up and walked a few feet away from Robbie-Lee. He said a few words, and she responded without turning around. He said a few more words, and she finally faced him again. She was crying.

Robbie-Lee went to her and hugged her for a long time. Then he took her face into his hands. He smiled.

And she smiled back. She might have said, "Brother."

Then Dora sat back down hard, like she was a sack of flour.

Suddenly it occurred to Bunny that they might come looking for her as soon as Dora caught her breath. Mercy, what an awful thought. She hurried down the stairs and out the front door. The river—her river—was calling her home.

Thirty-Three

This is what he said to me: "I have good news and bad news, Dora."

I sat down on Mrs. Bailey White's wrought-iron furniture. Moments before I had been thinking what a lovely garden this must have once been. Someone had been working on it—Plain Jane, maybe.

"What?" I said. "Just say it. What is it?"

"What do you want first?" Robbie-Lee asked. "The good news or the bad?"

"I don't care! Just say it!"

He cleared his throat and looked me straight in the eye. "My mother is the woman who gave you up for adoption," he said. He waited for it to sink in.

"What are you talking about?" I shrieked. My voice came out so shrill that I would never have guessed it came from me. "Robbie-Lee, that *can't* be right! How do you . . . What makes you think . . . That's just not possible!"

But, truth be told, anything was possible.

I felt like my skin had been bitten by a thousand fire ants, and I very nearly upchucked. I stood and turned my back on Robbie-Lee, just in case. I never, ever thought I would find out who my mother was.

Once I collected myself I turned around, tears flooding my eyes. "Was this the bad news?" I asked, confused.

Robbie-Lee chuckled. "Well, a lot of people would think so. You know she's not exactly Betty Crocker. I doubt very much that she's the type of mother you would have hoped for."

"Oh," I said. "Well, honestly? No."

"Okay, now I'm going to tell you the good news. Do you know what that is? This means that you're my sister!"

Despite everything else that was happening, I had to smile. This *was* good news. I'd always wanted a sibling. And Robbie-Lee would be the best. He was smart, funny, and an all-around great guy. We were friends. And now we were siblings, too.

"I have a brother," I said slowly, trying it out to see how it sounded. A wondrous thing, having a brother. My friends growing up complained bitterly about their brothers; Jackie's twin daughters seemed to dislike Judd heartily. But I always wanted to tell them, *You are luckier than you know.*

Suddenly I felt a little strange, like I couldn't breathe. I sat down again, trying to calm myself enough to find the right words. "Robbie-Lee, I thank you," I said finally. "I mean, thank you for telling me."

Robbie-Lee smiled a little sadly. "Well, I knew you had to know. I mean, she finally confirmed it. And you're an heir now. You and me both."

"Why didn't *she* tell me?" I asked.

"Because she was scared," he said simply. "I was scared, too, but not as much as her."

"How long have you known?"

"Oh, I've had some suspicions for a long time," he said. "Something she said once or twice when she was drunk."

I waited a moment, then, "Do you think we have the same father?"

Robbie-Lee surprised me by laughing out loud. "Not a chance," he said, adding quickly, "Does it really matter? I'm not sure we want to know any more secrets from the past, even if we could find out. I think we have enough to contend with."

"You've never known who your father is, right?" I asked. "I've been walking around for years thinking that Montgomery Witherspoon, wherever he is, is mine. So it's something else I have to accept."

"I'm so sorry, Dora," Robbie-Lee said softly.

I shrugged in response.

"Dora, I know this must come as a shock to you," he continued. "I know she's not a, um, *conventional* mother but she's a great person, she really is. She's a little rough around the edges, but if you give her a chance . . ." He hesitated. "I surely do hope that you give her a chance. Maybe not right away—that would be understandable—but maybe once you get, well, used to the idea."

What could I say? That my newly found mother scared me to death? That I was repulsed at the idea that my mother had been a dancer in a nightclub? That I was embarrassed by her? And that I wondered what this meant about me? I had thought I was a higher-class person than that. Mama and I were poor, I knew that, but Mama had been a nurse and I had two years of college.

"Want to hear something funny?" I said finally. "After I learned I was adopted I started dreaming that maybe I was Eudora Welty's secret love child. I was aiming high, wasn't I?"

"Well, now, that would have been something!" he said. "But that's the problem with real life, isn't it? Life can't live up to your dreams. I'm not saying dreams can never come true; sometimes they do, sometimes they don't. But one thing's for sure, once you start trying to make a dream come true you'd better be prepared that anything could happen. You find out you're adopted. You dream that your mother is a brilliant writer but she turns out to be, well, a stripper—or fan dancer, or whatever—turned alligator hunter. Good grief, Dora, I can see why you feel let down."

"I wouldn't say I feel let down," I said quickly. "That sounds too mean, and I'm not a mean person. I just need time."

Robbie-Lee nodded. "Let's go inside and get something to drink," he said, standing up. He took my arm and gently led me back indoors.

"ARE Y'ALL GOING TO TELL us what's happening?" Mrs. Bailey White demanded. I realized, once we were in the pantry, with Robbie-Lee chopping some ice for our drinks, that even a short person like her could get a peek at the garden as long as she stood on her tippy-toes.

"Mrs. Bailey White, were you spying?" I said with fake outrage, yet she reacted with guilty shame.

"Well, we all were," she said. "Jackie and Plain Jane, too. Only they ran off to the living room to pretend they weren't in here watching you from this here window."

Robbie-Lee and I looked at each other and grinned. After fixing lemonade for all of us, we commenced to finding the others, with Mrs. Bailey White trailing behind. Jackie and Plain Jane were in the parlor pretending to play cards.

"What have you two been up to?" Jackie asked.

"Dora and I have an announcement to make," Robbie-Lee said. "I have just informed her that we are brother and sister."

Jackie had been reaching for her lemonade and nearly knocked it over. Plain Jane let out a little gasp, and Mrs. Bailey White said, "Did I hear that right?"

"Yes, you did, Mrs. Bailey White," I said, following Robbie-Lee's courageous lead. "We have the same mother."

Jackie gulped. "*Dora, your mother is . . . ?*"

"Yes," I said, realizing that my face was starting to flush.

"Well, I'll be a monkey's uncle," said Mrs. Bailey White. "And here I thought he was proposing to you!"

"What? You know he's not the marrying kind!" Plain Jane said loudly.

"Well, just because he's not a man's man and not interested in women in the Biblical sense doesn't mean he might not get married," Mrs. Bailey White said defensively. "I mean, it happens all the time, doesn't it?"

Robbie-Lee seemed a little amused. "All y'all are something else!" he said. "Now let's go see Mom. She's upstairs resting."

But all we found was an empty room.

Thirty-Four

"R obbie Lee, you're going to wear a path in Mrs. Bailey White's Oriental rug," I said, watching him pace back and forth. We had to decide if we were going to go after her.

"I need to get back to New York," he said, "but I'm not leaving until I see her. You know she's back at her place, probably talking to that bird and drinking up a storm. I'm worried."

I had told Robbie-Lee about the night heron but he hadn't seemed surprised. He liked the fact that she had named the bird Peggy Sue because he used to sing that song and make her laugh.

"Well, you could go see her and then tomorrow you could catch the morning bus northbound," I said. "I'm sure—"

"I have a better idea," Robbie-Lee said, a little impatiently. "Let's you and me go see her together."

"No," I said firmly, "I'm not ready to see her."

"Well, fine," he said. "I'm going there now."

Great, I thought, *we're already quarreling like brother and sister.* The others wisely stayed out of it.

• • •

I SPENT THE AFTERNOON PLAYING with Dream. Mrs. Bailey White was resting; Jackie went back to her house to be with her kids, and Plain Jane puttered around the garden. I was glad for a chance to be with Dream, who was beginning to warm up to me. She liked it when I played on the floor with her. I had not spent much time with an infant since my babysitting days in high school.

I got to thinking how strange it is to be alive in this world. It's not like anyone asks to be born; you just arrive whether you like it or not. You've got no say whatsoever in who your parents are. And yes, life is good and even wonderful. On good days you say to yourself, "My, it's good to be alive!" or "Ain't life grand?" or "Thank you, Jesus!" But other times, when things go badly, you say, "What the heck is this thing called life?" or "What exactly am I doing here?" Or even, "Lawd, what kind of trick you be playing on me?" Now the last is sacrilege, of course, but I bet there's not a human being alive who hasn't had moments of despair.

Of course, Dream was a long way from having thoughts like these, good or bad. She was still living in her own world, as yet unformed as an actual person, her future a question to be answered in time. What questions, I wondered, would Dream ask her mother one day? Would she be angry at Priscilla for going away to college and leaving her behind? Would she demand answers about who her father was?

By the time Robbie-Lee returned from his hike to the fishing shack, Dream was fed and asleep. I was waiting for a chance to talk to Robbie-Lee, but I must have dozed off, too, because when I awoke in Dream's room it was dark and I heard the sound of his voice coming from the kitchen.

As I came quietly down the stairs, I said a little prayer. I wanted to clear the air with him before he went back to New York.

He had showered and changed his clothes, and was sitting at the kitchen table with Mrs. Bailey White. The remains of a Key lime pie—one of Mrs. Bailey White's specialties—sat in front of him.

"Why, hello, Dora!" he said, sounding like his old cheerful self. "Mom is doing fine. I gave her some money to buy some things she needs. I wish she had let me know she was so tight on money! But that's Mom—she's nothin' if not prideful and stubborn."

"So . . ." I said, searching for words, "she's okay then?"

"Yes," he said. "And it's up to you if you want to see her. She and I talked about it and of course it's your decision. I'm sorry I tried to push you. I was wrong."

"So I should—"

"You should do what you want to do, whenever you're ready to do it," he said, taking another mouthful of pie.

Hearing the commotion, Plain Jane, wearing an old plaid bathrobe, joined us in the kitchen. The only ones missing from our old book club were Jackie, who was at her home, and Priscilla.

Mrs. Bailey White left the room for a moment and returned with a copy of *The Adventures of Huckleberry Finn* and, just as we sometimes did, back when the book club met regularly, we took turns reading it aloud, passing the book around the table.

Just like old times.

Thirty-Five

Robbie-Lee left the next morning for New York City. I watched him walk down Mrs. Bailey White's long dirt driveway toward the Tamiami Trail until he disappeared from sight.

An hour later I was dressed and heading to the fishing shack.

I told myself little tales as I began my walk. *I could turn around at any time. I don't have to go.* I wasn't really going to see *her*. I was just going for a walk in the swamplands, by the river. . . .

I carried a copy of the *Naples Star* with a headline that screamed, SWAMP QUEEN PREVAILS IN COURT.

So much had happened. The river and the land surrounding it were safe from development.

I was adopted.

And this strange woman named Bunny Ann McIntyre, of all the women in the world, was my mother.

Once Robbie-Lee had stopped asking me to see her, I thought it through and I knew that nothing would feel settled until I did. But it had to be my idea—my choice.

I wondered if I got this stubbornness from her? Pride and stubbornness, Robbie-Lee had said. Oh dear. That sounded mighty familiar.

I stopped and drank from a canteen that Mrs. Bailey White had given me. The water was hot and metallic tasting, and I spat it out. I was suddenly angry at Robbie-Lee and I wasn't sure why. I should have gone with him yesterday to see her. I could have let him do all the talking. I could have . . .

But I couldn't go back in time.

It would have been nice if there was a way to run away, to reject all this new information, these inconvenient facts. It was a burden. I had been forced to rewrite the story line of my own life.

And yet I had to do it. I told myself: *Sometimes the hurricane hits south of you, and sometimes north, and once in a while, the dang thing smacks you head-on. Well, Dora, this is your hurricane. And if you hang on for dear life, you just might make it through.*

I didn't know what to expect when I got there. I thought she might be sitting in her favorite spot on the dock, maybe whittling as she had that first day when I responded to her telegram and she'd said, "It's about time you got here." It made me laugh to think about that now. In retrospect it sounded like something a mother might say to a daughter.

I had no idea what I would say to her. A few things went through my mind, but none of them were right. I'd just have to pray that the right words would come to me. I hoped to keep it brief and, well, *manageable*. Tidy. Just a few words for now. I'd tell her that I had to go back to Mississippi for a spell but that I'd be back. No promises. Just an acknowledgment of what had occurred between us.

But that's not how it worked out.

I arrived to find her in full uproar. Something—something

terrible—had happened. I mean it had *just* happened, seconds before. She was wailing and carryin' on like somebody had up and died. When she spied me, she reacted as if I was any old person, no one special. I could have been anyone. "Look, look what happened!" she cried out. She was pointing up at the tree where the night heron had been keeping her nest.

Apparently sometime during the night the nest had been disturbed—a bobcat, maybe even a panther. The nest was hanging at a sickening angle; part of it appeared to be missing altogether. Bunny must have just woken up, come outside, and found it that way.

"Peggy Sue is gone!" she hollered, and I didn't know if she meant dead or flown away.

As I walked toward her she turned her back to me to hide her weeping. She was crying so hard she had to gulp for air, which scared me to pieces. After all, it was *just a bird.*

And then I thought, *No. It's not just a bird. It's not "just" a bird any more than Norma Jean, my Everglades snapper, is "just" a turtle. Once you love something, it owns a smidgen of your heart. That's the price we pay for giving our love away.*

I took her arm, but she yanked it away. I watched as she sat down on the dock with her back to me. I could see her shoulders heaving with sobs.

I examined the nest, or what was left of it. I found no sign of Peggy Sue. There weren't even any scattered feathers, so hopefully she'd been able to fly away.

I poked at the debris and jumped back when something moved. At first I assumed it was a snake or some other swamp critter. But then I realized I was looking at something wonderful. I was nose to beak with two helpless chicks. I had never been so happy in my life.

"Hey!" I shouted. "Lookee here, two babies!"

Bunny stopped wailing. She was by my side so fast it spooked me.

So there we were, me and my mother, peering anxiously at the tiny chicks, which, bless their little avian hearts, were the ugliest things God ever put on this earth.

We named them Lamar (after a skinny-necked guy who sometimes worked at the Esso station) and Liz (after Elizabeth Taylor, of course). We took them into the fishing shack and spent the next hour arguing about the best way to feed them and keep them warm.

Once we got them situated, Bunny poured herself a small glass of gin. "Want some?" she asked.

I shook my head.

"Robbie-Lee's gone; now even Peggy Sue is gone," she said bluntly. "And if these little babies don't make it, I won't have nothin' at all."

"Well," I said finally. "You've got me."

AND SO I BEGAN TO accept that I had two mothers—the one I called Mama, who had raised me, and who had died; and the one who had given birth to me, who was standing before me, puffing on a small cigar and fussing over two baby night herons—the heiress of the river.

"I don't suppose you'll want to call me 'Mama,'" she said, loosened up by the gin.

"Well," I said slowly, "the fact is, I won't call you Mama, because I had a person in my life who will always be Mama."

She flinched ever-so-slightly. "Well, Robbie-Lee has decided to start calling me Mom because that's what he always wanted to call me," she said. "You know, I always insisted he call me Dolores." She started to say something more but stopped. "I guess you can call me whatever you want."

"I need to think about it," I said. "Maybe just Bunny." I felt like I was being a little snippy but, mercy, I'd been through enough. At least I could think this over.

"I just have one thing I want to say," she said, slurring her words a bit. "I want you to know that I admired your mama as a person very much, and I think she done a durned good job raisin' you, if I may say so myself. I couldn't have done nearly as good."

"Well, you did a good job with Robbie Lee," I said. And it was true.

"If you don't ever want to call me Mom or Mother or nothin' like that, I understand," she continued solemnly, as if she had practiced these words. "And I agree you have only one 'Mama.' She may be gone, but she'll always be your mama."

I felt tears stinging my eyes and blinked them away. "Thank you," I mumbled.

"And if you don't want folks to know about me, or you don't want to be part of my life, I will git used to the idea," she said, with a sniffle that might have been for dramatic purposes but I couldn't be sure. She added, "You have that right."

That's how we left things. I wasn't about to make any promises, except for one: "I'll be back," I told her. "I'm leaving for Mississippi for a spell. But I'll be back. And I hope these little critters"—I pointed to Liz and Lamar—"are big and strong by then."

As I hiked back to the main road, all I could think of was getting back to my little cottage and seeing my turtles. I understood Bunny's attachment to Peggy Sue; herons, like turtles, don't talk back. They just listen.

Whether I ever really got to know Bunny or not, I was determined that it would have to be on my terms as well as hers. I would take my time. This situation was going to require a whole lot of thinking and forgiveness, which was not going to happen overnight.

I'd have to forgive Mama for her secrets, and I'd have to forgive Bunny for being who she was, and for giving me away.

On a much lesser scale, I was annoyed—just a bit—at Robbie-Lee for not telling me long before that he knew, or suspected, that he was my brother. But then that thought led to another: I have a little brother! This was a dream come true. And while our mother was, well, a lot to handle, at least we could handle her together.

As I came near the end of my hike, it began to rain. I didn't care that I would get wet—soaked to the bone, even. This made me almost as happy as discovering those fragile baby herons. I kept moving but I listened. The rain, making its way through the thick tree canopy, made its distinctive sound like an audience applauding—first a few claps, then growing to a thunderous roar.

And I thought, *That is Mama, speaking to me from the Spirit World.* For the first time I realized something important—crucial, even. As a nurse, Mama had always seemed to find room in her heart for damaged souls. She didn't fault people for their mistakes. She recognized that we were all worthy human beings.

Bunny Ann McIntyre was precisely the type of person Mama would have been kind to.

And she would have expected me to do the same.

Thirty-Six

After all of the hullabaloo died down, a couple of things happened.

Darryl offered to buy part of the river from Bunny but she refused. And although Mrs. Bailey White told Bunny she could move into her old Victorian house, Bunny declined, preferring to live in her fishing shack. When Darryl offered to buy a different section—the part that included the Negro settlement—that got on Bunny's last good nerve, and she threatened to shoot him if he set one foot anywhere on her property.

The night heron chicks, Liz and Lamar, survived.

Robbie-Lee continued to thrive in New York City. He began studying acting with a famous teacher. He even got an understudy role in a play, and although it wasn't on Broadway, we were ecstatically happy for him. Maybe this would be his big chance.

Priscilla continued to get straight As at Bethune-Cookman College in Daytona Beach, and there were hints that she had met someone special. She came home as often as she could to see the baby as well as her grandma, whose health had begun to decline.

Jackie still had regular arguments with Ted about all the time he was spending on the road while trying to launch Wild Blue Yonder Airways. The business continued to be rocky, and Ted didn't help matters when he misspoke at a Chamber of Commerce event in Tampa. "We have a dozen frights, er, *flights*, a day," he said. The audience burst out laughing. For a while, people referred to Mr. Toomb's pride and joy as White Knuckle Airways.

Jackie and Plain Jane continued their plans to start a home for young, unwed mothers at Mrs. Bailey White's house. I could see trouble on the horizon already; there'd been a heated discussion about what the residence would be called, with Jackie insisting on the Collier County Home for Exceptional Girls.

We never did find out who vandalized the Welcome to Dreamsville billboards with paint. Not that it mattered. Perhaps it really was the ghost of Seminole Joe. Some folks thought it was Judd Hart, but I never believed that. My money was on Mrs. Bailey White.

Darryl got into some trouble when authorities asked him to explain where and how he got the idea that he could build Dreamsville Estates on what was, in fact, Bunny's land. Darryl claimed to have bought the land from a fellow in Kentucky who, as it turned out, didn't exist, but charges against Darryl never materialized. Meanwhile, Darryl began work on a different development, this one called Pirate's Landing. He convinced the state to build the roads but after losing in court to Bunny, he lost his Basking Ridge, New Jersey, investors, along with the fiancée—kinfolk, we learned later, of our mayor's wife. The abandoned roads of his new development eventually became an ideal landing strip—*for drug smugglers coming to the U.S. from Central America.* Way to go, Darryl.

I went back to Jackson on a late November day with barely a dime left in my pocket. I'd been gone three months and didn't expect anyone to forgive me for being gone so long. To my surprise, my job at the library and my room at Mrs. Conroy's waited for me. I worked at the library long enough to pay Mrs. Conroy the money I owed, plus a little extra on account of her being patient with me. I wrote a brand-new short story called "The Book Club" and showed it to Miss Welty in her garden. This time she not only liked it, she suggested that I write more.

When it was time to say good-bye to Jackson, my new friends implored me to stay, but this much was clear to me: I belonged in Collier County. I wanted to say farewell to 1964, and welcome 1965, by singing "Auld Lang Syne" with my book-club friends. I had always known Naples was home but now I understood my deep attachment. Of course, nothing would be the same, knowing what I now did about Mama and myself. My life had changed; I had changed. There was no going back but taking steps toward the future was necessary, even if it sometimes felt like running barefoot in deep sand. I had learned that dreams have a life of their own, propelling us onward even when they don't come true or are realized in unexpected ways.

Now there would be time for new dreams, though, and I had a feeling that Mama, up in heaven, would have liked that. Mama used to say, Open your heart to the future, Dora. You can either be afraid of what's to come, or embrace it, *come what may.* I was so glad I could still hear her voice.

Back at home, near the mangroves, the herons, and the turtles, and sleeping soundly in my little cottage by the sea, I would start the next chapter of my life. This new beginning would, no doubt, include writing and storytelling. Only now, thanks to my recent journey, and the encouragement of Miss Welty, I had the confidence to value my own experiences. My stories were my own, and I would tell the stories I was meant to tell.

Come what may.

Acknowledgments

I am overwhelmed with gratitude to thousands of readers, including book clubs across America and beyond, whose love and enthusiasm for my first novel, *Miss Dreamsville and the Collier County Women's Literary Society*, inspired me to write this sequel. I am humbled and deeply moved by the support of each and every one of you.

Both books are works of historical fiction inspired by my long-ago experiences as a fledgling newspaper reporter in Florida. Thank you to the people of the great Sunshine State, especially in Hillsborough and Volusia Counties, where a key part of my life was launched.

And, of course, thank you to the people of Collier County, where my wonderful and devoted husband, Blair, grew up. It's safe to say that this book and its predecessor would not exist if not for Blair, whose stories from life in Naples in the 1960s captivated my heart and imagination.

Collier County folk who have been enormously helpful include Robin DeMattia, Sandy Linneman and the Friends of the Collier County Library, the staff of Sunshine Booksellers on Marco Island, the librarians and staff of the Collier County Library System, and the volunteers at the Museum of the Everglades in Everglades City.

I must thank my parents, Dorothy S. and Lee H. Hill, Jr., for encouraging me to become a writer. I would be nothing without my parents. Thank you for (among other things) reading to me as a child; putting up with me when I was a highly annoying teenager; paying for my college education; and teaching me (to quote my old friends, the Delany Sisters) to reach high! Thanks also to my brother Lee, a race-car driver; my brother Jonathan, a cultural anthropologist; and my sister, Helen, a musician and elementary school teacher. I have learned a lot from each of you. Thank you, also, for my nieces and nephews, who are my joy!

Professionally speaking, I am very grateful to Carolyn Reidy, president and CEO of Simon & Schuster, Inc.; and Judith Curr, executive vice president, publisher, and founder of Atria Books (an imprint of Simon & Schuster, Inc.), for unwavering support and enthusiasm. My editor, Sarah Cantin, is a gem, with whom I look forward to many future adventures. Thank you, Sarah, for editorial insight, which brought out the best in me as a writer.

More than any other publisher with whom I have worked, the staff of Atria Books works as a team. I would like to thank the production, marketing, publicity, and sales staff. Your talent and dedication are deeply appreciated. Together, we have created something special.

Very sincere thanks to my longtime agent, Mel Berger at William Morris Endeavor, who is not only the best literary agent in the business but also a very funny guy and a great friend.

I must also thank my dear friend and longtime publishing attorney, John R. Firestone, of Pavia & Harcourt in New York.

ACKNOWLEDGMENTS

I owe a huge debt of gratitude to Kathy L. Murphy, founder of the Pulpwood Queens, the largest book club in the known universe with more than six hundred chapters. Kathy is a whirlwind of book-loving enthusiasm. All are welcome at her unique, annual authors-and-readers retreat called Girlfriend Weekend held each January in Texas.

I have visited many book clubs in person or via Skype/Facetime. The list is very long so I will just mention a few: the Stonebridge Book Club, Kensington Book Club, Harborside Gardens Book Club, Olde Cypress Book Club, and "The Runaways" Book Club, all of Naples, Florida. Elsewhere in Florida: "The BookEnds" of Pinellas County, the Glen Lakes/Weeki Wachee Book Club, the "Caloosa Readers" of Fort Myers, and the Everglades City Book Club. Other book clubs I've enjoyed include groups in Baton Rouge, Louisiana; Columbia, South Carolina; Woodbridge, New Jersey; Wall Township, New Jersey; Baldwinsville, New York; and Tyler, Texas, home of the "Tyler Well Read Roses."

I must thank nine women novelists with whom I share a phenomenal group blog, *Southern Belle View Daily:* Lisa Wingate, Julie Perkins Cantrell, Denise Hildreth Jones, Kellie Coates Gilbert, Shellie Rushing Tomlinson, Nicole Seitz, Jolina Petersheim, Eva Marie Everson, and Rachel Hauck. Thank you for welcoming me to the porch!

Last (but never least), thanks to the members of my local writers group, the Sisterhood of Atomic Engineers: Pat, Caren, Janet, Audrey (who kindly read this manuscript and provided insight), Gwen, Denise, Joanne, Lillian, Nina, Frances, Jen, Kim, Leah, Kris, and our emerita member, Jo. Y'all keep me sane! Thank you for sharing the milestones, both good and bad, in this writer's life.

Miss Dreamsville

and the Lost Heiress of
Collier County

AMY HILL HEARTH

An Atria Paperback Readers Club Guide

Introduction

It's late summer 1964, and members of the Collier County
Women's Literary Society are shocked to learn that a large
development is planned for the edge of the Everglades along
a stretch of tidal river that is cherished by several members of
the book club, including Dora Witherspoon, the book's narrator.
The development also threatens Gun Rack Village, a hideaway
in the swamp where the residents include book club member
Robbie-Lee Simpson's mother, Dolores, a recluse whose life re-
volves around her small fishing shack.

In her first novel, Hearth explored what life was like for outsiders or "misfits" in a small, isolated community in southwest
Florida in 1962. By forming a book club, they band together
and thrive.

In this sequel, Hearth addresses how our identities are closely
tied to the places we call home, and the stresses and conflicts
that arise when great change is on the horizon. It is also a story
of how long-held secrets, once revealed, can have unexpected
consequences.

Questions and Topics for Discussion

1. Secrets can shape our lives in peculiar ways. Do you believe that keeping a secret is sometimes necessary, or is revealing the truth always the right thing to do?

2. Book club member Priscilla is away from her baby, attending college in another part of the state so that she and her child will have a better future. This is an enormous sacrifice and Priscilla is conflicted. (page 152) Do you think she is making the right choice? If you were in her shoes, would you make the same decision?

3. Hearth explores the different treatment that an unmarried woman could expect to experience upon finding herself with an unplanned pregnancy. (page 62) What did it mean for a poor teen compared to one who came from a family with resources?

4. The tension between Northern and Southern states is illuminated by the experiences of Jackie and her husband, Ted, who are from Boston. Jackie, in particular, makes many mis-

steps while adjusting to life below the Mason-Dixon Line. Do you think the "North-South Divide" has improved or grown worse since the 1960s, and why?

5. In a post–9/11 era with Homeland Security, would Judd's Cold War experiments with volatile chemicals and rockets be interpreted differently? Would Ted be allowed to privately settle the matter with his son? How have both political views and parental roles changed in fifty years?

6. Were there any historical facts about Florida that surprised you? Were you aware that Florida was a Confederate state during the Civil War and that the KKK was very active in the state into the 1960s?

7. Society tends to judge women like Dolores very harshly. Often, a stripper or "exotic dancer" is viewed as a simplistic, stereotypical character. Hearth, however, shows Dolores as a complex human being, an overlooked or "invisible" person worthy of our attention. Should Dolores's past life be considered in court as a way of judging the veracity of her testimony?

8. There are several ardent fans of the actress Elizabeth Taylor in the book. Are you a "Liz" fan? Have you ever watched any of her movies? Which of her movie roles was your favorite? Can you name an actress on a par with her today in terms of influence and iconic stature?

9. The Everglades region could be said to be a main character of the novel. Did the book change the way you "see" that part of the country?

10. Throughout history there have been many debates over the idea that real estate actually can be owned. At various times and places real estate was owned: by individuals, by corporations, by kings, in common, or by the state. Some view real estate as entirely owned by an individual, who has the right to preserve, develop, or destroy it (and whatever lives on it). Some see real estate as being held in trust for future generations, regardless of who currently owns it. This debate is woven into the fabric of the book. As you read it, where in the debate did you find yourself to be?

11. How should society decide whether to allow development of places like the Everglades? Does the kind of development change the equation? How much economic benefit does there need to be to outweigh individual property rights versus ecological benefits, such as oxygen production, water conservation, and species protection?

12. Some people (like Jackie) welcome change. Others (like Dora) fear it. Which do you think describes you?

13. Seminole Joe is Collier County's boogeyman. The concept of a ghost who seeks revenge is commonplace in many cultures. Can you think of an example of a famous boogeyman? Did your hometown have a boogeyman? What was he called?

14. Jackie creates confusion by wearing mourning clothes for an unusual reason. Were you aware of the strict societal rules about wearing black, and for how long, after a death? What was expected of you during that time in the culture in which you grew up? How has that changed today?

15. Dora "got to thinking how strange it is to be alive in this world. It's not like anyone asks to be born; you just arrive whether you like it or not. You've got no say whatsoever in who your parents are." (page 282) How much of our lives is a result of circumstances over which we have no control? Does destiny, or free will, determine our lives?

Enhance Your Book Club

1. Visit Amy Hill Hearth's website at www.amyhillhearth.com to learn more about the author and to read her essay "Why I Write." Contact her through the link on her website and invite her to "Skype" or "Facetime" with your book club.

2. Play some of the music mentioned in the novel, including "Another Saturday Night" (Sam Cooke), "Where Did Our Love Go?" (The Supremes), "The House of the Rising Sun" (Eric Burdon/The Animals), "Everybody Loves Somebody" (Dean Martin), "I Want to Hold Your Hand" (The Beatles), "Oh, Pretty Woman" (Ray Orbison), "You Don't Own Me" (Lesley Gore), and "Peggy Sue" (Buddy Holly).

3. Prepare and share food and drink mentioned in the novel, such as Jell-O wine, pineapple upside-down cake, Collier County cheese grits, Mrs. Bailey White's Died and Gone to Heaven Cake, and Boston Coolers. Visit www.amyhill hearth.com for recipes!

4. Pick one of the books that the Collier County Women's Literary Society reads (or plans to read) in the sequel, such as *To the Lighthouse, Cross Creek, I Never Promised You a Rose Garden,* and *A Moveable Feast.*

5. Dora Witherspoon talks to her pet snapping turtles. Dolores Simpson chats with a heron she calls Peggy Sue. Have you ever found yourself talking to "critters" as if they were human? Have you ever given a wild creature a name?

AVON PUBLIC LIBRARY
BOX 977 / 200 BENCHMARK RD.
AVON, COLORADO 81620